T0277538

In the House of Wilderness

In the House of Wilderness

A NOVEL

CHARLES DODD WHITE

Swallow Press / Ohio University Press
Athens, Ohio

Swallow Press
An imprint of Ohio University Press, Athens, Ohio 45701
ohioswallow.com

To obtain permission to quote, reprint, or otherwise reproduce
or distribute material from Swallow Press / Ohio University Press
publications, please contact our rights and permissions department at (740) 593-1154 or (740) 593-4536 (fax).

Printed in the United States of America
Swallow Press / Ohio University Press books are
printed on acid-free paper ⊗ ™

28 27 26 25 24 23 22 21 20 19 18   5 4 3 2 1

Library of Congress Cataloging-in-Publication Data
Names: White, Charles Dodd, 1976- author.
Title: In the house of wilderness : a novel / Charles Dodd White.
Description: Athens, Ohio : Swallow Press, Ohio University Press, [2018]
Identifiers: LCCN 2018025366| ISBN 9780804012102 (hardcover : alk.
paper) | ISBN 9780804040976 (PDF)
Subjects: | BISAC: FICTION / General.
Classification: LCC PS3623.H57258 I52 2018 | DDC 813/.6-dc23
LC record available at https://lccn.loc.gov/2018025366

For

A., E., and I.

These lonesome people in the wild places, it is their nature to speak; they must cry out their sorrows like the wild birds.

–Frank O'Connor

Wilderness. The word itself is music.

–Edward Abbey

Part I

1

THESE THREE had survived by charity and deceit for the better part of the winter. Two women and one man, all young and adrift in the turns of the American South. They'd left the wilderness preserve the autumn before, hitchhiked down into Charlotte, and stood around bus stations telling fictions of abandonment to any kindly face. Taking the dollars with self-abasement, saying God's blessings and crushing the money into their rucksacks until they collected enough for food and weed and the means to find a new place to hold them.

In the cold they stood in evening lines at the shelters and moved around the streets through the sunlit hours, bound always to the next alcove, adopting whatever stray dog they could for the day so that they might beg more profitably.

Still, their eyes grew hungry. Their faces took on great depth.

They called themselves Wolf, Winter, and Rain. The names they'd taken when they met and fell in love in the forest, married one another by their own decree before they came back to the cities where they'd learned this new kind of survival and what it exacted.

Things had taken a turn in Knoxville. March held onto the cold and the shelters overfilled. They'd headed east of the river to find abandoned homes near the interstate they might occupy, but there was little to be found that wasn't already claimed. Wolf told Rain that she could make some money for them if she walked Magnolia Avenue after midnight, and she had and they had all slept for three of the coldest nights of the year in a Holiday Inn, bathing and laughing, and drinking boxes of wine while sleet tapped the windows fogged from the heat of their presence. They made love together and forgot the need of anything other than the comfort of skin and languid days.

It became an unstated routine. Sometimes Rain, sometimes Winter, would go with the men who offered them a means to survive the streets another week or two. Money accrued. Gradually, the season warmed and the banks of the Tennessee River began to green and bloom Easter colors. They moved farther east then, outside the city, strode past the billboards for gas stations and Gatlinburg amusements. When the women asked where they were going, Wolf told them that they were finding the paradise that was intended.

Out past the truck stops the green hills began to rise. On the highway shoulder they learned another world of detail. Castoffs and leavings of rapidly passing traffic. Tires blown like exploded eyes. Busted crates of rotting produce. Roadkill, bloated and flung in comic postures. From this they picked what they could use and resumed their march. Within three days' hard walk there was little more than the inclining mountains before them and the highway at their backs.

And then on the fourth day, when they had walked the sun up into its highest zone, Wolf turned from the roadside and plunged into the woods. The ground was stony and steepened as they cut for the Pigeon River. They stopped and studied the water for signs of a ford, but the current was too strong and they made slow progress as they continued upstream, crossing finally at twilight when they had to make a basic shelter of river cane and cut laurel at the mouth of a dripping cave.

That night there was a close moon and they all stripped and played in the cool shallows. Wolf sang love songs to them, and it was as if the forest had given up its secrets of pleasure, erasing all that had happened to get them here. As they lay beside each other that night, he asked them what suffering was to compare with this calm.

In the morning Wolf led them up a foot-trod path, unwilling to tell them where he was taking them. Still, they followed, in love with what he had promised.

And then, deep in the heat of the day, the abandoned village appeared, a presence amid overgrown vine and broken boardwalks. A town of clapboard and old brick, the interiors heavy with shadowed heat. Some few had been vandalized but much remained untouched. This was where they would make their new life, he told them. Each woman would tend her own home, which he would visit in turn, and in this they would find the secret heart of contentment.

They lacked seeds for gardens but there was a surplus of forage: blackberries, fiddlehead ferns, poke sallit. This they supplemented by occasionally scouting the interstate shoulder where they would cull the meat of animals freshly struck. At night they divided the shares equally before Wolf divided himself from one of the women's company as he joined the other for the night.

At the first hard rain they learned every ill fit and gap in the rotted ceilings. Water came in and stood in pools. They watched the downpour for any pause, and when they had half an hour or so, they would fetch what scrap from the unused buildings they could find. Much had been picked over. Much had been burned by those who had found this place and squatted here across the derelict years. But sometimes there would be a beam and a reasonable sheet of plywood. They patched their homes together, made them as whole as the materials would allow.

The wet season then gave way to early summer drought. The days were spent by the river or under shade where the small crawling creatures harbored alongside them. The waterline lapped the cutbanks lower each succeeding day. In those weeks they saw copperheads as they came down from the high terrain to take to the river. Wolf killed three of the snakes and they ate the meat after it had been spitted and turned over blinking campfires.

Evenings were long and humid and thick with mosquitoes. They closed themselves up inside the buildings to escape the worst of the infestation, but even there the bugs circled and lit, drew welts out of unprotected skin. Their chemical sprays were soon gone and they slathered river mud to salve the inflammation and escape further stings, but this was insufficient.

One afternoon it became too much. Wolf rose without a word and took the hatchet from his rucksack, tossed the scabbard free, and began to pound and chop into the wall until daylight punched through.

"You all get whatever makes smoke," he told them, pointed vaguely at the encroaching summer forest.

The women went out and gathered leaves and green firewood, great armloads of torn grass and the smaller broken elements of the unused buildings, dumped them all in a pile beside where he worked. A lump of fuel that fattened under the weight of its increase. Still, he told his wives to bring more while he continued to hack, to true out the edges of his hole.

By the last minute of daylight he was satisfied with the gap and stacked the materials to burn. He burned the grass first and then the dried wood, pulled the smoke over him with great inward sweeps of his arms. Once the fire steadied and sustained he placed the leaves and the broken and cut greenwood branches in the flames. The fleshy wood boiled sap from the ends and the smoke thickened. The women crawled down on the floor beside him where they could catch modest sips of clean air.

When twilight had gone over to full dark they no longer needed the fire and he let it flutter and die. For the first time in many days they could sit together without clawing blood from new bites. In the dark their voices guided them toward one another.

They talked not of particulars that night. Instead, the veil of darkness allowed them to speak without knowing if the others listened, as though they were addressing different segments of themselves kept secret in daylight but permitted in this strange anonymity. They talked of dreams and what they signified. They talked of the wisdom of communal living. They talked of the zodiac and sex and how the stars were made from the same elements as skin.

Wolf did not know when his wives had fallen asleep, only that they had grown silent. He had spent many nights like this, aware of his guardianship of the two women, a burden he welcomed though a burden still. He rolled a small joint for himself. As it took hold he recalled how far he and the women had come, how much they had accomplished based on their own resources. It had been no easy matter holding them together, but the hardships had wedded them far closer than any tendered document could have. There was a kind of philosophy in that, wasn't there? A recognition of indisputable value measured not by currency but by risk and trust and shared sacrifice.

Sleep descended on his chest and lit there, squat as a cherub. Perhaps the cherub was part of a dream personified, a dance of surprising weight that sunk him into a pit of his own design, ever receding. A phantasm then, a broached inner world. Let that have its own share of time.

He bolted from sleep unable to breathe. Smoke swelled and filled the room. At the edges he glimpsed the distorted flash of stuttering firelight. The beat of a blown heart. The heat was spreading. He tried for a breath to call out for Winter and Rain but the smoke put itself in his throat and his voice was wrung out by the stinging fumes. He tried to stand but he felt his head grow light and he collapsed.

It would go like this then. Fast but no so fast that he couldn't perceive the chaos. Part of him had always expected this final outcome, undone by events beyond his comprehension. He had wanted his wives to understand this and he hoped that they had been given the gift of consciousness when the smoke took them. He wanted them to see that the impossibility of resistance was its own kind of mercy. There was great friendship in the eye of what killed you. His only regret was that he could not hold Rain's hand when it had come for her. That girl that was as much a part of him as his child would have been. To touch her as she died. That would mean everything. That would be the end of all lack.

There was a sense of being lifted, which surprised him. He had expected extinction only, the purity of oblivion. But instead, he felt his weight ease. Some trick of the brain, he assumed. Even now he wouldn't have pursued the escape hatch of a spiritual life. And yet the sensation continued, not lifting him, he realized, but dragging him, slowly and with great effort. There was pressure as well, sharply felt beneath his arms. His feet knocked across the floorboards and a tunnel of sight appeared to him as he was hauled clear of the burning building and could see the night sky overhead. Each of his wives had hold of him, had survived, had fought to make certain he survived as well. He looked back at where he'd just been. The smoke assumed everything into its greater shape.

His coughs came with sure violence. Breath forced its way in. The women offered him water when he could take it. It was as warm as something from a body, but it was easier to swallow for that. He tried to speak, but his voice was cracked and Rain and Winter told him not to try. In time, he obeyed their counsel, and they all watched the building burn. Their faces glowed by the pretty animal of fire.

2

STRATTON BRYANT met the man who meant to rid him of the house. It was late and a crash of rain had touched off the present noise and spasm. He stood on the porch, waited to see when the headlights would flood the drive. It did not take long. As soon as the Chrysler appeared he lifted his hand. The car engine balked and stilled in the rain, ticked. The night seemed to hollow itself while he stood there against the bulk of the farmhouse. He thought of all that was behind him, all that there was still to hold on to. Only a year had gone by since Liza had died, though the time had rolled and rolled.

The silver-headed real estate agent got out of the car and came at him through the weather, snapped his hand out like some tool made to cut.

"Sorry to bring you out here in this," Stratton told him as he took the hand to shake it. "I would have come to town to spare you the trouble."

"Not at all. No trouble. Here, let's step inside."

He could hear in the agent's voice something from up north, vaguely Midwestern. Ohio likely. Practical and measured. A man, like him, not native to the Tennessee hills. He closed the door and the din subsided. They walked up together through the hall with its bruised wood and talking floor. A warm span of light brushed across from a lamp at the living room entrance, and they went on through it into the farther darkness, the space smelling faintly of dust and furniture oil.

Stratton took him on to the kitchen where he often ate his meals over the sink, now that he was a widower and free to his own brand of neglect. He was aware of the broken puzzle of dirty saucepans and dishes on the draining board, marinara viscous as engine grease. He did not explain or apologize. He did not care to justify the way he went about hurting.

"Can I get you a coffee? I've got some decaf in the pot."

"No, that's fine, Mister Bryant. I just need you to go over these papers with me and we'll have you listed by the beginning of next week."

Stratton tipped the carafe above his mug and drew out a chair across from the real estate man, saw on his hand the gold wedding band with encrusted diamonds. Big and expensive but handsome. A man who wore his money like a tailored shirt. Stratton went through the papers without comment, initialing and signing where he was told.

"You're sure this is the price you want to list?"

"Yes. I want to sell as quick as I can."

The agent nodded, pleased.

"I can't promise anything, of course, but we'll do what we can. There won't be any repairs to worry about. Maybe some paint, put down as many personal items as you can. People don't like clutter. They like to be able to see themselves in the home. Reduce as much as you can stand. I've heard there's another structure on the property. Is that right?"

"Yeah. An old homeplace. Something left over from the Great Depression. Not much more than sticks and a tin roof now."

"Well, that's fine. Might even be a selling point. There's a certain type of buyer who might even find it romantic. We'll be sure to include a note about it in the listing."

Stratton saw the agent's eyes take in the counters and shelves before they worked across the walls with Liza's pictures. The burned-down mountain home up around Pigeon Forge. An orphan girl in a field of chicory. Liza's father's face the morning after he died.

"Your wife was famous for what she did, wasn't she?"

"Yes," he said. "People admired her photography."

Neither said anything more for a while, just sat with the company of the images. When people became aware of Liza's work it often resulted in social awkwardness. Her view of a profoundly flawed and compromised world. She'd once told Stratton she knew she had a photo right when the viewer looked sorry to have seen it. Surrounded by her pictures, Stratton felt he knew his wife better now than he ever had when she was alive.

Once Stratton had seen the agent to the front door and watched him drive off he went to the kitchen to tidy up, tossed what remained of the coffee. He tried the television but at this time of a Friday night it was all melodrama and local news. It was still too early to sleep so he went into the library and rooted through his collection of CDs until he found the Philip Glass, his Violin Concerto No. 1. He sat and tried to place himself in that soundscape of vista and repetition until there was little of this world left to him. He'd tried to explain to one of his music theory classes at the community college that there was a particular advantage in understanding what music made of the listener, what new space it could create, though he doubted that they had listened, had truly desired to understand. He was glad that he now had the summer break to escape the pressure of dealing with students and what they expected him to solve for them. This annual rhythm of teaching was strange in that it seemed he was always trying to catch something that remained elusive. The year took a lot from him and these periods at the end of a semester were a chance to collect himself, to remain beyond the scorch line of final burnout. But the breaks depressed him too, all that time without specific containment.

He woke sometime past midnight, sitting up in his chair, the tabby cat tucked into the crook of his arm as if it had grown there. He carefully lowered it to the floor, tried not to make it fuss with arthritic pain. It was supposed to have been her pet, a shelter rescue kitten from when they lived in Berea. More than fourteen years ago now, just as her work was beginning to get serious attention. Liza sneezed whenever the cat nosed her, called it "that damn cat," which in time became its name. Now, Damn Cat was grinding his decaying teeth against kibble in the next room and Liza was nowhere at all.

He knew he should shut down all the house lights and go up to bed while he could, find the rarity of untroubled sleep, but there was a warmth in the downstairs silence that kept him there. It was in the timbers of the house, the life still locked up inside. This had been their realized hope, finding this place in the woods, with all the folded land around them, the Smoky Mountains at their backs. How was it possible for a forty-seven-year-old man to feel this old? And yet here he was—geologic—covered up like something to be excavated at a later point in time, some remnant to unlock the problem of a future history.

Upstairs, he took the pistol out. Studied it as if it belonged to a symbolism he couldn't quite solve. The ritual: the loading and unloading, the snug clasp of the magazine into the receiver, the snap of chambering, the cool kiss of the muzzle against his temple. Then he placed it on the pillow beside him, the pillow where she'd lain her head, available if he decided he had no other choice but to follow her.

HE DROVE in early the following morning to gather what he would need to dress up the house. The roads were emptied of commuting traffic and it was easy to slip into the Lowe's, where he wandered around for a few minutes in its sheer warehouse enormity before he began piling paint buckets and brushes into his cart. His hand fell to whatever brightly advertised itself as a bargain. He considered it a virtue to trust in the marketing that had gotten the product this far, considering he had no expertise to rely on.

On his way back, he stepped into the Hardee's just off the I-40 exit and ordered a coffee and sausage biscuit. Inside, there was a clutch of retired men wearing caps with stiff brims and glasses held in place with nylon cords or rubber bands. They were tacit and workmanlike about their meals, hands smoothing wax paper on tables, eyes sidling even as they spoke to one another. They discussed upcoming planting schedules, the chances of a furniture factory moving into

Jefferson County, the Braves' likelihood for a wild card berth. He caught himself thinking absently about Liza, was confused by it for a moment before he realized it was because she would have loved to have come out here and talk to them, follow them back to their homes, their lives, and photograph what she found there, either good or bad. Odd that he had never told her about them, about this quiet routine he played out when he was on his way up to the college to teach. He wondered why he left certain things a secret between them, covetous of something that could never belong to any single person.

By the time he got back to the house it was already hot and the cicadas were screaming. He carried all the supplies to the front porch and went inside to pull the furniture away from the living room walls. There was no air-conditioning in the old farmhouse and within minutes he was slick with sweat from the work. He went back to the bedroom to change into a faded pair of swim shorts and sandals, threw all the doors open, swept what he could.

By noon he had cut in the corners and rolled a clean coat over two walls, careful that Damn Cat didn't scamper through the paint tray and leave his signature on the tongue-in-groove floors. Stratton acknowledged his progress with a tallboy of Budweiser and a half hour sitting on the shady side of the house while he watched songbirds at the feeder. Finches mostly. The infrequent Carolina wren. He crushed his can and cracked another one open as he kept working through the long green heat of the afternoon.

Later, he got around to bracing himself for what he meant to do. In the carport he turned up a couple of broken-down cardboard boxes that he shaped and duct-taped into solid cubes. From the recycling he gained a short stack of old newspaper to use for wadding. He worked through the living room first, taking down the pieces that were some of her most famous works. *Teenage Girls Skinny Dipping on Troublesome Creek. Dulcimer Burning. Old Preacher at His Pulpit. Unsolved Arson. King Coal.* As he took each one down and wrapped it in the paper, he tried to keep his eyes on the next picture, wary of being drawn into contemplation, but he found that nearly impossible. It was like taking down parts of Liza's mind, this purging, this deletion by his own hand.

It took both boxes to finish the den and he hunted around for a while for a place to put the rest, but he would have to buy some more boxes. There was just too much to store and he didn't want to risk the framing by trying to fit too much into a tight space. He took down all of what remained, spread them out on the sofa and kitchen table, any surface at all until he had succeeded in bringing down the walls to the bare paint which he would need to repaint. The whole house would need a new skin, and it would be so much easier now with the pictures gone.

Knowing that he was too tired to face it but unable to resist the pull, he went into her study, stood in the darkened doorway for a while before he gathered himself and crossed to switch on the desk lamp. The desk was all in a jumble, just as she always left it when she worked—pieces of correspondence, travel receipts, promotional material for photography equipment, all turned over by the circumstances of the moment. Her hands always busy as a sewing machine, selecting the next project by a need for perpetual motion. It had been her way of retreating from obligation, and, he suspected, the routine of him.

He sat at her desk and studied the twinned specter of himself in the window pane beyond the burning cone of light. This was the version of his appearance he liked best, this hologram compressed into two dimensions. Perhaps this inclination was a vanity, though he doubted himself capable of something so material. It was this second self in a middle space of canted light that suited what he had become, an image outside of form, incapable of the many small concerns of being fully realized within its frame.

In the top drawer he found the picture he had first seen there last winter but not looked at since. It was in black and white, heavily shaded by what appeared to be evening sun coming through a background balcony window. Liza rarely shot interiors, preferring the bold and vivid play of outdoor lighting on her subjects. A realistic way to lift the varnish of habit, she'd explained in one of her guest university lectures. The harshness of nature held up to itself as proof of what time costs the human heart.

The trick of the photo was the way in which it held the viewer's gaze into this rich background light, obscuring for several seconds the concealed subject, the shadowed figure that stood blocking the left third of the composition, golem-like, shoulders dipped from holding something in front of its waist, suggesting an appendage of wings. Only by close scrutiny could one begin to make out the musculature of a bare chest and legs, and the towel hanging from the midsection of a young man. His face was smeared, of course, a simple monster in its anonymity. In the bottom right corner she had penciled in its title: Adultery.

He returned the photograph to its place and slid the drawer shut, committed this part of her to a place he would not touch.

3

THEY FOUND the abandoned homeplace the day of the solstice. It had been a hard day's walk through open meadows and burning sun. With their high-slung rucksacks, they looked like wayfarers fresh from the Appalachian Trail, a disguise that they relied on to avoid the curiosity of those who might view their trespass.

The house was far back from a barbed wire fence just beyond a huge pin oak and an encircling camouflage of scrub. Built on mortared bricks, much of its original clapboard siding remained in place, though one panel had been pried open long ago, exposing a now dormant bee colony that appeared to run the length of the entire back wall. Wolf marveled at the sight, said that what the hive would do with the elements of the earth owned a greater symmetry than anything men might realize by hand and iron.

Within, the floor joists remained in place though the tile had rotted to the point that they could not support the weight of anything heavier than a child. Nail points bristled everywhere. The window's glass panes were gone and the sound of air coming through the house was that of a bad rumor in the ear.

With so much daylight left, they grounded their packs and began to work. They employed hatchets and hands to get what they could from the timbers of the house and a collapsed outbuilding some fifty yards distant under a wig of kudzu. Winter and Rain drew the nails from the wood and passed them down the line to Wolf, who beat them as straight as they could be beaten. Once they had collected enough salvage from the back end of the house they carried it forward and ripped the decay away, installed the improvised flooring of clapboard, slats flush as the rough hew would allow. By the hour of starshine they had covered the parlor and the front vestibule. They got all their gear off the ground and away from the hazard of snakes and built a cook fire in a hastily scratched hole a few feet beyond the granite stoop.

Their only food was oatmeal boiled in a Coleman skillet. Wolf squatted over it and eyed the burbling fare. A mood of exhaustion had come over him. Speech stopped as they watched the meal, waited for it, unable to talk until they conquered the obligation of their own bellies.

Wolf divvied the portions and they ate, finishing nearly as soon as they commenced and then wiping their fingers into every circle and slight contour of their bowls to glean whatever residue they might. The food was not much but still enough to tend them toward sleep and Wolf was the first to succumb, kissing both his wives goodnight before climbing the steps to the front of the house and collapsing on his sleeping roll.

The two women sat close and held each other. When their voices came they were like something ill-maintained put to use.

"I don't know what we're going to do."

"I don't either, baby. It's okay."

"Are you still hungry?"

"Yeah. You?"

"Yeah. Real bad."

The wood fire rollicked and sprawled, flung out a parody of shadows against the brush.

Winter was up before the others the next morning, stoked the flames so they would serve for heating some water she'd fetched from a nearby spring, a thin dance of stream that she hoped was as clean as it appeared. There was only instant coffee to boil and pour out in their tin mugs. Everything else had been eaten to the bottom and the containers burned.

"We'll need some things from town," Winter told Wolf as soon as he stumbled into the sun of midmorning, having slept for the better part of twelve hours. He nodded, yawned, called Rain over to him. He looped his arms at her waist and drew her thin body toward him, nuzzled her at the nape of the neck until she began to twist against his hold.

"Hey there, Little Bit. I need you to resupply while me and Mama work on the next room. Think you can handle that?"

She said that she could.

"Good girl. Here, take this and be smart with it, okay?" he said, pressed a greasy roll of cash into her palm, slapped her lightly on the ass.

Rain tucked the money into her rucksack after emptying out her possibles on the floor next to her sleeping roll. She told Winter goodbye before hefting the pack onto her back and setting out toward town.

She walked down through the hardwood brakes until she came to a clearing that bordered a dirt road. Already the cicadas were sounding their tidal clamor. The noise was overwhelming and she imagined she could locate herself in relation to it, entangled but guided by this disaster of sound. She regretted the lack of water as soon as her sandals touched the dust of the road. For so long it had been one road after another. She wondered how many miles she had walked in the time she had been joined to Winter and Wolf. Not just in transit from one camp to the next, one home to another, however short lived, but all the steps in between. The lone hikes through the deep woods in search of a vision. The burning in the legs and the damaged soles of her feet as she walked out to the edge of herself to find the bright rim of pain where truth was purported to lie. How could she calculate and weigh that and what did it signify if she could?

After a while she caught a ride into Newport in the back of a pickup hauling a small tractor in a wagon behind it. She had to make room amid tarp and assorted farmhand tangle, and every bone in her frame rattled as the vehicle gained speed on the rough back road, teaching her gratitude for pavement. Then there were the smells too, of grass and gasoline and horseshit. When the driver turned onto the macadam ten minutes later it all eased and thinned in the quickened slipstream, everything then lost to speed.

She thanked the farmer for the ride at the parking lot of the Food City, offered him a five-dollar bill for the ride, which he refused before he wished her luck in this hot day that promised no respite and was gone on his way. She discreetly counted what Wolf had given her. Forty-six dollars. A strange and painful kind of wealth in itself. In her hand it felt like something ready to detonate.

The air-conditioning attacked her. The coolness was extraordinary, exposing the outdoor heat for the enemy it was. She had to pause to steady herself, understand what it was to be human for a quick moment in this world of controlled climate before she unslung her ruck and stowed it on the bottom rack of the shopping buggy. She strolled forward, her skin raising goosebumps.

The aisles, overburdened with product, were like an accusation. She laughed quietly, knew how absurd that would seem to the people around her that something as simple as twenty variations of bread and bowtie pasta could create panic, but it was true. To reconcile herself to it required everything she could summon. She wished that she had thought to write out a list, give herself a scaffold to build from, but she'd lacked paper or pencil. It was strange that Wolf had entrusted her with this errand. Was he simply disposing of less-efficient help at the homeplace, or was this supposed to be a compliment to her competency, a belief that she was the right person to provide for them all? She liked to think so.

He couldn't have known, of course, how apt his choice had been, what kind of experience she'd had gathering food with so little in her pocket. She had learned that well as a girl when her mother would be pulled under by one of her depressions and everything about the house would have run to permanent ruin if it hadn't been for her. All she had then was what could be scrounged or what some man might have left in the cushions of the couch or on her mother's bedside dresser. Many meals of beans and salted meat cooked down in the Crock-Pot sent one Christmas by her grandparents, a pair of aloof Mississippians who never once deigned to cross any threshold between them and their child and grandchild. Tall and broad Presbyterians who observed the semblance of propriety by sending letters each season on watermarked stationary the color of warm butter, saying nothing really in the correspondence other than the affirmation that they still acknowledged their daughter and her bastard offspring as relation, poor and misbegotten though it may have been.

She threw in a couple of bags of pintos, along with split peas and black bean soup, some yellow grits. She picked up onions, potatoes, and carrots too, knowing that it would be nice to have something to put in the broth. She stood in front of the butcher's case for a while, weighed the tantalizing promise of red meat before she realized it would be impossible to justify, given the budget. She did get two cases of Natural Light, more for the guarantee of clean water than the negligible alcohol it contained. Once she checked through she had ten dollars left, a good buffer against future privation. Wolf would be pleased with her thrift.

She declined bags when the clerk offered, packing everything into the ruck herself before she cinched and secured the flaps, tossed it over her back, and tightened the straps until the freight rode high across her shoulders. She set out.

Once she cleared town she stuck out her thumb each time she heard the approach of a vehicle. The sun was starting its long afternoon decline, but the heat was still prime, and as soon as she came to a shaded spot of two mimosa trees near the interstate access ramp, she dropped the pack and clawed inside to get at one of the cases of beer. The can was so cold in her hand that she nearly dropped it, but she managed to thumb the tab down and sucked a long and clean pull. Her throat simply opened and it was all gone in a matter of a few seconds. She crushed the can, stuffed it deep in the sack and opened a second, enjoyed the cool taste this time now that she could sense something more than the basic need for water. She fought back a wave of guilt at tearing into the supplies prematurely, promising herself she would deduct it from her share as soon as she got back to Wolf and Winter.

A black Honda SUV stopped on the shoulder and the electric window went down. A man in sunglasses and a green T-shirt leaned forward and asked if she needed a ride. She hesitated for a moment, halfheartedly screening the beer can from his view as she weighed how much she could trust the unsolicited offer.

"Don't worry," he said, tried a smile that seemed aware of its own awkwardness. "You can finish your drink on the road if you like."

He was easy in his speech and unhurried. Had there been the faintest note of desperation or a need to convince, she would have bolted. She registered too the slim gold band on his left hand and this further eased her defenses.

"You got somewhere I can stow this beast," she said, dragged the ruck upright.

"Sure. As long as you can spare me one of those beers."

She fished another one out and handed it through the window to him. The back hatch clicked and sighed open. She loaded up and got in.

The road made smooth noise as they merged onto the interstate and he ratcheted up the volume on his stereo, some harmonica and folk lyrics. He opened his beer and sucked at the brimming foam.

"You not worried about the cops?"

He shrugged, turned the can up to get a good pull, then pocketed it in the console's holder.

"I should ask you the same thing."

"What, for hitchhiking?"

"No, buying underage."

"I'm not. I'm twenty-two."

"Bullshit you are."

She was used to men studying her for something, but his attention seemed different. Less obvious than most, more penetrating.

"I'm nineteen. Most people think I look older. The cashier didn't even card me."

"Well, that's one advantage of living out in the sticks, I guess. How far am I driving you, by the way? I'm not going all the way up to the Carolina line, if you're trying to jump on the Appalachian Trail."

"No, it's not that far. I'll tell you when we get on up to the exit. Just a few miles."

He was satisfied with that, dropped the questions. From the corner of her eye she studied him, tried to get some idea of him in turn in order to balance out where they stood. On his jeans were several white ragged islands of paint that looked to be recent, but he lacked the squared hands of a manual laborer. His long fingers tapped lightly on the steering wheel as he kept a meticulous count against the music and the wild voice of the singer, a voice that summoned a kind of lonesome bluegrass wail. She could smell him, that stench of work on a body. It called back the stink of those men who had passed her money for a quarter of an hour. Used her like a tool for something they couldn't do on their own. Maybe that was what he had in mind. Make her into something that submitted, something that didn't matter.

"So, your wife approve of you picking up young girls on the side of the road. Hot little things to keep your motor tuned up?"

He released a smile so thin that she doubted whether she had actually seen it. He said nothing.

"Here, this is the exit," she said a few miles later.

He slowed and coasted up to the crossroad.

"I can get out here."

"No, this is my turn too. I can take you on a little further."

And he turned then without waiting for her agreement. She sunk back into the seat as they cleared the nowhere of the rural road and climbed up toward the foothills, turned off the pavement and bounced over the gravel and dirt. He slowed and turned into the driveway of a farmhouse set back beyond a grove of mixed hardwoods. The vehicle settled into park.

"Hope this gets you pretty much where you're headed."

She couldn't quite tell whether he was making a statement or posing another question.

"Yeah, we're camped up the road just a little ways."

"I see. Well, good luck."

"Thanks."

The hatch popped open and she went around to gather and bear the considerable heft of the pack.

"Hey."

"Yeah?"

"Could you spare another one of those beers? You know, for the taxi service?"

She made a face he couldn't see in his rearview.

"Sure. Hold on a sec."

She got another sweating can from the box and secured everything down before tossing the ruck on and coming around to the driver's side.

"Thanks. You take care, okay?" he told her.

"Sure."

He flipped the unopened can into the empty seat beside him and crunched up the driveway. She watched him swing behind the screen of trees, his flat hand stuck out the window in farewell.

She stood a moment staring there at where he'd gone, sipped the rest of her beer before she went around to his mailbox and stuck the can inside. Then she turned to the road and headed back toward family.

4

STRATTON SAT in the rocking chair on the front porch long enough
to drink the second of the gifted beers. His mind hadn't left the
girl since he'd dropped her at the end of the drive. He knew the
rest of the road up the way she had gone and there couldn't have
been more than half a dozen places she could have had in mind to
go to ground. It had to be the old homeplace at the back end of
his property. They were all farms up that way, owned by the kind of
good country people who would have hated the sight of her blond
dreadlocks, the stink of her patchouli. She didn't belong to any of
them, that was for sure. And even if she had, there would have been
no reason to carry that pack filled with beer and whatever else she'd
got in town.

   He went out to the CR-V and hauled in the few buckets of paint
he'd picked up in town to finish off the back rooms, shifted some
furniture around, and worked until an afternoon shower moved
in and cooled things off. Damn Cat came in and circled his shins,
tacitly demanding attention. He scratched the old tom on the top
of his head until his ears saucered around, his expression of mo-
mentary satisfaction.

   "Run off, now. I'm done with you."

   The cat slowly shuttered his eyes and ignored him, sliced each of
his cheekbones into his ankles.

When the sun was gone but there still remained good enough light to walk by, he slipped on a ratty pair of sneakers and stepped around the side of the yard, made for the back trail that ran past the untended garden. He paused there at the tree line a moment, considered the problem he might be making for himself before he breached the woods.

The path narrowed almost immediately until it petered out into a game trail so that he had to stoop and pinch back low-hanging branches to pass through. Almost at once there was the staccato of flushed birds and ground squirrels. Later though not much later, the occasional serious break of something larger, deer hide flashing like a patch of shade made suddenly animate. And then after a while the sounds and shapes of startlement began to diminish as the woodland absorbed his trespass into its larger confusion.

The ground gently rose and hardened into shoulders of granite, protruding at times where the natural goblet of rock held a stream. The water circled and spoke and he passed his hands through it to drink. It tasted faintly of a woman.

He had to place his hands on gritty knobs of overhanging stone as he raised himself above the bank, careful but untroubled by the concentration the movement compelled. He had to remind himself not to muscle himself up but to use his legs and patiently crawl forward until gravity swung back to his advantage. His eyes remained on the close purchase of ground.

Once he achieved the top he took a minute to rest and draw away the sweat from his hairline and eyes. He was having to breathe harder than he should and this caused a wave of vain anger. To contemplate getting older was bitter enough without having to fight the physical restraints his body seemed anxious to impose. He forced himself to his feet and drove on.

He heard the sounds of hammering long before he could see where the woods cleared. He moved along behind the deep border of scrub so that he would have the advantage of whomever he might find there. Progress was restricted by his desire for stealth and it took him half an hour to cover the distance.

At first it was only a pair, a woman a few years older than the girl he'd picked up on the roadside, hair dreaded like hers though a shade darker and perhaps a few inches longer. Her carriage too was more vertical, heron-like, as she pried nails from boards laid flat on the ground. As she worked, her slim biceps jumped like something nervous beneath her skin. Standing a few feet away was the man, darkly bearded and tattooed across his pale chest and down the length of both arms. He wore a blue bandanna tied around his head to catch his sweat as he nailed good pieces of siding into the house's frame. Occasionally they would pause from this and speak quietly, intimately, and his hand would stray to her bare shoulder where it would rest for a while. She did not appear anxious to have him remove it.

Then the girl appeared, coming down from the interior of the house, said something to them that Stratton couldn't hear, and it was then that he could smell something cooking. The woman and man put down their work and followed her around the side of the house, mounted the stairs and vanished from sight. For a long time he listened to the sounds from within, the creak of the floors, the laughter amid the vines and standing heat. Eventually, he withdrew.

HE HURRIED home in the dark, took the road the last half mile now that he didn't have to be concerned about being seen. He passed no neighbors on this back end of the dirt road. Everyone was already locked up safe for the night in their family homes, electric lights burning behind shaded windows, the lives they lit contained within the larger fact of darkness. He recalled how he had once given himself to their common peace and how simple it had seemed at the time to behave that way.

Once home he showered and dressed in a pair of clean shorts and a T-shirt, poured a tumbler full of whiskey that he carried into his office. Tonight was suited to John Adams's *Christian Zeal and Activity*, and he turned the small silver sun of the compact disc against the light to check for smudges and scratches before he loaded it into the player. The sound staggered a few brief times before the track came alive from the speakers with the reassuring score against the frantic overlay of the preacher's sermonizing, his rhetorical "What's wrong with a withered hand?" repeating like errors too beautiful to correct.

In the bottom drawer beneath a sheaf of exams graded but never returned to students at the end of the semester, he found the property documents rubber-banded in a manila folder. He pulled them out and spread them on the desktop. There were well reports and original home inspections, everything maintained from the time he and Liza had bought the property. At the bottom was the tissue-thin trifold of the plat. Here were written the details of ownership, not only of the house but of the secondary holdings as well, the fifty acres of land that belonged to him alone, paid out fully now since the disbursement of Liza's life insurance policy. He placed his finger where the derelict homeplace stood, the oil in his fingertip leaving its faint fading shape.

He refolded the plat and set it aside from the rest of the house's papers, sat looking at it for a while as he finished his drink, his eyes lifting occasionally to regard the walls of the house, the blue portal of the window trained on the night. He took some quiet pleasure in the physical presence of the place itself, the real alignments of architecture and décor that comprised the structure anchoring him to this specific point in time. The abstraction of the plat told its own kind of truth, presented the science of azimuths and acreages, but it lacked the living experience of being at home among one's private things. Impossible to explain that to someone who might come out to have a look around with the idea of buying it all in order to transpose their lives into what had already been lived through. Impossible also to explain the feelings this made him have for these people trespassing, his desire to wish their presence unknown because ultimately it would force an action he had no appetite for.

The CD ended and it was getting late. He shut off the office light and went into the kitchen to pour out a saucer of milk for the cat, warmed a small cupful of the same for himself. Like two old friends, they drank their simple nightcap while they watched over each other, companionably silent.

5

RAIN SLIPPED the light cover of the summer sleeping bag and walked naked down to the stoop where all the sandals were piled. She sat and listened to the sounds of Wolf and Winter asleep, coiled into one another atop the inflated sleeping pads. She had lain with her back to Wolf, remained awake after they'd eaten supper and made love all together.

Without knowing why, she began to walk away from the house, followed the moonlight to the clearing beyond. Her solitude gave her courage against the night. As a little girl she had been terrified of darkness and what invisible threats it held. But now she felt protected and insulated by it. She couldn't remember when that change had taken place, when solace overtook fear, but it was written indelibly in her now. She did not need to evolve some further defense against the dangers of the world because she carried the gift of living so close to the earth. What most people feared losing could never belong to her and this was a distinct freedom. She had known that on her own but Wolf had been able to articulate it in such a way that it was a part of her character. He had retailored a piece of her and it was impossible not to admire him for that.

She thought about when she had left home, those last few months in her mother's house. How time had eaten her like something it kept in a trap and portioned out. She'd watched a show on TV once, one of those cable reality dramas where the camera went into the worst state penitentiaries and you got to see how men lived in the prison underworld, thieving and raping and torturing one another while the guards did their best to stay clear of the cultural undertow of it all, and she'd remembered one of the prisoners, a thin Mexican kid with a tattoo of a Henry David Thoreau quote on his neck. This kid had said how after what he had seen that he was going to survive just by keeping his head down. And that was how it was with her and her mother and that last man who had been there, Robbie, who never did actually come out and *do* anything to her exactly, though she knew it was more because he was afraid of getting caught with his hands on her than because he was morally opposed. All that time, those six months, she'd managed to put away enough money from her Burger King job until she had what she thought would be enough to get her clear of Elizabethton, Tennessee, and maybe get a cheap apartment up over the mountains near Asheville, find work there waiting tables or maybe on the Biltmore Estate. That had been the plan, at least, until her momma or Robbie had found the scratched-up flap of carpet where she'd hidden the money. Full withdrawal, close to eight hundred dollars. She didn't say anything to her mother about it, knew it held no purpose now that the money was gone, likely already spent. That was what surviving by putting her head down had gotten her.

She left that night in her Escort, a vehicle older than her by a decade. It coughed and quit not much longer after she made it over the state line mountain pass, not too far from the town of Mars Hill. She'd sat inside and cried for a couple of hours, slept badly, then got out and began walking, the new mountains coming up around her from behind the complete wall of darkness into something fractured, lovely, and pale. She caught a ride into the city and was walking around its streets at midday.

She spent most of the summer in Asheville, bussed tables at a Japanese steakhouse on the west side of town, roomed with a hippie couple that flew a Che Guevara flag from the front of the disheveled bungalow they rented. But the couple argued and fucked in a relentless cycle that was maddening. Then an apartment on her own fell through at the last minute and then she was fired.

There seemed to be so many And Thens. So many.

When it got bad enough she called her cousin in Boone who worked waiting tables at a downtown pub, told her she could set up something in the kitchen there for her, but after spending her last money on a Greyhound ticket to get there the hiring man said he wanted cooks, not bussers. Her cousin let her stay for free for a while on the couch, but she was married and it didn't take long to see that her husband had no use for her being there.

To get out of the house she sometimes went to the university library, pretended she was a student there. She walked each of the floors, breathing it in like it was a more exotic kind of air. She talked to the librarians some, asked them questions about what was good to read, what was new. One handed her a book with the picture of a handsome man squinting off into the sunset called *The Last American Mountain Man*. She sat down at one of the long tables and read the entire book, learning of Eugene Connors and his Falling Sky Preserve just a few miles outside of Boone city limits. Falling Sky was a wilderness school that was entirely self-sufficient, growing its own crops and raising livestock to sustain those who worked and trained there. No one who was accepted had to pay with anything other than their labor and an openness of mind to Connors' strict tenets. Hard work was expected, as well as unquestioning obedience. But the potential rewards were undeniable. This was a place where you could learn to live truly off the grid, where you could shape your future. Connors believed in the value of the young and their commitment to making the world a better place through discovering their inevitable connection to the land. Rain couldn't imagine anything more perfect. That night she went home and told her cousin she needed to borrow a few camping things she'd seen in the garage.

She showed up at the front gate of Falling Sky with everything she owned or had borrowed strapped to her back, considered turning around for a half hour before she finally went on to the receiving building. The young man behind the counter took her information with a cold efficiency, asking her next-of-kin, her blood type, her religious affiliation. When she joked that she didn't realize she was enlisting in the military he told her that no she wasn't, what she was doing was much harder than that.

She was issued a pair of gray wool blankets and a surplus sleeping roll, assigned to Quonset hut "C" up a ridgeline road flanked tightly by Canadian firs. Above the lintel post hung a hand-painted shingle that read "Mama's House." Inside she found a tangle of shouting, laughing women getting ready for the supper bell. Her sisters, she was told.

"Come on, Little Bit, throw your shit over here," said a woman with pigtails. She showed her an empty cot and helped her put her few things in order. She was not pretty exactly, but there was something in the woman's face that attracted her. When her hand brushed her hip as she reached past to tidy her ruck at the head of the mattress, she felt a nervous warmth in her neck, coloring.

"Winter," she introduced herself, told her to come on or she'd miss the best pickings at supper.

After settling in Rain noticed that there were no men aside from those few hanging around the administration building. She asked Winter about this.

"Oh, they're on working party," she said. "That happens a lot. They work apart for a couple of weeks at a stretch. I think Connors thinks it makes them work better, anxious to get back home to the honey pot," she said, laughed. "Don't worry, though. They're around. When they get back I'll get you to meet Wolf."

"Wolf? Is that your man?"

"I don't think Wolf is anybody's man, but we mean something special to one another, if that's what you mean. We met up here last year. He's been working on getting things together to move out on his own. It's beautiful the way he sees what all this is and how we're supposed to fit in it," she said, motioned generally at the woods. "Like it's something prophesized."

For those first few weeks she continued to use her given name though she'd noted several of the girls had adopted their own. Riverstone. Mockingbird. One odd girl with green hair called Lichen.

But it was Winter who steadied her hand, who looked out for her on the long days when they'd be sent out to mend fence or clean stables, earning their rooms and meals through the endless work of the preserve. Sometimes Connors would come and oversee their work.

She grew a new kind of toughness, a physical accompaniment to the inner strength she'd learned as a girl. Her hands changed shape and texture. Pain began to mean something different when the tools of this new life shaped her.

One evening as she was sweeping out the hut she saw the men coming down in single file from the high country, axes scabbarded and slung, timber saws balanced across shoulders, the metal speaking in its soft voice as the blades bounced with each downward step. They were all beautiful to her, these men who seemed to belong to something larger for the first time in their lives.

That night they gathered around the bonfire, their beards and grime showing the wildness of their time in the higher country. They talked of their weeks clearing the dead timber, promised greater achievements when they would bring it down to the building sites, assemble the cabins for the wilderness school before the winter deadline. All the work behind and the work still ahead, a pledge as well as an enticement.

Winter introduced her to the one called Wolf. He was older, more aloof than the others, as if he was amused by the general mass of humanity and paid it only scant notice. Still, he spoke kindly to her, asked her what she expected to gain from the wilderness education program. When she answered his questions his eyes stayed on her as if they were locked there. It confused her, but wasn't unpleasant.

The next day she volunteered to join one of the working parties that would support the timber detail, hauling up water and medical supplies. They left early and walked out into graying weather. There were only four of them to carry everything and it was slow going because of the weight and narrow trails. She felt her lungs tighten and she began to cramp, falling behind, her voice croaking when she tried to call out for the other women to slow. And then, so quickly, they were gone and she was left alone with no sense of where she was. She fought down panic, breathed it away, resumed the march, paused to hear any signs of the other women, though there were none.

There was a turn somewhere, a choice among the rocks that misled her. She soon realized she had left the trail and began to go back, but her foot missed purchase and she felt the overwhelming topple of the weight on her back, the swing of something beyond her control.

Pain was everything when she struck the ledge below. She lay there for a while unable to fully take in the injury. Turning her head she could see the mountains in the distance, a shadow cut from the granite sky. She kept her eyes there for a long time, not wanting to see what the fall had made of her, but eventually she looked down. Her right leg was twisted in a way she had never seen on a person and with each breath the ache traveled until there was no part of her body without hurt. She tried to move but when she did she felt a sudden wave of nausea and everything she had eaten that morning came up from inside her in a warm wash. She was humiliated to think she could die like this.

With slowness and care, she raised onto her elbows and propped against a stone outcropping so that she could see over the ledge and into the valley below. It was a terrible chaos, this loss of where she was, something akin to madness. She called for help, but even as she did so she could hear the frailty of her own voice swallowed by the mountainside.

Memory had thrust down then into her brain, something she'd not recalled in a long time. It had been when she was thirteen and her mother had left her alone in the house for three days, chasing some man or some other easy fix. At first she'd turned out the cupboards for food, found a couple of cans of Campbell's soup she heated and drank that first day. By the second evening she was sick at her stomach with hunger and she turned the garbage can out looking for something left over, but there was nothing. She prayed, though she damned herself for doing it even as the words were in her mouth.

That third morning she decided to find help. She went down to a place on the Watauga River where a piece of storm-broken tree jutted over the water. She'd seen out-of-town fly fishermen down there many times, geared out expensively, and she knew if one of them saw her there they would have no choice but to try and help her. She didn't care what they'd want of her in return. Hunger didn't care about virginity. Hunger only knew and feared itself.

She edged out on the log, tested each inch of advance until she was suspended above an avalanche of whitewater. The dam had been let go that afternoon and the pool below her was too deep to see bottom. It was dangerous being there and the thrill of being that close to something she couldn't stop was like looking into the seductive eye of nothing.

For hours she waited there, waited to be seen, waited to be sought out by anyhow who might have noted her missing, but there was no one and as she recognized this something greater than hunger over-took her. She was utterly alone. When she got back to the trailer her mother was passed out on the couch. She covered her with a blanket from the front closet. In her purse there was a twenty-dollar bill. She had lifted the bill, left quietly and walked into town for what she could find.

And now, lost and hurt here on the mountainside, she felt she was reliving the ache of being forgotten. Perhaps she'd been fooling herself to think that anything she could do would make her any less alone. Perhaps loneliness was an inheritable trait, an infection. Her mother suffered from it as much as any person she'd ever known. Why would she believe she would be any less subject to its injury?

She would not pray this time. At the very least, she still had that much she could refuse.

Then, there were voices. Distant but nearing. She called out and they answered, came faster and more urgent. Two faces, Wolf and Winter, peered over the ledge. Blind love crowded in her until she wept.

So much time in so few months since that day on the mountain and this night at the Tennessee homeplace. Sometimes Rain was unsure when she let go of herself, when it was no longer she alone but Winter or Wolf who thought a thing, who *felt* a thing. Was that what love was, this gradual resignation of what she believed to be distinct? She had read in the university library that some scientists believed that the dimensional world we live in is in fact an illusion, that the concept of space and time can be compressed down into a flat surface of information—one thing or another, this or that. In the world of the tiniest things there was a basic buzz that rendered the plans of God. If that were true then couldn't her mind be its own deception, a product of contraries that needed one another to exist at all? Perhaps this loss of herself in her marriage to Wolf and Winter was what made it possible to really love.

The night had cooled and she was ready to go back, but she lingered a while still, felt the brush of sedge and vetch against her bare legs, the earth's lightest touch. She wanted to be cold before she returned to her lovers. She wanted to know the hurt of not having what she desired.

6

STRATTON LEFT early for Knoxville. He got up in the warm summer dark, fed the cat, and stood on the porch with his coffee. There were many songbirds out there in the concealment of the tree line; their voices seemed to testify to the belief that they could dissuade nighttime air. In a while it seemed to be the case, the old parchment gray of the hour filtering in.

When the light was full he went back to where he'd boxed so many of Liza's pictures. It felt wrong to keep them like that, even given what the real estate agent had said. He hung many where they had been before and the rest in the back bedroom. If he were to have his way, they would soon disappear, but it was better to have them where he could see them for now. Better to deal honestly with what they were.

I-40 was flanked with occasional crosses to mark the highway dead. Semis pressed from behind, headlights in the rearview mirror like threats. Things slowed as he came into Knox County, the glut of commuter traffic rising up as suddenly as something sprung from the ground. There were stalled vehicles on the shoulder, yellow roadside assistance trucks flashing code lights. At a halt, he quick-timed the intervals of traffic, plunged his foot on the gas so hard that his heart bobbed up to his ears and then the gridlock fell away.

There was a spot on Volunteer Boulevard on the university campus; he fed the machine with all the spare change he had and tried to remember how to get around. In a quarter of an hour he found himself standing in the waiting room of the office for the art and photography program. The woman behind the front desk was on the telephone. He took a seat and waited.

"Can I help you, sir," she said a few minutes later in a tone that suggested the very prospect grieved her.

"Yes, ma'am. I was hoping to talk to John Easterday. I wanted to see him about some photography he might be interested in."

"Let me check his schedule."

She made a face that was less than encouraging before turning to consult her computer monitor.

"It looks like he's on campus early this afternoon and has an office hour. From one to two. It's an open hour so he should be available to walk-ins. I suppose you might need to know where his office is?"

Stratton said that he would. Without a word she scrawled an abbreviated title and a number on a pink Post-it and stuck it to the desk counter. He peeled it off as carefully as he would a bandage, thanked her, and left.

He wandered down to the banks of the Tennessee and walked the greenway for a while. He had not been to the city in well over a year, and it was always a pleasure to come and spend a little time here where the river flowed under the old iron railway spans. It provided the perfect opportunity to empty himself, to walk beside something of magnitude.

An old spaniel with a gray muzzle popped up a few feet in front of him and wolfed. His owner, a sleek black man in a battered fedora, told him to hush as he flicked his fishing rod toward the water and the reel sang.

"Don't worry," he said, "he don't eat white meat."

"I'm glad to hear it."

The man spoke a few words barely audible and the dog relaxed, his tongue rolling brainlessly from his mouth. Stratton patted him on the head and the tongue went to work. When the dog was done Stratton wiped the back of his hand along his trouser seam.

"I should have brought my rod."

"You should have. There's plenty to catch in there."

Stratton took a seat and watched the man fish, cast after cast, with the elegantly slow retrieval, the rubber lure fluttering in the brown water. Patience and commitment to pattern made into its most essential shape.

"If you don't mind me saying. You look like somebody that ain't in the right place," the man said.

"There's a fair chance," he said, and despite his desire to say something more to the man, he felt awkward and prohibited. He remembered the ugliness of his father about Black men and what he would say when he would see them sitting beside some bridge or overpass fishing. Street bait niggers, he had called them. Even as a boy, it struck Stratton's ears with its low violence, its idle hate. But he'd never been able to tell his father his thoughts and now they passed through him with a haste to be gone. He said his farewell and went on.

On farther up the landing he passed a few people out on a midmorning stroll. College boys and girls running in close file, made of little more than lovely muscle and tans. He marveled at the fact that the young women stimulated only the lightest whisper of lust. Was he that far into oblivion that he could sign the receipt on his own broken libido? He sat on a bench and watched the river for the small fishing canoes working in close along the banks, their pilots scruff of face, their paddles tilted like medieval lances. They reminded him of McCarthy's Suttree, of the man who forsook everything promised for everything abject; he suspected real genius in a man like that, though he would be hard-pressed to say why he thought so.

He ate lunch at a riverside restaurant called Calhoun's. The waitress seated him in a glass room overlooking the water. His table was cut hard down the middle by a stripe of sunlight from overhead, but he liked the view and the relative quiet. He ordered iced tea and a hamburger and watched a long snaking barge crawl with the current, its burden under black tarpaulins. On the opposite bank big cranes were unmanned but appeared to be staged for demolition of the old hospital. The barge came even and blocked his view with its slow dream of gradual movement, setting all surrounding things into their relative contexts of time.

He finished his lunch and paid his bill, went back up toward campus to tour the McClung Museum, derelict this time of the week. It was cool and dark inside, the exhibits maintained with a kind of clinically imposed silence. He started on the bottom floor, walked past the displays of different primate ancestors, rigidly patient in their artificial skeletons. Next door he found the Civil War display with its sabers and bullet-torn tunics, its soft maps of temporary conquest, proof that progress across the ages had been altogether dubious. He liked the display of indigenous Tennessee gems the best, preferring their resistance to becoming anything more than what they were—beautiful pieces of self-sufficient geometry. On the top floor he found the pottery of Egyptians and scale models of their sacred cities, but it was the exhibit of the Mayans that he liked best and where he lingered. He read of their classical period, saw the stone art and the elaborate calendar.

He wondered what would be made of this time he lived in. What would historians write of this life built around objects glowing with the magic of electric power? A world made up of billions of small parts that most men and women walked through without the faintest idea of how they actually worked. What kind of exhibits could be arranged for men like that?

He realized that he'd lost track of things and was late to meet with Easterday. He hurried out through the front doors and past the sculpture of dinosaur bones, bumping into a security guard and speaking a quick apology. When he arrived at the office, he found the man already gathering his things to leave.

"Excuse me, Dr. Easterday, but we've met once before," Stratton began. "At an exhibit of my wife's several years ago."

Easterday crammed a sheaf of handwritten papers into his leather briefcase and snugged it by a pair of belted straps. He had not bothered to glance up.

"And who was your wife?" he asked, stroked the slight whiskers of his chin distractedly as he turned to shut off his computer monitor.

"Liza Bryant."

Easterday's eyes rose briefly, made a weak effort at smiling.

"Yes, I believe I remember. It was in Atlanta, wasn't it?"

"Savannah, actually."

"Yes, that's right," he said, caught in the awkwardness of how to go on. "I know it means very little, but my sincere condolences. I didn't know your wife but through a few professional contacts, but I was upset to hear of her passing. Her work was important. How can I help you?"

"I wanted to talk to you about her pictures. About donating them."

"Donating them?"

"Yes, for a collection. For the university to house."

Easterday seemed to weigh this a moment.

"I was just on my way out for the day, Mr. Bryant, but why don't you let me buy you a drink so we can discuss your offer."

A quarter of an hour later they were sitting at the bar of the Bistro at the Bijou Theater drinking whiskey highballs. Stratton had parked his car in an overnight garage and walked down, followed Easterday's directions. They had the place to themselves this time of the afternoon. Gay Street was all busted concrete and cyclone fencing from some work on the sewer system, so the tourists avoided coming this far down the avenue. Nothing but the dark solitude of the leather stools and the reliable attention of the man behind the bar, the full clash of sun on the facade, while quietness enclosed them.

"You're making a mistake," Easterday began. "I hope you realize that. It's foolish to just give these pictures to us. They're worth a great deal more than we can afford. Now, I'm not about to turn my nose up at a windfall, but I do want you to explain it to me. Otherwise, my conscience might develop a bit of a rash."

Stratton felt odd to find himself in defense of his intended charity. It wasn't what he had expected to have to do.

"It's about her legacy," he said finally. "If you were to pin me down about it. I want this part of Liza to have a life of its own. I think it deserves that."

Easterday absorbed this over a philosophical swallow of his whiskey. "Yes, well. That certainly *sounds* good, even if it is only about half of what is going on. Listen. I'll be willing to take you up on this, get the materials housed here and get you at least an honorarium that saves us from looking like a bunch of cheap criminal bastards. Given one condition. Sleep on it. If this still sounds viable tomorrow morning then I'll get the wheels turning."

Stratton could see no reason to not honor Easterday's request. They agreed over a second round and did not talk of it again.

He made reservations for a room at the downtown Marriott and took a cab over, promised Easterday he would see him the following morning. Though still early, he was exhausted by what he'd accomplished, and he drew a bath for a soak in the deep tub. He turned the water as hot as his skin could endure and eased into it. The heat was like being born into something and it released all that he had carried into the day. He would be glad to be relieved of Liza's pictures. Like selling the house, it was what was needed if he was to find out what it meant to live on his own. Some men could live as ghosts or votaries, hang their fortunes around the throats of the dead, call up the pieties of grief. But Stratton had come close enough to that kind of sacrifice while Liza was still alive. He wouldn't shoulder it in her death. People who survived shouldn't have to suffer the curse of common virtue.

HE LEFT for home early, but even so when he got there he saw his professor friend from the college, Josh Callum, sitting in his truck at the end of the driveway smoking a cigar. In the pickup bed his red kayak was stuck in amid a jumble of camping gear. Out here on one of his rescue missions, no doubt.

"Was on the verge of getting the bloodhounds after you," Josh told him. "You heard the water report?"

"No, I've been busy. Some of us are grownups even."

"Doesn't excuse negligence, bud. They got a bona fide deluge over in Carolina. Plus, this weekend coming up is *Deliverance* weekend. The boys just thought we'd hit it a couple of days early. Get the hell out of Dodge, make a run that was worthwhile instead of scraping bottom the whole way. I told them I'd kidnap you if you refused, so they'd think a lot less of my manhood if I turned up by myself."

Stratton toed the truck's front tire, thought if there was any way to say that he couldn't do it, though he knew he had to come out from time to time. Otherwise, people started to notice, and he didn't want to have to face that.

"Yeah, okay. Let me feed and water the cat and get my boat."

"You take care of the cat. I'll grab your boat. How is that old tabby bastard doing, anyhow?"

"About as well as all of us."

"That bad? Damn."

For a sane man it was two and a half hours to the river, but Josh slashed a good twenty minutes off that. After they went up the I-40 gorge and passed over the state line they cut through the slim western finger of North Carolina and took Highway 107 through Cullowhee and made the winding shot up into the higher mountains, slowed through the wealthy second homes of Cashiers and then descended the South Carolina grade with its panorama and occasional general store. They were at the Chattooga North Fork put-in by noon and were ready with all their gear stowed in the kayaks and down on the river half an hour after that. They'd beaten their paddling partners, Cliff and James, who had a few domestic chores to tidy up before they'd left Clemson. They checked everything to make sure they could duck into the water at a moment's notice before they cracked a PBR tallboy and passed it between them.

"Camp beer," Josh said.

"Damn right."

"Not for reasons of hipsterdom, mind you."

"Hell no."

"Just economic practicality."

Of all of the river trips Stratton had made, the Chattooga three-day run was his favorite. Josh always referred to it as the *Deliverance* trip because many of that film's climactic scenes had been shot along the river and while running the rapids it was easy to recognize some of those landmarks. Stratton had read Dickey's novel for the first time after his inaugural trip but was disappointed when he saw that the writer had used a fictional name for the river. Since then he had always preferred the movie.

They'd finished the beer can and crushed it when Cliff and James pulled up in Cliff's battered Cherokee. Though a scholar of Irish literature who had published monographs about Flann O'Brien and Frank O'Connor, Cliff liked to pretend a kind of rustic machismo that included his choice of automobile. Every facet of the vehicle carried knocks and concavities from aggressive off-roading, stripes of pine pitch where he'd blazed trails untried. Cliff said it was the natural product of living a stripped-down existence, close to the bone. James had said it was because Cliff would forget what made him a man without it.

"You tenderfoots ready to take your chances on this goddamn beauty of a river?" Cliff called down from the parking area.

"I think we might be convinced to hazard it," Josh answered.

They exchanged embraces, stood talking for a few minutes until they walked the paddles, supplies, and kayaks down to the water. With their gear stowed and battened, they lowered themselves into their boats, closed the skirts and pushed down the soft grassy decline. They slipped into the water with the strange grace of smoke.

The river was slow this far up the fork, the wooded banks a constriction of half-tumbled pine pinned back from the waterway by large hanging loops of overgrown poison ivy and a barrier of mixed scrub. Stratton picked up a line behind Cliff, just a few yards off James's right bow, and paddled softly, getting used to the newly quiet world this close to the weightlessness beneath him. He felt settled by the compliance of water, as if it needed him there to run true.

"Makes you almost feel human again, huh?"

This from James, spoken in his companionably soft voice. Unlike Cliff, he preferred to speak when he had something to say. Stratton had known him for a dozen years and had only a superficial knowledge of his life away from the river, but that didn't seem to matter. What they knew of each other out here held greater consequence.

Within the first half hour, they scooted over three downed trees, crossed the timber's wet backs and pivoted through the shallow runs, rocky entrances that required a technical handling of the boats. They made the main branch of the river within two hours, the sun running long fluttering shadows as they moved on toward late afternoon.

As they rounded a deep curve, two herons dropped from a close branch and flapped upstream, passed overhead. Their thin legs were folded up and as they flew their bodies seemed to lope despite their grace. Without being able to name precisely why, Stratton watched them with the sense that it was important he remember every detail he could.

They reached the island where they intended to camp not long after the river fell to late afternoon shadow. There were perhaps two hours of daylight left, but it was a good time to settle and build a cook fire. Stratton dragged his boat up, shucked his life vest, and dug out a length of loose chainsaw with corded grips at each end. He and Cliff crossed the island and forded a brief feather of whitewater before climbing up the mucky shore of the main bank.

"We're in Georgia now, son," Cliff said. "You and sister-wife are full legal in this country."

Cliff was ever testifying to the frequency of incest in Georgia. Stratton suspected that it owed much to his loyalty to the Clemson football program. His mouth kept running until they found a downed white pine straddling a broken hemlock. The end had been sawed off smooth and it didn't appear anyone had tried it since this same trip the year before.

"Let's hit this bad boy a few licks," he said.

Stratton pulled the loose chainsaw to its full length, handed the other end over the log where Cliff took it and they began to cut together, kept tension as they pulled. As they worked the chain tightened in the cut and sawdust snowed into a small mound of powder that collected at their feet. Within five minutes the heavy timber, big around as a man's waist, cracked and thumped to the ground. They set back three feet farther and did the same thing, working like men born to this life and nothing else. A few minutes later that length too was cut and ready to be hauled back to camp.

Twenty minutes later the mosquitoes got bad. Having had enough, they teamed up on each log, carried them balanced on their shoulders, made four trips while Josh and James trued up the pile of small and medium deadfall they'd gathered.

When the fire was burning well they all found sturdy branches and opened their Buck and Case knives, whittled cooking sticks, and stuck their steaks on. They seared the meat quickly before putting it between hand-torn hunks of bread. They ate and passed two plastic pint bottles of George Dickel whiskey.

"To that great man of the Volunteer State," Josh intoned as he raised one of the bottles. "Mister George Goddamn Dickel."

"Hear, hear."

"A poor man's solace, I'm afraid, gentlemen," Cliff countered, though he did not refuse the bottle when it was passed his way. "You Tennesseans would do better to look to your white liquor and leave the manufacture of brown spirits to your northern neighbors, despite their late lamentable status as a border state."

Stratton could tell that Cliff had been taking early samples of whatever personal ration of alcohol he'd brought along. When he was into his drink he had the habit of adopting the speech patterns of a wounded Confederate cavalry officer tolerating the ignorance of his benighted lessers. One of his favorite subjects of debate was bourbon.

"Now, Pappy Van Winkle is the beverage of a true Southern gentlemen," he drawled. "Why, I picked up a bottle the other day for the modest sum of four hundred dollars."

"That right?" Josh said. "I'd not give a damn for your Pappy Van Winkle up against this Dickel. You want to know why? Because Dickel is here and Pappy ain't."

"One doesn't bring liquor of that caliber amongst heathens like yourselves," Cliff concluded.

The talked passed around like that a while, half-joking and companionable. James told of a visit he'd made over into Clayton, Georgia, where he'd met the banjo-strumming boy from *Deliverance*.

He was middle-aged now, of course, and worked as a greeter at Wal-Mart. James said that he was pleasant and gave his autograph freely. Stratton thought how strange it must be to be that man, forever famous as something that was as much a part of imagination as fact.

As the whiskey gradually disappeared Josh and Cliff went off to their tents. Stratton sat up with James while the fire thinned. They heard a screech owl and Stratton whistled to it a few times to draw it closer but the bird remained out in the dark somewhere. He tried to remember the last time he'd called one up within sight but it had been too long and his desire to recall doing so may have been a lie to cover the truth of what may never have happened. He wasn't sure that he'd ever seen a screech owl in the wild at all. Perhaps what he remembered was from some documentary he'd watched as he was falling asleep in front of the TV, *National Geographic* or *Planet Earth.* There was no way to be certain. He whistled again.

THE SUN was up under a screen of gray that saddled the valley. From it a fine mist fell. The men all sat in a small circle around Cliff's camp stove as he heated water for coffee, and they listened to the light rain tap the tarpaulin stretched from the tree branches overhead. Stratton had succumbed to a mere tolerance of the morning, the night without sleep on his shoulders like something that had him in its grasp. He took his canteen cup of coffee and carried down his dry bag of compressed gear to the kayak on the island's mud shore. Once it was all aboard he sat on the bow and lowered his face to the steam.

They met the braided water and shuttled through the runs. The sunlight flattened everything into a perpetually moving image that drew them toward the best entrances and sometimes the worst. The bottoms of their boats ground over submerged ledges and narrow traps until they rocked free and paddled into stronger water.

It was all as wild as it was supposed to be.

Stratton tailed James, watched his entries closely and tried to match them as best he could. The river was not as high as he had expected and the rapids were toothy with stones normally rounded by the smooth carve of whitewater. Still, they ran hard and fast and true, met the high spray and paddled hard into the laughing riffles as they glided out from beneath the tall figures of white pines and the crows at early roost under a sky that pended storm.

Shortly after noon they entered The Narrows, turned into the currents that pushed them clear of the dangerously undercut boulders to the left and dipped into a pool of calm water halfway down the rapid. Cliff beached first on the sand and stone beach and everyone came in close beside him in the notch, pulled their boats halfway out of the water before they turned out from their dry bags what they would eat and drink. Stratton tipped up his Nalgene bottle of water, felt like he could empty all of it into him as easy as if it were air.

They climbed up to an overhang and sat there overlooking the river while they sheltered from the passing shower, dipped their fingers into peeled-back tins of sardines and tuna with crackers, legs dusty with pale Gatorade powder. Stratton unbuckled his life vest and set his helmet on a flat ledge of stone beside him, felt the breeze touch him with a slight trembling. He sat and ate, though he did not taste anything. He was thinking only of how little difference there must be between him and a man passing through this place a thousand years before, how that man, like him, would have stared into this rushing water with awe and respect.

"You hanging in there, bud?" Josh asked, offered a nip from his leather flask.

"Yeah, I'm good. Boat's good. Not much else to ask, is there?"

"No, I don't really guess there is. You know I'm not just asking about the boat though, don't you?"

"Yeah, I know."

"All right. I won't beat you over the head with it then."

"I appreciate that."

Stratton tipped back the flask, felt the burn pass his lips and spread out in his stomach like it meant to colonize him. In the end, it was enough to make him talk.

"I've been wanting to ask you something, Josh, if you don't mind."

"Hell, you know I don't."

"I wanted to know what you think about why we try to keep ourselves away from suffering. We all know it's coming, don't we? I mean, there's really no possibility of avoiding it, but that doesn't stop someone from trying. And we tell ourselves that we are the only ones who could have possibly hurt from something to the extent we do because it wouldn't make sense otherwise. Because when it happens it feels so unnatural to us, so specific, that we can't make sense that everyone has the same thing to deal with."

"You want to know if I think universal damnation is something to get in a tizzy over? Sure, of course it is. That's what we do best as people. We bleed. Look, bud, I know what you've got on you is something I'll never understand. That doesn't mean that you aren't still yourself inside whatever it is you're going through. You still exist and you are the only one that will ever get to live inside your skin. You get to build that church of meaning wherever you decide."

Stratton considered telling Josh that was the coldest kind of comfort but didn't see any gain in mocking his friend, especially as this friend was doing the best he knew with a question that was unanswerable. He would have done as well to ask the rock beneath him, perhaps better.

They paddled that afternoon, made camp on a broad flat stretch of Georgia shore with many hours of daylight left, hung from a rope swing left there by teenagers. Stratton watched as his friends took turns sprinting and flinging themselves from the bank. They flew like trapeze artists and screamed like happy children. He watched it all with eyes he wished belonged to another.

7

RAIN LED them up in the dark toward the house. She regretted telling of the man who had given her the ride back from the highway and of how close he lived. Foolish to believe Wolf wouldn't see the opportunity in that, what he would call the inevitability. She had been right, of course, to regret. When she protested, Wolf pulled her close to him and his mouth had been in her ear as he talked, more breath than words.

"Come on, Little Bit. You know we've got to do this. This isn't a matter of wanting. This is a matter of *surviving*."

Winter had tried to gentle the demand, to point out that no one would force her to do anything, but Rain realized the imperative. The world they lived in afforded no room for the convenience of conscience. The real way of nature was to self-preserve, and it was that course they had committed themselves to long before.

So she had conceded, kept them behind her in single file as they stayed out of the road and close to the tree line so they could drop to the other side if headlights appeared. With all their time on the roads and along trails they had mastered the ability to move quietly.

They stayed to the edge of the yard, gazed up at the lit windows for close to a quarter of an hour, saw nothing inside.

"His car's here," she said.

"He's gone, I'm sure of it," Wolf said.

He scooped his palm through some loose driveway gravel and cast it against the closest window. It clattered down but no one came to see what had caused the noise.

"Come on."

They came around to the back and went up the porch steps, stepped farther in and looked through the windows there. Wolf tried pulling up on each frame, but they were locked. He went down into the yard and took a small pile of broken bricks to hand. Crashed one through and with another chunk tapped back the jagged edges before he reached his hand inside and unfixed the deadbolt. The door swung wide and bumped softly against the backstop.

"You say something," he whispered to Rain. "Less likely to be nervous hearing a woman's voice."

She didn't imagine the pitch of voice would make much difference following the sound of breaking glass, but didn't bother to contradict him, calling up softly at first, then louder. Still, there were no sounds within. She was the first to step inside.

They passed through a mudroom with a coatrack wearing a rain jacket, a peacoat, and a pair of neoprene waders slung by black elastic suspenders. Past that was a high-ceilinged kitchen cluttered with several closed and taped cardboard boxes. The smell of fresh paint came from somewhere farther on like the scent of something newly slaughtered.

"What are we looking for?" Rain asked.

"We'll know when we see it," Wolf answered as he strode past and entered the darkened front room. Winter shrugged as she mounted the stairs and walked slowly up to see what could be found there. Rain remained alone in the kitchen, suppressed her impulse to rinse the dishes stacked in the double sink. The mess of it bit into her sense of trespass.

"My God, you've got to see these," he called back, loud enough that she jumped. She hurried out to keep him from speaking again.

"Shouldn't we try to be quiet?"

"Here, look."

She followed the line of his finger to the far wall. Along it was an array of photographs. Almost all were portraits of some kind, though the eyes of the subjects were rarely fixed on the camera, abstracted within their own interior framework. Their faces, regardless of sex or age, shared some kind of similarity, not of feature or expression as much as exposure. They did not pose; their faces simply opened.

"Amazing stuff, huh? Your boyfriend looks like he knows what he's doing."

"He's not my boyfriend."

"No? Don't worry, I'm not jealous. Man's got the gift."

He went back toward the office, stuffed what valuables he could into his cloth bag as he moved through the hallway. His footsteps trod on the floor's complaining bones. Rain did not follow him, let herself be drawn to the photographs instead. She took down her favorite, a picture of a young woman like herself, blond hair dreaded but loose around her face, watching something beyond the frame, something permanently unknowable. Rain held the picture and saw the glancing reflection of her own face overlaying this counterfeit. She slipped it into her backpack.

Wolf hooted and clumped back to show off a brace of whiskey bottles still sealed. The cloth bag swinging from his shoulder swelled as tight as a belly. Rain went to him to help relieve his burden.

They burst back into the quiet night with the whiskey at their mouths and a strain in their shoulders from all they could carry. It was a pleasure to counter the pain and the struggle as they walked up clouds of dust, marched the back wilderness and farm fronts as if they were native to them. What a thing to belong somewhere, to feel the place sink its teeth into your heart, when every step you took was another gentle worry and shake that cut in a bit deeper, made the good deep pain of being home do something big inside your chest.

That night, when they had returned to the homeplace, they filled it with what they'd stolen. Though it would all have to be quickly consumed or sold, that night was large enough to fill with whatever arrangements they could imagine. It began as a kind of play, moving the silverware and television, swapping the assorted jewelry and the Bose stereo, finding the different combinations of all these things that were supposed to matter and putting them in absurd new relationships to one another. But the longer she watched, the more Rain began to be sickened by it, not at the materials themselves, which were supposed to be the object of their mockery, but of the growing hysteria, drink fueled, that seemed to be descending on them, as if the trivia of plastic and metal wasn't at stake as much as their own compliance and greed. She left Wolf and Winter to their game and went through the back-broken rooms to find a place to hang her picture of the girl.

She hung it in a small bedroom where the floor was still solid and a glassless window overlooked a rash of kudzu. She retrieved the hammer and drove one of the straightened hobnails into the clapboard. The wood split but held firm and when the hanging wire snugged itself in place you couldn't see any tell of damage. She stood back and studied to make sure it ran a level line, which it did. Moonlight striped the top corner of the photograph, lent it a glimmer. She thought about talking to the picture, perhaps asking it a fortune or demanding a proverb, but that would have ruined what she really thought of the image and the girl inside it. So she just sat with it a while, let it reside.

HE CAME to her that night after Winter had fallen asleep, touched her on the shoulder wordlessly and led her to what had once been the family room. Her bare feet moved with caution over the spaced boards. Lantern light reached down and showed the stuttering filter of their shadows as they passed over the deeper shadows beneath. She liked this museum of a place, the dark below. She liked how it held her at the bottom of something she could not escape.

"I've missed my private time with you," he told her. "I don't want you to think I've forgotten what I said."

"That was a million years ago," she said. "Promises don't last that long."

He took her by the shoulders, turned her into the gentle heat of him.

"Don't say that, Little Bit. You know we're the future. We see things as they are, as they have to be."

"What about Winter?"

She wondered if he'd made promises to Winter like this. Sometimes, she would see an understanding pass between them about their lives together at Falling Sky before her. A quick smile at a memory briefly mentioned, or a change that would come across their faces when they thought they were alone together. Like everyone who loved someone, their loving was done without knowing if it might end, and loving like that was capable of saying and promising anything.

"What about her? She's part of the family, yes, but that doesn't mean things will always stay as they are. She changes just like we have, like we're *meant* to. Listen, now," he said as he took the fine point of her chin into his hands. "We are pledged. Do you understand what that means, how that matters?"

She remembered the weight of the child that he'd put there, how he had told her it was what proved his entwinement to her. She remembered too after the pregnancy miscarried how he had wanted to take her over with his hands, force himself inside as if he sought something of himself withheld in her sex. The look as well. The glazed eyes of some mania for her that was its own fulfillment of sore need.

She surprised herself by biting him so hard on his hand that blood salted her tongue. He closed his free hand around the slender column of her throat. Her mind went light under his grasp and came back when he let go.

"You're tired. You need to lay down."

Without understanding why, she agreed, allowed herself to be led to his unfurled sleeping roll. Neither did she protest as he lifted her tank top from her shoulders and tugged her shorts and underwear to the floor. As she watched him she was aware of a perfect numbness in the center of her gut. She could have just as easily dreamed this.

He had laid her out now, arranged her with a kind of professional boredom. That was better, she realized. Better to be the object that receives the act rather than the woman who expresses permission. He was in her before she could become slick. As he worked over her

she felt like something might give way but it would not. She closed
her eyes and smelled the night, listened to the crickets.

No hope of rest once he was done. Not for her or him either.
The accomplishment of the thing hung over them like the promise of pain. He tried to touch her lightly, to stroke and whisper to
her, but everything seemed desperate and errant. Worse even than
when either she or Winter had prostituted themselves and they
all pretended an emotional indifference that did not stick without
drugs or wine.

"We shouldn't have stolen from that man," she said.

"No, maybe not. Too late to fix that now, though."

"Yes, I guess you're right about that."

She sat up, covered herself.

"Why are you doing that?" he asked.

"Because that's what you do after what we've done."

She thought he was going to try to argue, to lecture, but he
didn't; instead, what she'd said stayed in the air between them until
she had to get up, get dressed, and make some place for herself back
in the deeper rooms.

8

THE HOUSE was overturned the evening he got back. He did not realize the extent of the damage until he had walked to the kitchen and seen the back window smashed. The office next: the liquor stolen and the drawers deprived of their contents. A few small things pointlessly broken. Overall, a kind of violence for its own sake, as far as he could tell. The spite and meanness of vandals. He added the expenses of the damage in his head, wasn't concerned until he thought to check upstairs.

He went up and saw that the bedcovers had been stripped, the pistol taken. He removed his telephone from his trouser pocket, considered calling the sheriff's office, then Josh, but put it on the nightstand without punching the numbers.

He stood at the opening of the crawlspace. He thought he heard something down there and went back inside for a flashlight. He circled around the opposite side, practiced what he imagined to be stealth, though his pulse hammered a disco beat in his temples and he was unsure how covert his approach really was. The light showed a pale nothing until it found the far wedge of foundation and banked earth. There, a pair of iridescent eyes and the pale snout of a possum. Stratton switched off the beam, left the creature alone.

After picking up the tines of broken glass on the back porch, he sealed the window with flattened cardboard and duct tape. He went through the house once more before checking the locks and taking a beer with him to bed. Though not expecting to find sleep, he went down fast and remained in bed well past daylight.

While he drank coffee the next morning he made notes for repairs in a small moleskin ledger. It was a book he'd kept for some time, a kind of diary that he'd never managed to use regularly. Instead, it had become a convenient volume of bound scrap paper, practical bits of life encroaching on more abstract concerns. The disagreement of his inner and outer lives made into a more complete disagreement and held in the insufficient shape of a book.

He drove into town and then out to the Lowe's, picked up the boxed window panes, the measured and sawed length of sill molding, some touch-up paint. Once he had it stowed in the back he locked it up and stepped across the street to Wiley's Lounge on the river.

It was a slumping horror of a place with green indoor-outdoor carpeting over a tumored floor. God knew what crimes lay beneath it. Stratton preferred to press that thought to the back of his mind, along with his faith in the building's overall structural integrity. Every time he took a step he braced for the inevitable soft give beneath his feet, the feeling of proximity to infection. It was hot inside, sun pouring through the riverside picture window; the bartop box fan was a negligible comfort. Buck Wiley stood at the far end of the press-wood bar, drinking coffee from a big Darth Vader mug that said I'M YOUR DADDY. He had a birthmark shaped like a country on the right side of his face.

"The regular?"

"You got it."

Wiley went down to a small black cooler and pulled out some pre-mixed Bloody Mary mix, poured a shot glass's worth into a pint glass, cracked an egg after that, filled it to the top with beer from the tap and stirred it once with a long spoon. The egg yolk circled like a small sun.

"Run a tab?"

Stratton answered with a thumbs-up and lifted the drink to his lips. He watched the run of the river out the window for a while. High and hectic amongst some rocks before a quick wash down to where the channel ran deep and the current braked. The waters ran down through town and then on to Knoxville where it fed into the Tennessee. Men had come in flat-bottomed boats long ago, come from as far as New Orleans to find this notch in the green hill country. More to prove that it could be done than for any sustainable interest of commerce. The sheer taunt of difficulty compelling them even when the reliable principle of greed failed. Something about this place turned up the dregs of other places, brought a kind of person here that had nowhere else to claim a hold on life. There were other geographies like that, Stratton knew, had known more than a few of them in his own life, but this was the one he lived in and he knew that so much of his life now belonged to this river and what it brought in its long ancient slide. It didn't matter if one came from upstream or down, only that one was confined to perpetual waters that drained the land of its surplus. Men caught in the shedding of what should not be contained.

In time Wiley grew bored of the drunk he'd been talking to and sauntered down, pulled up his stool and started that casual and elliptical approach of his where he talked as though he had no mind for the purpose of the words, just talked in the ceaseless and patient way of an old man tired of facile wisdom. It was all entrapment, of course. His way of getting others to betray themselves.

"So, I've been vandalized."

"That right?" Wiley said, wrenched up a hairy eyebrow as he brought out a couple of shot glasses and poured them both full with Buffalo Trace. "Illuminate me."

They toasted and took the shot.

"While I was out of town. Somebody got in and tore through things. Having to fix it myself."

"I'm sorry to hear that," Wiley said, though it was clear he wasn't. "Any idea of the responsible party?"

Stratton hesitated then said that he didn't. He could see Wiley take this in.

"You calling the police?"

"To hell with it. It's done."

"Sure. That's good philosophy. You want another bloody beer?"

"Load her up."

Another pint glass appeared. He thought this not at all an unpleasant way to take a meal. When he drank hard and early he felt the distance to Liza bridge. Being drunk in the daytime was its own act of faith, a wading into the deep ocean of what it meant to exist. Even the other side of death exacted some kind of pull on what remained behind. Or so it seemed when the liquor took hold. The give of this world for the take of what didn't come next.

He liked Wiley's company after a while. It was a natural thing to feel warmth to those sharing your quarter of hell. Then too, he could feel a squall come on him and there was nothing in him that didn't despise the man.

It was getting later now, close to four in the afternoon. The bartender's gossip had gotten ugly. He'd talked with contempt of several men he served, often to their faces, as if they were all enacted some quiet theater of mutual loathing that depended on a sequence of insult and boozy consolation. Stratton was still at his place at the bar, getting up only to piss as the day had come on and the weak daylight gradually slanted through the riverside window. He'd leaked on himself as he stood over the urinal and when he now moved his legs he could smell the reek of it rising from his lap.

He sat back down, studied Wiley's ugliness.

"How many lives you think you managed to ruin?" Stratton asked.

"What, you talking out of your head too, professor?" Wiley said. When he talked his teeth showed like a line of small and pointed hate.

"I'm just curious what drew you to this line of work. Why a man would want to surround himself with as much suffering as he could. Must take something in the gut, some kind of a thing that feeds on itself. One in a million, I bet."

"Okay, I'm pretty sure we can get a cab out here for you. Let me just get out the phone book."

Stratton swallowed the last of his drink and stood.

"Did anyone ever tell you," he said as he leaned in close, "that your smile looks like it's made out of equal parts Crisco and horseshit?"

Stratton looked into the man's animal eyes to see if they would blink or swerve, but they did not.

"Sit your ass down," Wiley said. "I'm going to get you so drunk you won't know who you are."

Stratton accepted the whiskey for the damnation it was and sat back down.

Hours dropped by and he began to fold in on himself. The successive drinks set off this quiet and insistent and familiar war with grief that would so often arrive without preamble. No reliable sign that it would come, just knowing that it would, that it was as much a part of him now as any physical trait ever could be. A companion without compare, eclipsing everything. He thought of Wiley's curse, that he would get him drunk enough not to know himself. What a hard deceit that was. He had tried that on his own too many times to have faith in such a promise.

Suddenly, it was dark outside and voices surrounded him with their hot fog. He found it difficult to hold his head erect or look anyone in the eye. He sensed other drunks come and go. A woman sat next to him. She smelled like something that had been closed up indoors for too long. She wanted him to buy her a drink. Said she'd sing a song for him. She did, too. Céline Dion. Someone's heart claiming to go on and on. He wasn't sure if he ever ordered the drink, but eventually Wiley brought something for her. Stratton remembered seeing the bartender leer when he left the cocktail.

"You can drive me home, right?" she asked.

His tongue crawled over the words, but he told her that he could. After another drink.

They left when the lights came on. She put most of her weight against his shoulder and cried a bit. He didn't want to ask her what was wrong. She dried it up by the time he got her to the car.

"It's not too far. I walked."

The car reeled across the center line, gradually eased back.

"Just tell me how to get where we're going."

"Stay on this road a while. It's not far."

The night swallowed them for a bit before she motioned him off to a flat sandy shoulder with a trailer set back maybe a dozen yards. He nosed in along the back of a small deck leading to the entrance. Together they sat in the car for a while. He listened to her bad breathing.

"Are you going to be sick?"

"No," she said. "Come over here and help me up."

He came around, opened the passenger door, and hoisted her by her underarm. She turned her face toward him in a simulation of romance before she let her head loll as free as if it were attached to nothing at all.

There was no need for keys, as the lock had been busted and the striker plate pried off. The door surrendered to them with little more than a nudge, bounced hollowly against the hollow wainscoting. Stratton tried the light switch to no effect.

"Got turned off last month," she explained, managed to bear her own weight as she guided him down the hall to the bedroom. There was little to avoid, the living room empty except for a battered couch and a short row of cardboard boxes.

"You just move in?"

"Hmmm? Oh, yeah. No, I've been here a while. Keep meaning to get moved out, but it never seems to catch, you know?"

The bed was a mattress on box springs without a frame. She sat down on the edge and removed her earrings with deliberation, deposited them in a soup bowl on a stepstool placed at the head. The jewelry chimed thinly as it went in. She patted a place beside her and lay down without waiting to see if he would join her.

Stratton's eyes adjusted to the dark. He turned and looked at her single bookcase with its books of broad and glossy spines. Textbooks, he realized. He wanted to ask her what she studied but realized there was no reason to feign interest in her life. He hoped to God she'd never been in one of his music gen ed classes at the college and he'd not recognized her. Better to remain strangers to one another than to attach any significance to this sad mutuality.

He undressed and stood looking at her, unsure if she had yet fallen asleep. Her breathing was coming more evenly now and she seemed to be feeling better. A blue arch of shadow concealed her face and neck, so he couldn't tell if her eyes were open and watching him there above her. It was the power she held, hidden in this recess among her things, these poor and weak pieces that made up what she called home.

He got down beside her and felt her good and warm body. That was all they needed of one another in a time like this, sleepless and afraid, subject to the awful sorrow that could attack someone in the long hours of an unknown night.

THE NEXT morning he stopped at C&C Pawn, looked over the shelves, asked the man behind the counter if he'd had a whole cache drop in his lap from some hippies he'd not seen before. He looked like he wouldn't have told him if he had, but Stratton didn't see anything familiar anywhere, even after he checked the gun case. He went next door to the gas station and bought a big Budweiser to kill his hangover. He sat in the car and drank it in the parking lot, gave his mind over to the problem he meant to bring to its conclusion. Once he finished, he drove back over to Lowe's and picked up a buggy full of cleaning supplies.

When he got back to the house Damn Cat rose from his sleep in a sunlit nest of newspaper and wicker basket. He stretched and blinked.

"Miss me, partner?"

He blinked again, then circled the outdoor food bowl. Meowed one dolorous meow to get his message across.

"All right. Hold your horses."

It was hard to pour in the dry food without dumping some of it over his knobby and impatient head stretched across the bowl. Some of it bounced and sprangled and some of it actually made it in before the cat began to crunch the kibble down. Stratton sat in the rocker and scratched him behind the ears for a while.

He went up to the second floor and wheeled down the attic ladder, tested its flex and weight bearing under his hand before he stepped up and stood in the dusty and dark heat of the roof's steep angles. Slumped and sheeted piles surrounded him. Castoff overlaying castoff. A facet of light crept in at the eaves, and this was what he moved by as he sifted through the packages, felt through the bundled shapes.

Dust came away in a small rolling cloud as his hand touched the canvas gun case. He found the leather handle and tugged the case free of the weight pinning it. Under his arm the shotgun felt the same as it had as a boy in Texas shooting doves, like a piece of awkward iron better handled by someone else.

Downstairs, he unzipped the case and lay the 20-gauge on some unfolded newspaper on the kitchen table. It was an old Remington pump gun that had gone to patchy rust along the receiver. He tore rags, wet them with WD-40, ran the oil over every metal surface until the disuse brightened into something like the shotgun's original luster. The release button gave way under the solvent and the slide opened with a brisk and savage noise. He worked the action back and forth to introduce the oil, then he loaded three old yellow shells of bird shot that had been shoved into the bottom of the gun case. From the front closet he dragged out his biggest backpack and loaded it full with all the cleaning supplies he had bought at Lowe's.

He went on foot, took the same path he had that first time he had discovered them squatting on the homeplace. The noon sun was unkind, like something that meant to hurt him. Even in the woods it seemed to come from everywhere, stabbing in between the hot shade like there was some repeated riddle in its persistence. When he came to the creek he doffed the pack and drank from a pool, tasted the minerals and mud that bled into it, splashed his face, then went on.

He stood in the bordering tree line for some time to see if there were any signs of current occupancy. He had expected to see it, had expected to need the shotgun, but the old house was empty. After grounding the pack, he walked around the front where the fire circle showed recent scorch. Some spilled food, some empty liquor bottles. Inside, he found where they'd pieced together a rudimentary living area, including their backpacks and sleeping rolls, some personal effects scattered like a child's abandoned tea set. He leaned the shotgun against the front door sill and grabbed the bottles of bleach and ammonia from the pack, covered his face with a dishrag and began dumping the cleaner into the timbers of the house, let the poison make its own signature. He left the bones of the place to those who would have it.

9

THEY HAD fenced the stolen goods across several pawnshops in Knoxville and rented a motel room just off the interstate for two days. Rain had remained in the room, kept the DO NOT DISTURB sign hung from the door handle so that housekeeping wouldn't see anything to stimulate curiosity. She watched TV and drank Diet Coke, flipped the window blinds every quarter hour to see if Wolf and Winter had returned or left her there. It was dark before they appeared, smiling and high.

"Hey, Little Bit. Have we got something sweet for you."

He produced the weed and papers, rolled one nearly big around as her pinkie. Lit it and smoked once himself before passing the joint to her. Winter leaned over and kissed her on the cheek, showed a neat fan of bills.

"Not too bad, Little Bit. Wouldn't you agree?"

Winter collapsed on the bed next to her, bemusedly studied the television, apparently confused by so much light and movement. She closed her eyes, held her hand and veed fingers out for the joint. She took it and inhaled. Wolf went into the bathroom, closed the door and ran sink water.

"All of it sold?"

Winter held the smoke as she nodded and let it out in a slow tumbling breath.

"Yeah, most of it."

"Most? What's left?"

"You need to ask Daddy about that. It was his call."

Wolf came out with a damp hand towel pressed against the pink skin of his face. He drew it down so that it covered his beard and mouth like a half-realized disguise.

"Everything copasetic here?"

Rain shrugged, concentrated on the television. *Jeopardy* was on.

"What's this? Little Bit seems like she's not too happy with us. What do you think, Mama?"

Winter coughed, waved a bank of lung smoke away, didn't answer. Wolf circled around and sat on the edge of the mattress. The springs took his weight. His hand touched her under her chin and lifted up so that she had to look at him. Her eyes were like something that had been pulled out from deep inside, something that could cut.

"That's a look that some men might answer with a hand."

"You should try it and see what happens," she told him.

"What's at you, girl?"

"I don't like having to wait around here all day for you two. There's nothing in this town I forgot the last time we were here. I thought we were going to find a place to settle. I thought we had. Until you ruined it."

"Ruined it? Nothing's ruined. We're going back, don't you worry. That place is ours, understand? That place belongs to those who need it. That's what the world is for. To receive those that have the willingness to seize. It sure as hell doesn't have anything to do with property deeds."

"No, it's ruined. It was ruined as soon as we stole from that man."

"Goddamn, you're hardheaded."

He hooked an arm around her waist and drew him to her. She did not yield but did not fight him either.

"What is it that you've still got?"

"What do you mean?"

"Winter said you still had something to sell."

He straightened, but left his hand resting on her leg.

"Yeah, we didn't sell everything. It's best to keep it, I think. For now, at least. Until we know how things might work out."

"Oh Jesus."

"Calm down. It's necessary right now."

"Where is it?"

He leaned forward, patted the small of his back.

"Do you want to see it?"

She said that she did, unsure what compelled the desire. He removed the pistol and dropped the magazine. She had never held a gun before, and she was surprised by its weight despite the cleanliness of its lines. Her finger wanted to curl close to the trigger but she refused the impulse. Strange how a thing could seem to have a way of talking to you. She handed it back. He stood up and shoved it to the bottom of his rucksack, drew the cord tight and strapped the flaps back in place.

They checked out of the motel the next morning. Wolf, feeling expansive, left a five-dollar bill on the nightstand for the maid. They got a ride a bit of the way down the road before being let out in the parking lot of a Bass Pro Shop superstore, the gargantuan striking cartoon fish affixed to the side. Wolf wheeled a shopping cart down the aisles, piled in camping gear on top of three enormous dry bags he meant to tote it all in. Outside, they stripped the electric lanterns, batteries, tarps, camp stools, folding shovels, and other small effects from the hard plastic packaging and stuffed everything into the dry bags that filled into tight burdens. Wolf hefted two on his shoulders while Winter got the third. Rain was tasked with carrying the fishing rods. She held them canted at her shoulder so that they danced like aerials as she walked. When they stood at the interstate access ramp with their thumbs in the air they looked like a family embarking on deranged holiday. The passing motorists remained wary and after half an hour they had to set off walking.

"Shit, it's hot!" Wolf said half a mile down the road. He let the bags slide from his shoulders and thud to the barren shoulder just off the emergency lane.

"Well, it is summer," Rain said, sticking her thumb and a bit of thigh out at a semi. It honked once but didn't slow.

"Nobody likes a smartass, girl."

It was twilight before they caught a pickup ride as far as the Sevierville exit. They thanked the driver and cut for the woods and pressed through the clouds of mosquitoes, the freshets of poison ivy. The shade and the evening offered little to cool them and they drank bottles of water and Gatorade until they had nothing left. None mentioned the need for building a fire.

Painful welts woke them in the predawn before the heat had its chance. Wolf tossed the thin covers of his summer sleeping bag and cursed a creative arrangement of obscenities as he scratched blood to the surface of his skin, blood that could be seen inking his neck and arms even in that sunless hour. Winter too was covered with inflamed skin, though she tried to ignore it to keep from opening sores that might later infect. Only Rain remained unblemished.

"Must not be allergic," she observed, to Wolf's renewed curses.

By ten in the morning it was ninety degrees and the air throbbed with cicada screams. Three times they'd walked the extreme edge of the highway shoulder to scout for signs of any creek that might offer water to pass through the emergency water filter they had bought at the camping outlet. Each time they had found clay banks and pine straw, the earth gone dry and brutal.

"You all shouldn't have drunk all that fucking water last night," Wolf said through his teeth.

They came to an exit that had a country highway passing and a Marathon gas station in sight. Wolf counted out ten singles and told Rain to get them some bottled water while he and Winter rested in the shade. She grounded her pack and left it with them, willing to walk on alone for the simple reward of being left to her own company.

When she returned with a half a dozen bottles she found Wolf and Winter sprawled beneath a pine tree like a pair of casualties. Each took one of the bottles and drank and made no further effort to stir.

"We need to get on," Rain said. "It'll get worse out here before it gets any better."

They came to a kind of slow and demoted form of life, wrestled their rucks on and staggered toward the familiar highway march. A turkey vulture flapped up enormously.

Night had found them once more by the time they reached the homeplace. The evening had made a kaleidoscope of the woodland, a flex work of shadow that manifest the thousand variances of time and light, an invitation into a reality lifted inversely from what could be recognized and named. Wolf insisted that he knew the way, and he plunged on through the eerie country. The women, though they knew him lost, followed without argument.

The moon finally gave the abandoned house to them. The world lay bare before its rise above the tree line. The triangular peak of the pitched roof stood against the soft whiskers of tree limbs. Wolf hurried on then, did not wait to see if his wives could breast the brush that separated them from their rest.

It wasn't a smell so much as the air itself becoming hostile. The fumes made bitter work of their lungs until they first coughed then gagged and staggered back from the ruined house. Wolf tried to enter from the opposite side but was immediately driven back, the entire structure sealed behind its impossible chemical barrier. He flung his gear down and tried once more, held his breath and tried to take sips of air, but he soon began to retch and lose whatever he had on his stomach. He came back smelling of his own sourness.

"That sonofabitch poisoned it," he spat.

Winter tried to place her hand on his back to quiet him, but he cast her back, as if he would damage under empathic touch. He sat alone bent over the humped shapes of his discarded backpacks, a man paying tribute there to his own sorrows before he would see what new ones might be lying in wait for him.

"Come on," he said after a long while. "I think I remember seeing a clearing back here somewhere."

THEY CONTINUED east the next morning. Wolf had stopped speaking altogether, refusing conversation even when one of the wives would question him directly. Once back to the interstate he didn't bother trying to flag down a ride, striding on with the grim regular pace of someone destined. It was midday before he deviated from the road shoulder, cut for the same path they'd taken weeks before.

Something freed in Rain. She knew immediately that he meant to lead them back to the forgotten village in the wilderness where he had nearly burned them all alive, and she knew too that nothing could ever lure her back there.

"Where are you taking us?" she called forward.

He did not pause or acknowledge her. He moved down through the shallow game trail, idly scratching his scabbed neck.

"I asked you a question, motherfucker."

He slowed, put his head over his shoulder, one passionless eye locked on her.

"You do what I tell you to do, girl. That's how it's always been. And it's going to be how it stays. Don't think anything changes just because you want it to."

She braced her hand to a tree, as if it could hold her against his words.

"I'm not going back to that place, Wolf. I'm not."

She looked to Winter for support, but she would not meet her gaze. When she glanced back to Wolf she saw that he had made the pistol appear his hand, as if by some dark art.

"Get your ass up here," he said.

She obeyed. He motioned her farther ahead with a casual toss of the gun barrel. She noted how natural it seemed in his hand, as if a simple extension of him rather than a wrought prosthetic. His footsteps behind her took on a new and fearful tone. Each crunch of pine straw matched the jumping beats of her blood.

The descent toward the river was made along a stony ledge that approached the sound of running water long before they caught sight of the white boulder rush of rapids. When finally they could see the river bend they were close enough that they could feel the change in the air as well, the cool elemental brush of so much water draining from the high country.

"We're crossing here," he told her. "You go on ahead."

She nodded, tugged up tight on her ruck straps so that the pack rode as high across her shoulders as she could make it. The entry was sandy and the water cold, but the shoal soon ended and by the time the water was as high as her knees it was all slick ledge and potholes. This was no true ford. It was where a mistake could catch you in the current and hold you under until you didn't exist anymore. Midway across she turned back to see that Wolf and Winter were struggling through the underwater rock traps. She quickened, made the opposite bank, grabbed hold to a branch of thick rhododendron, eased the straps from her shoulders and let the heavy pack splash into a ribbon of current.

Her body was strong and young and she trusted in her animal advantage, her ability to survive when that was all that mattered. She ran and ran. Told herself never to stop. His shouts could not slow her.

Part II

10

HIS FLOWER garden had failed. Never his strong suit, Stratton had turned a poor hand managing the beds along the front of the house; the summer drought had demanded he water, and he'd been distracted. Many of the blooms had blistered in the full sun. It made for a poor realty advertisement.

He drove out to the greenhouse and garden center and walked down the aisles spilling every variety of decorative shrub that might be bred. He knew nothing really, and the immensity of his ignorance forced itself on him in a dizziness amplified by the greenhouse's trapped heat. He tried reading the little hard plastic tags stabbed into the soil of each pot, but he couldn't grasp colors and arrangements. He stuck his hands in among the ferns, the caladiums. But it seemed a science beyond him. In the end, he decided on a copy of a magazine called *Garden and Gun* for a model of inspiration. That and a garden gnome.

When he got home he took a beer from the fridge and went around to the shaded side of the house where a hammock was stretched. He warily entered, aware of the tender balance needed to keep himself righted and his beer unspilled as he found equilibrium. He thumbed through the magazine, tried to pay close attention to what the experts were saying about the yard arrangements that were said to demonstrate true elegance and sophistication, what really set apart a mere amateur scratching in the dirt from meaningful floral architecture. Yet he found himself drawn to the articles about bourbon cocktails and a story about some writer with a dog dying of cancer that made him actually weep and wet the page with his tears. As if sensing this possible betrayal of loyalty to a warring species, Damn Cat appeared from the back of the house and leapt up gracefully into the hammock to install himself at Stratton's hipbone. He scratched the old cat behind the ears and sipped his beer until they both closed their eyes.

He woke to a disturbed sense of time. It was still light but in that confused moment of waking he had to turn hours inside his head to get an idea of whether it was morning or afternoon. Then he heard voices coming from around front and he remembered that some people were coming to see the house.

As he circled around to the porch he could see a bobbed-haired young woman in professional attire with a smile that looked like it could open a can.

"You must be Mister Bryant. It was our understanding you wouldn't be in," she said, weighing heavy at the conclusion of her sentence, as if she thought very little of some fool who would stick around and get in the way of her doing her job.

He took her hand and shook it, followed her gaze down to the empty beer can in his other hand. He self-consciously tucked it behind his back. The young couple had already mounted the porch steps and were putting their faces to the newly installed window panes, chancing a look inside.

"Sorry, I forgot someone was supposed to come and look at things. I'll get out of your hair. Everything's opened up anyhow."

"Thank you, Mister Bryant. I'm sure we can manage from here," she said, made it plain that she was done with him.

He went out to the car and got down the drive as fast as he reasonably could. His presence contaminated the place. No one would bear a stranger preceding them into a house they intended for themselves, for the good life they planned to make there. People desired innocence, the perfect innocence that affirmed events turned out well in the end, even if it sometimes appeared that they wouldn't. There was a certain pattern that guided someone toward happiness. The shape of another man's disappointed hope could only be a poison to this innocence, to this faith in happiness, and people are never as unforgiving as when their best lies are held up to the light.

The driving helped free him. It was good to be on the road without significant destination and he wanted to stay with this aimlessness as long as the good feeling remained. He loosened his fingers on the steering wheel and bumped down the road until he came to an old white brick Shell station with a Budweiser light on in the window, a BBQ grill off to the side leaking a fragrant blue cloud of meat smoke.

Inside, an ancient man wearing a smock worked behind a glass case warmed by a heat lamp. His hands appeared orange by the steady glow. When Stratton asked what was good, the man said it was all better than anybody ever had the right to expect or deserve and he'd know the state of his own satisfaction only after he'd hazarded a blind decision. He then pointed at two papered squares.

"Those are the freshest, though," he said and smiled.

Stratton told him to box those and ring everything up. He took his pork sandwich and a bottle of Coke around to the side where a picnic table was set out beneath a pecan tree. He began to eat, his mind going vague in the simple occupation of taking on this basic need of keeping the body running with the self-care of food and drink. How ancient this was, to come and sit beneath the shade of an old tree and let a place inhabit you, to find a way to listen to that secret music out beyond the normal reach of sound.

He thought of Texas when he was a boy. Not a common thing for him much anymore. Not too much to lure him in terms of nostalgia. So many of those memories had been the ammunition he carried into his adulthood, a reason to escape the claustrophobia of his family and what they had expected of him, which was entirely too little as far as he was concerned. To follow in his father's footsteps, to take to the oil fields as he had. To make money. To stand in his forebears' land and make a living by the labor of his hands. But that life had never held much prospect for him. He had seen the price it demanded of a man, especially an intelligent man, and he refused to give away what even as a child he recognized as a vital part of his character. Namely, the ability to tune into the subtle currents of the world, to detect the occasional windows of real beauty. And though he had not recalled it in many years he now remembered one of those moments when he had seen what a crack in time was capable of revealing.

He had been riding in the truck alongside his father and a winter storm was coming in, a line of darkness pinned just above the horizon, a clouded vein of sunset slight and contracted. It was late in December just a few days shy of Christmas, but his father was on call for any parts that might be needed if one of the pump jacks broke down and needed repairs. As they had been sitting down to an early supper the call had come in as it so often did on those wind-blasted evenings and Stratton had asked if he could come along. Out in the fields with the edge of the world right there Stratton became afraid, as if he could sense how suddenly the earth could turn its eye of disfavor on a single man caught beneath a naked sky. His father told him to stay in the truck, that he wouldn't be but a minute. He did what he was told though his father remained gone much longer than that. To divert himself from his sudden and strange worry, Stratton began to count the nodding repetition of the pump jacks seesawing above the basin until it was as if he had entered a dream and the motion of everything slowed, aligned in an inexplicable harmony that suited not only the sublime picture of the landscape but the mechanical lapsing of the minutes as well, as if the enormity of the desert depended on that rhythm as physical antistrophe to explain its habitual stillness. It was simply lovely, this thing that was symbolic of what he hated most about Texas. It captured him, the graceful tilt of the machines, as soft and beautiful as the eyes of the blind.

He had fallen in love with music some years later when he had sat down to his first piano lesson and observed the similar measured pace of the metronome. The sway of sound and the lack of sound taught him to trust the patience earned between one note and the next as it built into something larger than individual strokes, a message surpassing what could be written down and recorded. Instead, it became the silent waiting that conveyed the truth of any meaningful piece of music. All of his life since had taught him to excel at waiting.

Once he'd finished his sandwich and sat for a while he was sure the real estate agent would have cleared out. He drove on back and saw she'd left her business card tucked under an empty pot on the front porch railing. He stuck it in his shirt pocket, noted that it was about as useful as any other piece of scrap. He stayed there on the porch as the evening light invaded, watched the yard take on its elongation. Hard to show someone what it meant to be witness to this gradual and needed change. Harder still to assign it negotiable value.

He heard the scratch of footsteps at the far end of the drive. A tentative yet determined approach. He leaned back against the front door to let the house's natural lines engulf him in the deep shade and bulk. A pause. A long pause before the sound came on and resolved into a human figure.

"I can see you up there watching me," a thin but not small voice challenged.

He moved his head, though he was unsure the subtlety of the gesture could be seen at that distance.

"I imagine I have every right to, considering it's my yard you're standing in."

Rain ventured another few steps until she came slowly up and sat on the edge of the porch, posed in profile, as if arranged there for a portrait.

"I wanted to apologize for . . . for what they did to your home. They had no right to."

Stratton let his arms stay crossed, said nothing for much of a minute.

"Where these friends of yours gone to now? They left you?"

Her head shook in the dark space.

"No, they didn't leave me."

"They coming back to collect you, then?"

Again, that slow and deliberate movement of her head, as if she were just getting accustomed to the idea of saying No.

"You look like you've come a pretty good way," Stratton commented. "I bet you wouldn't say no to a cold beer, especially since I could be said to owe you one. Though that little trick of leaving your empty in the mailbox might be enough to cancel out that debt."

She said, "You don't owe me anything."

"Well, we'll split the difference and pretend I do."

He opened the door and snapped on the front hall light. She followed him into the kitchen and sat down at the table, spread her hands out on the surface to register every detail of its temperature and texture. He set a can of beer on a coaster in front of her. He motioned her to drink when she saw that he intended nothing for himself.

"Don't worry," he told her. "I stay plenty hydrated."

She took the can in both hands and emptied a third of it in a single pull. The relief hit her so that she couldn't hold back a grin, though she tried to hide behind a flip of her hair. She wiped the foam from the can's lid and drank again.

"How long have you been out there? On the road I mean."

Her hand rose to the side of her face, tucked back a vine of knotted hair. A shy but collected gesture. Aware of the quietness of the setting and the desire to behave well.

"A while. Half a year now, I guess."

"How many nights you managed under a solid roof?"

She smiled, said, "Not many. How many nights you managed without a beer in your hand?"

He laughed, but didn't say anything.

"Where are you going to move?" she asked.

"Move?"

"I saw the For Sale sign out at the road."

"Yeah, I don't guess I'm sure yet. Maybe I need the money in my hand to make me decide."

"Is that what it takes? Money?"

"Maybe. What about you? What made you want to go out on the road?"

She shrugged, showed the palms of her hands.

"I'm still deciding, I guess."

"Well, there's nothing wrong with that."

"I couldn't help but notice your garden's not looking so great," she said once she had her voice again.

He glanced back toward the front door, as if he could see straight through the walls to the barren flower beds.

"I appreciate your attention to detail," he said. "I'm afraid I've noticed the same thing myself."

"What's that thing you've got sitting out there next to the steps?"

"That's Gordon Lightfoot."

"Gordon Lightfoot?"

"Yeah, Gordon the gnome. You like him? I thought he'd have more of a green thumb than me. Man's got to keep a bit of levity, don't you think?"

She had no opinion on this.

"I could help you get it fixed up," she said softly. "Could help you get the house all put together so you can sell it. If that's what you want."

"What's wrong with the way I've got the house?"

She glanced around, shrugged, as if that were refutation enough, and perhaps it was. Stratton thought about it a long while.

"If I said yes, if I was to be fool enough to think you didn't mean to rob me blind . . ."

"We could find a way to make it work."

Damn Cat slipped into the kitchen like the elegant twist of smoke that he was, meowed once at the stranger before wrapping himself around her ankles.

"He normally hates other people," Stratton said.

"That's all right," she said, scratched the tom's head. "Normally I do too."

11

STRATTON CLEARED out a bedroom at the back of the house and brought in a rolling cot, a box fan, a simple chest of drawers, and an old TV that only got a pair of public stations. Rain slept poorly the first night, hearing every tick and sway in the timbers of the old house.

She was up before he was and went out to tear the dead plants from their beds. They came up easily, as if relieved to quit the sham of their existence. She saw that the soil inside the raised beds was cheap and could be improved for the next batch, made some notes on a scrap piece of paper of what to buy later. She saw a good patch of ground along the side of the house that would gather midday light and knew that they should plant along there as well. Around back she found the outbuilding and inside it a spade and hoe.

The ground was stony and hard from the drought, so once she marked the dimensions of what she meant to dig it was largely slow work. Still, she warmed to the labor and her strong arms began to make discernable progress turning earth. By the time the sun was treetop tall she sweated freely.

"Looks like I hired somebody worth hiring," Stratton called down from the porch.

She smiled up at him. "I figured you wouldn't mind if I saw a way to improve the value."

"No, no, I don't mind that a bit. Why don't you take a break, though? I've got breakfast up here and I don't need any disability claims the first day I've got you."

She leaned the tool handles against the side of the house and followed him in.

Her belly went tight as soon as she smelled fried meat. She tried to recall how long since she'd had the taste on her tongue. It made her want to eat her hand.

"Here you go."

He flipped two sausage patties beside a yellow crown of soft scrambled eggs, a side of buttered toast, and handed her the plate and utensils. Coffee and juice too. An utter confusion of good things to consume. She tried to develop a method of approach to the food and drink to pretend this wasn't what she would have torn through a solid door to get to. How important it was, she understood, to have someone bring you a meal of delicious food. How much that mattered.

"Thank you," she said.

After breakfast he drove her out to the greenhouse and gave her free rein to buy whatever she thought would best suit the house. She appeared to know exactly what she had in mind, so he was content to follow at a distance. Every time she asked his opinion about one of the selections he waved the concern aside, told her that he trusted her better judgment.

Once they had filled two buggies with soil and flowers they checked out, loaded it all into the hatchback and drove home. He helped her set everything down and opened the house up so she could come and go as needed, explained that he had to drive out to the college campus for a couple of short meetings and run a few errands after that. He left her working in her newly turned field, this dreadlocked pioneering woman who seemed to have issued out of the ground itself.

THE CAMPUS was empty of students this time of the afternoon. Though there were summer classes in session, many had already run earlier during the day so that it was administrators and the few straggling faculty still on campus. He drove around the faculty lot twice in vain search of a shaded spot before parking in the midst of the scorched pavement, cracked his windows so that his CDs wouldn't melt, wondered again why the board of regents made war against trees.

His office was cool and windowless and held to the vague staleness of seasonal abandonment. The book spines of last semester's texts were warped out of square from having been dumped in a haphazard pile the last day of spring classes. Above that on a metal shelf were his own doubled row of books on music theory, composers, technique. Even though he rarely had time to read at his desk it was a particular comfort to be able to pluck one from the whole and pinch the cover back, scan a line or two, have those authors' voices rinse over him like a better version of his own. Occasionally one of his students stopping by during office hours would notice his small library and ask something out of genuine curiosity about one of the books, something not directly pertaining to grade percentage. Not often, but sometimes.

He shuttled through some neglected work emails, discarding most, before he stuffed a few relevant papers into his briefcase and went down to the conference room. He nodded at a few weary but friendly faces and sat down next to Josh Callum. After taking the better part of an hour to populate and schedule follow-up subcommittees designed to further lay out issues of curriculum and training, Josh pulled him aside, asked if he had time and the inclination for a cold beer.

"Sorry, I've got to get back to the house. For a man not working I'm staying busy as all hell these days."

Josh shook his head, made a big show of disbelief.

"They can go ahead and plant me in the ground. To say I was there when Stratton Bryant refused an afternoon drinking invitation. I guess you'll tell me you won't go down to Douglas Lake this weekend and help me haul some crappie into the boat either, will you?"

"Might be able to make that happen. You headed out early Saturday?"

"The earth hasn't stopped turning, so I see no reason to change my corresponding plans."

"All right. I'll give you a holler."

"You do that."

He started across the lot for his car, paused.

"Hey, you mind if I bring somebody along?"

"Somebody?"

"Yeah. My niece. My sister's kid. She's come out to visit from Texas. Helping me get the house ready."

"More the merrier, as far as I'm concerned. As long as she comes with a stocked beer cooler."

STRATTON AND Rain drove in the cool morning dark down to the Indian Creek boat dock, ate donuts and drank black coffee, rubbed sleep from their eyes. A pair of rods jostled atop some rain gear and what they had packed for lunch. In the cooler was a case of Coors Light and three strawberry cocktails in big cartooned cans. He had promised her a big time.

Josh met them down at the dock already loaded up and aboard the old Bayliner with the outboard softly purring. By the first band of dawn they had slipped their mooring and motored up the inlet, their wake a gentle cut in the calm water. Rain shrugged inside the fleece jacket Stratton had leant her, the cold shooting through as they gained gradual speed and the tight throat of the shoreline dropped away. She'd never been out on a fishing boat before and though she could see the faint outlines of second homes above the banks she felt as strange as if she'd landed on a new planet and traversed this smooth expanse before any other soul. Stratton had told her the lake was artificial, created in the 1940s when the Tennessee Valley Authority had dammed up the French Broad River for the sake of electricity and downstream flood control, but that did not dissuade her from admiring what surrounded her. She remembered once when Wolf had said the dams of the upper South had destroyed the essential wildness, the sufficient danger of the Tennessee landscape. That what we knew of the Tennessee River was a pale counterfeit of the unquiet creature it had once been. He would have wanted her to feel guilty for this present sense of excitement. Justly incriminated. But she could summon no disfavor about what had been made when the river had flooded this country, made something ancient into something new. This lake was its own kind of meaning, revived and altogether different than what had come before.

They slowed as they crossed beneath the interstate bridge, wake water slapping at the concrete stanchions. The bow rose once more as they throttled up and swung in a broad arc toward the eastern shore just short of where they could see bottom. Stratton handed her one of the rods and talked to her about how to fish the artificial lure while Callum dropped anchor. She paid scant attention, had no desire to catch anything. The water alone had been what had compelled her to come here. Still, she realized the need to act the part and she cast out, let the lure sink, and began the slow cranking retrieval. Too slow, she realized, but the men were otherwise occupied in rigging out their rods and wouldn't bother her. It contented her to be invisible there beside them.

Within half an hour other craft began to appear on the lake. Other fishermen still at this time of the morning, most waving good morning as they passed, though Callum told them to expect to see rednecks out for the sake of churning water from loud outboards as the day wore on. They would have to move into the corners of the lake then, find the narrow places and shoal water, nudge in where others couldn't follow.

"There's always a little extra room out there," Josh told her. "Always just space enough for solitude."

She liked listening to him talk, his easy drawl. She asked where he had grown up.

"Just over in Johnson City," he told her.

She started to say that she was from just down the road from there over in Elizabethton when she remembered Stratton had told her to say nothing about that, to keep to the deception of being his Texas kin. It made sense, she supposed, to not give away any more than she had to, but it bothered her too that she had to hold so much back, to keep a part of herself chambered deep inside so as not to spoil the part she was playing.

"Sounds like they must raise philosophers over in Johnson City then," she said. "All this deep talk about fishing and solitude."

He smiled over his shoulder at her, didn't mind that she had poked fun.

"Naw. I'm just a hillbilly that went off to school and learned to talk good. Your uncle here is the philosopher. Better be careful or some of it might rub off on you."

His rod bent briefly, but by the time he had set his hook the line turned slack.

"A hair too slow, I guess."

"Must be all that talking," Stratton offered. "Running off the fish."

"Naw. They like it when I sing to them so pretty."

Rain laughed, didn't make an effort to hide it.

"Look at her making fun of us old farts out here managing to neither catch fish nor tell good lies. I'm not sure I can abide a hostile audience, Stratton. We might be destined to maroon your niece here if this keeps up."

"Might be," Stratton agreed, cast once more.

"I'm not laughing at what you're saying," she answered. "Just, you don't sound like I'd expect a college professor to talk is all. Him neither, but you especially."

Josh lifted an eyebrow: his signature mock injury.

"The road to sophistication, my dear, is flanked on all sides by disillusionment. Speaking of disillusionment, I do believe the hour is presentable for libations, which would disabuse any ideas of my propriety, I'm sure. You would mind passing me one of those cold beers not too much, I hope?"

She reached one out of the cooler and popped the top for him. He winked as he took it and sucked with great savor at the ripple of foam.

They fished on through midday and into the early afternoon, emptied the cooler of the beer and baloney sandwiches while adding a moderate number of fish to the tally. It was time to head ashore when the water skiers started crowding them out. Callum turned the boat around and cut for the dock, bow raised high and the water flat and hard. He tried talking over his shoulder to Rain, but his words were torn by the wind. He seemed not to mind that he went unheard.

Callum followed them back in his truck and stopped off at the house on his way home. He said he'd help clean the fish they'd landed, though Stratton suspected it was something else. Rain went in to shower and tidy up inside while the two men worked shoulder to shoulder over an old picnic table set out in the backyard.

"You mind telling me who she really is or are you planning on lying to me for the rest of the semester?" Callum asked, his knife working up the tough fish gut.

"That obvious?"

"Only about as obvious as a nine-pound sledge."

Stratton put down his filleting knife, rinsed the blood and foul smell from his hands with a bottle of tap water.

"She's just a girl who seemed like she needed help. I don't think it would cost me anything to give her that."

"You sure about that, bud? Cost can come in a bunch of different ways."

"I'm not fucking her if that's what you're implying."

"Not yet you're not. Pretty girl, even if it does look like she just turned up out of a pigpen. There's a certain atavistic appeal about her, though. I'll hand you that. You ever watched that show *Swamp People*? She'd be the queen of the swamp people."

"I've got no use for your sex fantasies."

"Boy, I do though."

"Hand me that fish and shut up, will you?"

There was no way he could tell Josh the embarrassing entirety of it. That she was party to a group who had trespassed and stolen from him, who was as much an enigma to him now as when she first appeared stranded on the side of the highway. If he thought about it too hard he was liable to oust her himself, but no, he couldn't do that. Taken from a reasonable perspective, it was hard to disagree with the worst that could be thought of him for taking such interest in how the girl fared. And yet it seemed inevitable that she was now living there with him under the shoddy cover story he'd crafted. As if they had been destined to share the home for some reason and the problem of gossip held little sting considering how important it was to solve the question of his affinity for this seeming stranger.

Once they were finished and had put Stratton's share of fish in the freezer, they drank two beers from the fridge while they stood beside Callum's truck and talked the small talk of work concerns. It was dusk when finally they had exhausted the subject and themselves. Stratton told Callum to be good and Callum told Stratton to be bad and then he struck the truck engine to life and was out the driveway and down the road, a short blast from his horn answered by cricket song.

It was quiet when Stratton stepped inside and the only lights on were in the back of the house. He went to the kitchen and splashed some water on his face, the long day and heat on him like old skin that needed to be shed.

"Hey, would you mind coming back here," Rain called to him.

His chest clenched, just a little. Strange that his body could still act like a body sometimes.

"Yeah, just give me a minute."

She was looking at some of Liza's pictures that were up in the bedroom across from hers. A lot of them were older, what Liza would have called her sentimental stage, though to him they were about as sentimental as a hatchet head.

"When did you take these?" she asked.

"They're not mine. My wife took these. Same as the ones out front. A long time ago. Just a little while after we were married, I guess. Doesn't seem like it's been that long, but it has."

"You haven't mentioned her."

"No, I haven't."

The silence took up space in the room with them.

"They're very good," she said after a time. "I've never seen pictures like these. The faces seem like they're saying something that matters."

"You haven't asked me what happened to her."

"I imagine you'll tell me when you're ready."

He smiled, let it sink in.

"She was killed last year. She was riding with some men she was photographing for a magazine. Some men protesting mountaintop removal in Kentucky. It was late and they were drunk. Still, she was the only one that died."

She said she was sorry. Of course, he told her not to be.

"I don't think these should be kept back here," she told him. "Seems like they're hidden, you know?"

"Well, we'll see. I'm having a man from a museum in Knoxville come for them, so it's all temporary anyhow. I'm headed to bed. Turn the light out down here when you're finished, okay?"

He went back out the hall and up the stairs, left her there in the small room alone.

12

HE REMEMBERED often what it had been like when he and Liza were new to one another. When they had the same idea of what mattered when it concerned The Big Questions. She had not been drinking as much then either. A fair amount, a few glasses with each supper, a nightcap of cognac, but nothing that most of their friends wouldn't have fit into their idea of a social and artistic couple on the way up. Besides, she was so much fun when she drank, such an effortless wit. And it didn't affect her the way it did so many of the other women he'd dated who would begin to titter and slough twenty IQ points as soon as they nosed the bubbles of their champagne. She didn't become sloe-eyed and derailed or complain that she was ready to go to bed early. Liza absolutely thrived on drink. She would talk with animation and a careless verve, attracting anyone who would listen to her latest passion. She also, against all expectation and advice, actually worked better when she had a drink in her hand. It was as if she were more herself with alcohol than without.

They met when he was a visiting lecturer of music theory at Georgia State in downtown Atlanta, having come east from Midland, Texas, which he liked to tell people was little more than oil booms, football, and tumbleweeds. He had come up in a second-rate high school and then gone to a second-rate university in the Midwest and then a second-rate graduate school in the Northeast, giving him all the credentials he needed for a good career in academia but without the deciding pedigree. It wasn't a matter of test scores or general aptitude. Instead, it was his inevitable attraction to the periphery that kept him out of the line of sight. He had decided long before that he was willing to pay the price of obscurity for being able to remain clear-eyed about what was going on around him, not to be deceived by too much empty praise and easy satisfaction.

Liza was still a graduate student when he asked her out for drinks after meeting her at an end-of-the-semester mixer, an invitation that wasn't strictly within the bounds of appropriate student-teacher relationships, though he wasn't in a tenure line job and she was in no danger of ever sitting in one of his introductory classes, so the risk was minimal for either of them. The evening of that first date she called him at the restaurant to let him know she would be running a half hour late but was on her way, and would he mind waiting a while for her yet? He managed to keep any trace of irritation out of his voice (or hoped he did, at least) and said that he'd be waiting for her in the bar. He ordered a second martini, resolved to nurse it until she arrived, however late that might ultimately prove to be. All he could think of, though, was that she hadn't bothered to apologize for being late, a behavior that struck him as odd if not directly insulting. He gulped without realizing it and quickly ordered a third drink before she could show up to see how many he'd had.

It didn't matter, of course. Liza blustered in, tossed a backpack and camera bag on the stool to the other side of her, folded her arms deeply over the bar and rapped her knuckles hard on the surface to get the bartender's attention. It struck Stratton as both vulgar and a little charming.

"I should have ordered you something," he said. "I didn't think to, I'm so sorry."

She smiled, missed his sarcasm, and touched a wing of dark hair at her temple.

"Not necessary. Drinks are on me tonight, Mister."

Her gin came in a tall glass of colliding ice. She raised it in a quick toast and drank.

"So, am I going to have to dig it out of you?"

"Dig what?"

"You've clearly got some good news."

She shrugged, laughed at the awkwardness of her wanting to tell this to him during what was supposed to be a real date. It wasn't the right time, she said. But she soon softened under his curiosity.

"Okay, it's still top secret, though. *If* I tell you. Got it?"

He leaned forward, warmed by his drinks and enticed by being taken into a young woman's conspiracy.

"I got a phone call from some people at something I applied to back in the winter. I won an artist-in-residence position at a small college in Kentucky. It's just for a year, but it's really prestigious."

He congratulated her, though he already realized this meant she would be moving soon. He smiled tightly, ordered another martini. She downed her tall gin and matched his drink order.

Fifteen minutes later they decided they had both lost their appetites and would rather just stay where they were in order to avoid the hassle of being reseated. When she excused herself to the restroom, he ordered a bottle of champagne to split at the bar, told the bartender to bring something appropriate for a celebration. Just as she was coming back to sit next to him the bartender had popped the cork and poured two golden coupes full. When they raised their glasses, they felt the fizz snap their skin.

Then she had leaned forward and kissed him, touched off all the joy and damage that would become part of them as long as they remained together.

That first night they took a cab to her apartment, guided each other up the iron stairs and down the long hall, hands against stomachs, chests. Fingers drunk on touch. The dimness of her half-lit room immunized them from any missteps or mental complications. No sentences, just broken imperatives without clear source or subject. The sex was fast and chemical and athletic, a persistent desire to discover the utmost physical limits in the opposite body. And then the bodies became something more, though still attached to their conflicting anatomies. They moved through to the back of what was human in them, fucked down to the base elements by that

old and true clash of skin and angled muscle, yielded what survived
in a storm of sound and scent and cum.

The rest of the summer confounded Stratton. Even as he re-
signed his teaching position and gave notice for his apartment
lease, he couldn't make sense of the frail logic behind what he was
doing. He had been infatuated before, but this was something different, dangerously so. He felt parts of himself disappearing when
he was with Liza, and the onset of this change was more distressing
because of the way it seemed to attract his notice but not his care.
He found that he liked the sensation of being attenuated. It was
entirely at odds with how he had made his professional life, which
he now realized was a counterfeit of invisibility. In fact it had been
a consciously crafted way of positioning himself, like the teller of a
difficult story, at the margins. He recognized the advantage there,
the power to have the defining perspective on what was going on
around him. But Liza enveloped him, covered him up, made anything other than being secondary impossible. He had stretched his
throat before her blade.

They moved to Kentucky together, still relative strangers. He
found work teaching a single night class at a community college
half an hour away in Lexington with the occasional high school
substitute gig on the side, earning a pittance but still contributing
what he could to their household, a disheveled apartment in an
old divided Victorian, capacious and charming but really a teeter-
ing ruin of a place just on the edge of the Berea campus. It didn't
bother him at all to struggle and scrimp like this. To be next to her
as she was having the kind of success she was confirmed his resolve
to come with her. Everywhere she went she shined and he liked
nothing better than to witness it.

In time there were exhibits and receptions, invitations to speak
that had them driving many long weekends of the semester, often
down dark mountain roads so similar to the one that would kill her
those years later. In the car they would listen to the CDs that pulled
them through the evening miles and talk about what they tried to
believe was the limitless potential of their future. Sometimes they
would grow restless in the empty hours and initiate some playful

interest—a lingering touch on the thigh, a hand cradling the nape of the neck—and it would become febrile. A furious and emphatic rush to find a rest stop or dark lot where they could get at one another, shucking clothing in a confusion so absolute that it would have been comic if not for the sheer desperation and need to join the center of the other person. They often rubbed each other raw.

That winter Liza began to develop a consistent insomnia. She tried to slip from the bed without waking Stratton, but he could always tell by the unnaturally quiet register of her held breath and the special stillness that she was readying herself to get up and roam the apartment. He would not be able to sleep himself when she wasn't beside him, but he never let her know that he had been wakened. He liked watching her too much. It was a pleasure to see her when she thought she was alone and unobserved. She would pore over her work, set the photographs she'd recently taken in a complicated arrangement on the living room floor, sit down with her legs crossed and her night gown stretched across her knees so that she looked triangular and fixed above her images, a reliable trigonometry of the here and now by which she could judge her shots.

He didn't notice it then, of course, because it had been so gradual and so a part of how they lived their lives, but she would only come back to bed once she had settled all of the work on her mind with a shot of bourbon, perhaps more. The liquor disappearing down her throat like it was a voice going back where it belonged.

The following spring there was a gathering of successful photographers in Toronto and Liza was invited to participate. The art department at Berea was ecstatic that they were attached to her and by proxy internationalizing themselves. So much so that they offered to extend her residency for another three years. She took them up on the offer without asking Stratton what he thought because there was nothing really worth discussing, she told him. He agreed, as he was expected to.

They flew in late at night in a late March snow and took a cab in the city to a hotel on Queen Street. The city was bright and cold and safe. They left their bags in the room after they stood at the window looking out at the lure of what was before them. They knew they could not sleep without first joining themselves to it.

The wind off Lake Ontario was enormous. It made glass storefronts shudder and flex. The trails of snow ran the length of sidewalks in long spirals of movement, unwinding like some endless problem of whitened shadow. Stratton pulled his coat collar across his face but was embarrassed when Liza said he looked like a serial villain.

They drank whiskey at a couple of bars, dipped in just long enough to forget the cold, looked at the city with the eyes of those strange to it, saw its complicated procession of attractions, grew sleepy to its novelty before bracing for the long way back to their hotel room where they warmed themselves in exhausted sleep, limbs knitted into one another.

That weekend was the show. Liza had already been through the gallery twice to scrutinize her installation, to make sure her pieces were exactly where she wanted them. She was often nervous before the opening of an exhibit, but this time seemed especially exacting. In the days leading up she didn't eat well. She complained of a stomach ache though she took nothing for it. When Stratton tried to get her to come tour the city with him she said that she was too busy, that she couldn't spare any time in her schedule. During the days she drank black coffee and smoked cigarettes. During the evening it was wine and gin cocktails, the proportion of gin growing taller with each successive pour.

He met her at the gallery the night of the exhibit and immediately realized she was drunk. Yet she seemed the more possessed for it, as if the pressure of intoxication caused her to reach deeper into her reserve of poise. He tried to get her a cup of coffee, but she was politely dismissive of his concern, told him to get a glass of champagne and try not to ruin an important evening for her. He felt as though he were waiting for a whirlwind to tear the night in two.

He circulated at a distance, afraid that if he was too close to her he might do something that would make her self-conscious, something that would cause her to give up the game of sobriety she was playing. He tried to direct his attention to the other photographs, to listen to the ambient small talk through the half-lit gallery, but he could hear her voice rise unnaturally high when she spoke to someone about her work—the sound of a valve under too much pressure. He strayed out to the balcony for a cigarette.

There were only a few others willing to brave the outdoor cold. One was a man with thinning gray hair, wearing a tan overcoat and fashionable blue jeans. He stood at the edge of the balcony, staring at the city's lights and smoking. He appeared to be alone. Stratton realized from the exhibit brochure that it was one of the other photographers showing his work inside, Emmett Paul.

Stratton introduced himself, told Emmett Paul about his being there with Liza.

"Ah, good to meet you. Hell of a talent, that one," Paul said. "Easy on the eyes, too. You should hold on there, friend."

Stratton said that he intended to.

"It's good to see that she's made it up here. Good to see that I'm not the only wayfaring stranger that's being considered worthwhile. It's funny, you know. I've been doing this for nearly four decades and I always feel like they expect me to break protocol at any moment. Like I might ask one to yank my finger before I rip a catastrophic fart. All these art types that are supposed to separate quality from commercialism, they wouldn't recognize a serious picture if it bit them on the scrotum."

Paul finished his cigarette, stubbed it against the cement, said, "Shit, I'm philosophizing. My balls have shrunk to the size of concord grapes. Let's get out of this goddamn cold."

Stratton followed Paul in and walked with him a while, looking at his pictures when one of the other attendees would wander over to compliment his photography. It was all a daze, this movement of voices that spoke for their own benefit.

"Ah, here's the star of the evening herself," Paul announced. And, as if on cue, Liza was there, enclosed in Paul's professional embrace, though as far as Stratton knew this was the first time they had met. He trailed after them, not troubling to pay close attention to what they were saying, only nodding his attentiveness when Paul made some special effort to include him in the conversation. He swapped his empty champagne glass for a full one carried on a black tray by a woman in a tuxedo.

They escaped to a bar sometime later, just a few doors down from the gallery. The other people who were drinking there looked as crafted as their drinks. Paul said the first round was on him. As soon as Liza downed the Goldschlager and gave it back onto his lap he realized that his words had been more prophetic than intended. As he blotted the golden flakes with a cocktail napkin, he commented, "I've been anointed."

Liza tried to apologize before running off to the restroom, but Paul graciously refused to accept it, though he did call them a cab for their trip back to the hotel. Stratton thanked him for the kindness, but Paul dismissed it, said it wouldn't be a proper opening if some artist wasn't conflating body fluids and compositions. They parted without shaking hands at the sidewalk. As they pulled away, Paul turned on his heel and went back inside to finish his drink alone.

Stratton had little trouble getting her to the elevator, up to the room and undressed. He was becoming proficient at the routine. She sat up obediently for him, let him unzip and remove her dress over her head, then rolled over in her underwear and passed out half off the bed so that he had to carefully move her up, place a pillow under her head and draw the sheets and blanket over her chest. He sat up in the desk chair and tried watching TV for a while, the volume turned low. None of it could keep his attention, and the strangeness of the programming unsettled him. He fell asleep in the chair watching it.

ONCE THEY returned to Berea, Stratton found that it was as though the drunken episode in Toronto had never happened. All that was discussed in the art department was the fact that Liza had shown there, that the audience had been duly impressed by what she had exhibited. Another accent on her vitae. It was Stratton's first lesson in how success was guarded and maintained regardless of the individual price it demanded. Their invitations to faculty parties didn't diminish. Instead, they soared. He considered it a remarkably lucky stroke until Susan Cruz, a fiftyish landscape painter and part-time faculty member in the department, explained it to him. It was well if somewhat surreptitiously known that Susan was unhappily married to the college's dean of students, and she had a softness for Stratton's sympathy as well as his green eyes.

"Now you understand," she told him. "They're really hopelessly delighted with her now. Now that she's a perfect little monster."

He smiled, assigned her frankness to the drink. He had heard that Susan had a reputation for cattiness toward the younger female faculty, but this was the first time he'd seen it so boldly played out.

"I'm sorry?"

"No, you shouldn't be sorry. I imagine that you'd be rather delighted. She's managed something more important than luck or talent or vision. She's captured the most prized grail an artist can capture. She's figured out how to make people talk about her. Once you have that," she said, snapped her fingers. "You're the complete item. Your art is as much you as what you put down on canvas, what you put behind the frame. It's all framing of one kind or another. For some it's drugs, some it's drink, some it's sex . . ." She hesitated for a moment, darted a shrewd look before letting her mouth hollow into a wide bowl of a laugh. "But no, don't worry, I've heard nothing about that. Rest assured. It's just the drinking that's made the rounds. The Rose, I believe they call her."

"The Rose?"

"Yes. As in the Wild Irish."

After that Stratton had begun to notice a difference in the way they were received when Liza was invited to show her work or give one of her professional talks. She would be accommodated as frequently as before, but he detected a theatricality in how she was addressed, a certain pronounced deference to her that was aware of itself in the context of a larger narrative. It was no longer the simple matter of being a visiting artist. She had become a personality. A woman to be handled so that she performed up to expectations despite a defining flaw, this rather public pattern of drunken embarrassment.

Time began to take a toll on her ability to hide the effects as well as she had when she was younger. When the residency at Berea was

up Liza was forced to cast about for more temporary work and began
to accept more frequent freelance assignments from the national
magazines. This required her to travel frequently. Often, these trips
were made alone because Stratton's teaching schedule conflicted.
After returning from a job she would often sleep eighteen hours
out of the day, rising at midnight and drinking until dawn. For
much of it she was entirely solitary, surprised and somewhat irritated if she found him awake when she got out of bed. It became
clear that she preferred to walk the floors of her life without his
company.

One evening when he had been up late grading papers at the
kitchen table she came in, sat across from him with a bottle of gin
and watched him as she wrenched the bottle up by its neck, took a
steady pull.

"You want a chaser for that?" he asked.

She said nothing, watched him long enough that he went back
to the papers. His pen scratch was the only sound for a long time.
That and the lapping of the liquor against the side of the bottle.

"Why don't you ever play the piano anymore?" she asked, her
words like something unmoored in her throat.

"What?"

"The piano. You know? That fucking hunk of weight we've
hauled with us for the past three and a half years. It's an instrument, you know?"

He put down the pen, aligned the papers before setting them
aside. He took the bottle from her and tossed back a shot's worth.

"That's not an answer," she said. "Though it was a pretty good
try. I'll hand you that."

"I don't know what you want me to say."

"Just the truth. I like the sound of the truth once or twice a year."

Her face looked like it held some great pressure behind her eyes,
like something about to break.

"I have the feeling there's no such thing as a good answer right
now," he said.

She got up and went to the cabinet, pulled down a pair of coffee
cups. When she turned back to him her bathrobe had parted from

the loosened belt and he could see all of her there. He could only think how old she looked.

"Here you go, partner," she said, poured the cups full of gin, pushed one across to him. Her pose as the friendly barfly. The goodhearted tramp. "To your health."

The china clinked. He set the cup aside without drinking.

"So, I see you intend to let me drink alone. Afraid to let the knot loosen, I guess. Don't worry. I won't let it go to waste."

"I'm sure of it."

"All right. Be sure of it. I'm sure that makes you feel better. But stop deflecting. Answer the question." Her hand struck hard on the table as she yelled, "Why don't you play that fucking piano anymore? Why did you lie to me, huh?"

"You're not making sense. I haven't lied to you about anything."

"Of course you've lied. Everyone lies. But this one matters more than the others or are you that blind?"

"Blind?"

"Yes, blind," she said in a voice that seemed to come from deep within her, and only at a great effort. "You told me once that the piano saved you. Remember? When you were a boy and wanted to get away from your family. It was a passion. Something that allowed you to seek out who you were. Something that gave you purpose. Don't you see? That's what photographs are to me. My way of showing others what I make of the world. But you, poor thing. You have nothing at all."

Liza's closing note of pity touched off a rage in Stratton that he tried to quell with a long gulp from the china cup. He settled his voice before he spoke.

"And you, Liza," he said, aware of the heaviness on his tongue from speaking her name. "Have you not seen that everyone knows you are nothing more now than a drunk? A bit of wasted and spent talent."

Useless regret broke over him as soon as he had spoken.

13

HE SAT down at the piano and picked out a few notes, let them hang and quiver in the quiet of the old house. He could hear Rain digging around the side of the porch, her presence the past couple of weeks already something he'd begun to rely on.

When she came in at noon he set out a platter of tomato sandwiches cut into small triangles. They sat down together and he poured two glasses of sweet tea with mint.

"For a Texan, you've got the Tennessee lunch down cold," she said. "One thing my momma was always good for during the summer was vine-ripe tomatoes. That, Wonder Bread, and Duke's mayonnaise and you could keep a house full of rednecks happy all through July."

"I think that's the first thing I've ever heard you say about her, either good or bad."

"Don't worry. That's all the good I can come up with."

When he saw that she didn't mean to add anything further he simply ate, waited for her to finish before he took up the plates and carried them to the sink, stopped her before she went back out to the flower garden.

"I wanted to ask you something. About what you're planning now that the summer's almost done."

He could see her stance change, her posture stiffen.

"No, I'm not trying to kick you out," he told her. "I was just curious if you might be interested in taking some classes."

"Classes? You mean at college?"

"I believe that's what it's called, yeah."

"That costs money, doesn't it?"

"Not too much. Plus, I think we can advance whatever you might need. Anyhow, you're getting close to being done with the garden and what little bit there is to do to the house won't take very long. So, I thought it might be something you're interested in."

"What about the house? What if you're able to sell it?"

"Well, doesn't look like there's much of a threat of that at the moment. But if it happens, we'll figure it out when we need to. I'm not trying to force anything on you . . ."

"No, no. I was just surprised is all. Give me a little while to think it over?"

"Of course."

THEY RODE over to the college Tuesday of the following week. Rain had gone into town and bought a new blouse from the Dollar General with a little bit of money she'd earned from working on the house. She told Stratton she understood it was important to make a good impression on her teachers. He tried to explain that she wouldn't be meeting any teachers yet, that they were merely going over to get her tested for placement and then to register for fall classes, but this did not sway her.

He took her to the administration building's testing center and said he'd be in his office in the music building until she was done. Once he left, a short friendly woman with a hill country accent led her down the hall where she was seated at a desk with a computer. The woman asked her to surrender her cell phone and any calculators she might have on her person. She had neither. The woman smiled, punched a few keys on the keyboard to log in, and wished her luck.

The first test was multiple choice and involved reading short paragraphs and answering what the main ideas were, how they were supported. This gave her no problem at all since it was straightforward, and even if you did have a problem sifting something out you could go back and reread the words on the screen. Gradually, though, the questions got more pointed and technical. Grammar terms that she vaguely remembered from the tenth grade swam together. She eliminated the clearly incorrect answers and made guesses, hoped her percentages would play out.

Next was math—a clear disaster. She could feel her skin tighten at her hairline as she worked over the numbers on a shred of paper. Despite the air-conditioning, she soon sweat as much as she did turning ground. It was like trying to read a different language or play a game with rules somebody had forgotten to show her.

Once she had finished she was directed to return to the main office and wait for her results. A couple of other people were in line ahead of her, a woman with long yellow hair in her late forties and a tall, skinny teenager with pimples who had trouble looking anyone in the eye. The woman was talking softly on a cell phone despite the sign posted above her prohibiting it.

"Ma'am," the office secretary said. "Ma'am, I'm going to have to ask you to get off your phone, please."

The woman gave her a look sharp enough to cut, but she said she had to get off the phone to the person on the other end of the line and shoved the phone inside her purse. When her name was called to talk with one of the advisers she went back softly calling the secretary a goddamn bitch. Rain sat there staring at the wall for a while waiting for her own name to be spoken.

An elegantly dressed black woman came out and asked Rain to step back to her office. She said her name was Dawn and she had been assigned to get her registered for the proper classes.

"Is that your preferred name, honey, or do you go by something else?" she said as they sat down.

"I like to be called Rain."

"Is that a family name?"

"No, no it's just mine."

"Well, it suits you awful well. Now let's get you squared away."

She tapped a few keys on the keyboard in front of her. The computer tower whirred and faintly snapped.

"The good news is that you look fine for your English class, so we can go ahead and put you in a regular composition class. But, it does look like we might need to get you placed into a developmental section for General Mathematics."

"Developmental?"

"Uh huh. It's a class for students who will benefit from a little extra help. Do you have any special scheduling requirements or are we going to sign you up as a day student?"

"Just regular, I guess."

"All right, then. Let me get these put in and a couple of more general studies sections and we'll have you all set."

Ten minutes later she carried the printed schedule of classes over to the college bookstore, a tightly packed room with hardbound textbooks on the metal shelves and school tee shirts, shorts, and hoodies pinned to the wall, as if a few former students with excessive school spirit had been raptured directly from campus. She went down the first aisle trying to find the course tags that matched the numbers on her paper, rounded the endcap and saw the yellow-haired woman from the advising center.

"Hey, sweetie. You looking for the dummy math books too?"

"I'm sorry. What are you talking about?"

"I just saw you over there where that bitch told me to get off the phone, didn't I?"

"Yes. Yes, I was over there."

"They put me in the developmental section or some such bullshit. Dummy math is what my cousin said it really was."

They compared schedules and saw that they were in the same math course, as well as sociology.

"Here, I'll show you where the books are."

She said her name was Wendy Billins and that this was the second time she'd tried college after a two-decade hiatus. She wanted to get an associate's so she could become a paralegal, make a goddamn dollar that stuck, she said, though Rain wasn't exactly sure what she meant by that. Still, once she got used to her, she liked talking with Wendy, liked hearing things come out of her mouth that weren't weighed and measured for how they might settle with a stranger's idea of her. Instead, it was the fullness of her, of who she really was, delivered in a scattershot of speech.

Rain charged the books to her student ID account, the one that Stratton had told her to use, and Wendy asked if she'd smoke a cigarette with her while she waited for her cousin to come pick her up.

"She's about ten kinds of worthless, but I let Wes borrow the Corolla to go up to see his people in West Virginia, so she's all I've got to haul me at the moment."

"Who's Wes?"

She blew smoke, rolled her eyes.

"Just this old boy I know. Hey, you sure you don't want to bum one of these cigarettes?"

"No. Thank you, though."

Wendy told her about her family from around Sharps Chapel, how they'd been involved in the old coal miner wars farther north and been close with the Reece family, how her grandmother had sat in the same room as Florence Reece when she'd worked on her famous protest song, "Whose Side Are You On?" Rain didn't know that much about the history of her own people and couldn't have said much even if she had given her promise to Stratton to keep up the lie of their relation. But Wendy's stories interested her, made her see that there was more to where she'd come from than she'd credited.

While Wendy was telling about the Battle of Blair Mountain her phone buzzed in her bag. Without excusing herself, she put it to the side off her head and started talking, paced off a good distance so that while she couldn't hear the specifics, Rain could see that Wendy wasn't hearing good news.

"Sorry about that, sweetie. That bitch cousin of mine has gone off with some friends of hers and said she won't be able to come get me for another three hours. Blood apparently ain't thicker than bullshit."

"You could maybe get a ride with us," Rain told her. "I don't think my uncle would mind. We're about set to go anyhow."

"You think so? You think that would be okay?"

"Yeah, I'm sure. Come on."

They found Stratton in his office just closing down his computer and going through his rows of classical CDs, putting them in order, he said, though it appeared he was playing with them as much as anything, prying the plastic cases apart and studying the pictures inside. He said hello to Wendy and agreed it was no trouble at all to take her along home, especially as it was just the right side of Newport.

The CR-V's air-conditioner was slow to dispel the confined heat inside the vehicle, so they rolled the windows down to let the breeze in as they merged onto the highway.

"You might need to take her in, get some Freon in the system," Wendy counselled. "Wouldn't expect a car this new to have too many problems cooling down. I've got a friend runs the oil change place up by the interstate. He could cut you a deal."

"That right?"

"Yeah, you should. You just give them my name and he'll take care of you."

He let that sit for a minute.

"What you planning on studying, Wendy?"

"The law."

"Paralegal, huh?"

"That's right. I figure it's a hell of a thing to go through the world without sense of how those sonofabitches up in the court-house think. Plus, I understand it's pretty good money."

"I understand that too."

They drove along for a while with the sound of the road alone carrying them.

"Hey, Wendy. You mind a little music?" Stratton asked. "This afternoon sun is about to put me to sleep."

She said it was his car, so why should she have anything to say about the radio. He reached down and popped a ripped CD in the player, skipped up a few notches until Jason Isbell started singing about Decoration Day and spitting on his daddy's grave.

They took Wendy to some brick apartments not too far off the river. A scarred dirt lot and a basketball hoop hanging netless above a patch of cracked concrete. She got out, thanked them for the ride, and slapped her hand down on the roof before she turned and bounded up the wrought-iron stairs. Stratton wheeled around in the parking lot and pointed them toward the house, made the pavement beneath them blur with speed.

"Where'd you dig her up?" he asked.

"What?"

"What do you mean what? She's as clear a case of trouble as I've seen in a while."

Rain crossed her arms, leaned toward her window.

"I don't know what you're talking about. She's opinionated is all. Otherwise, I think she's perfectly nice. Plus, she has some interesting stories. About the history around here."

"Well, I don't doubt she's got some history to her."

There was that slight moment that she considered saying nothing before her voice snapped out, "You don't get to talk to me like I'm your child, you know. You don't get to do that."

He gripped the steering wheel until the tops of his hands whitened, said nothing more the rest of the way home.

SHE STAYED in bed late the next morning, turned her head on the pillow and listened for the midmorning birdsong even as he came down and tapped at the door to see if she was getting up. He stepped back through the house and made a lot of noise in the kitchen for a while before he went out front, started the Honda and drove off.

She put some of her clothes in the laundry and started them going before she found her work shorts and tank top, wrestled them on, and went out to check on the flower beds. At the side of the house she filled a plastic watering can from the hose and watered all that required it, then put everything away before she set out for the old homeplace.

This was the first daylight hour she'd gone to the site since moving into the main house with Stratton. Normally, she would have waited until he had been drinking too much and gone down to sleep in those dark alcoholic waters that wouldn't turn him loose until well into the next day. Then she would venture out into the starlit country and learn the paths that connected the two houses, trace the distance between so that it took hold of her in a way. But to see it in daylight was a deeper accomplishment. No trick of illusion could upset her sight when there was so much light and rambling air, so much of the full bloom of the high season. This was the only way to own the place, to have it fully comprehended. She came finally to the clearing and saw the ruins that were but a boneyard of their former shape under the church-white sky.

The place made her wild. That was why she came here, not to betray the kindness that Stratton had shown her, the life he was trying to make possible, but to restore something she felt being cut away with each new day she lived between walls. Wolf had once told her that the greatest ambition she could ever have would be to fill her eyes with beauty. How seductive that idea had been. To seek out beauty at the cost of safety. That, for her, was at the heart of wilderness, was what drove her through her most desperate hours in the hope that some better sense of what bound things together could be found, held, and known.

She circled around to the front stoop and though time had passed that should have dissipated the chemical fumes, she drew her tank top over her mouth and nose as a mask as she approached. The sun broke through the perforated roof and cast bright holes on the floor. She was careful not to tread across these, as if crossing them constituted an obscenity. With each further step loneliness built up inside her chest, one that touched on Wolf and Winter but which did not only involve them.

She found the photograph where she had placed it above the lintel of the bedroom door. She looked at it a while, saw the girl captured there with her gaze fixed beyond the frame. Rising to the tips of her toes, she took it to hand, lowered and hugged it to her chest and walked back out the front.

It was the next day before she and Stratton spoke again. He came out to look at the flowers with her, put away some paint roller extensions and brushes from the work he'd been doing inside. He asked her to come in a minute, that he had something he wanted to talk to her about. When she was done she washed up around the side of the house, let the water hose's arc splash over her shoulders and neck, then she cupped her hand, filled it, and drank.

She found him in the living room drinking something from a coffee mug. Maybe even coffee. He gestured for her to sit in the recliner across from him.

"I got you something I figured you might need," he said, pointed to a white box with a picture of a cell phone on the front. "It's not too fancy. Just a flip phone with a pay as you go plan from Wal-Mart. I'm sure it'll come in handy."

She held the box, read a few lines of description, set it back on the table.

"Thanks, Stratton, you didn't need to do that."

"Well, I kind of did. I need a way to get a hold of you and vice versa. There's something else too that I've been realizing, and that's about getting back and forth to school. That'll be tough to match up with my own schedule without you having to sit around and wait all day long for me to be done. Plus, now that the house is about done I thought you might be looking to pick up some part-time work to have a little bit of spending money."

"Stratton, you've done enough already. You don't need to worry about this."

He put his hand up to have her hear him out, reached for a folded-up piece of newspaper and handed it across. She saw that he'd highlighted a couple of ads for used trucks.

"Now neither one of these is too fancy from what I can tell, but they're both affordable and good working trucks, will be able to get you back and forth even if the weather is bad."

"Stratton, I can't . . ."

The hand came up once more.

"Look, the reason I found something cheap is because you can pay me back. I'm just advancing you the money. I've got it, so I might as well spend it. Plus, it'll make things easier on me as much as it will you. When it snows I can't get my car out of the driveway, so I've been needing a truck around here anyhow. You don't want me to starve during the next snowpocalypse, do you?"

She smiled, said, "No, I'd be ashamed to have that happen to you."

"Good. Well go ahead and get changed into some clean clothes. We need to get out of here pretty quick if we're going to make our appointments."

"What appointments?"

"The truck appointments. I told them we'd be by this afternoon. So, chop chop and all that happy horseshit."

She met him outside in five minutes, and they headed toward Sevierville, where both of the vehicles were advertised. The first address led them to a two-lane road that dipped down to a creek bottom where several trailers were gathered in a horseshoe. They saw the truck pulled under a mimosa tree with the hood up and a pair of skinny legs dangling out from the engine block. They parked and got out.

"You must be Loyal Turner," Stratton said to the ponytailed boy with gaged earlobes.

"Yessir, that'd be me," he answered, dropped down from whatever last-minute tinkering he'd been doing, shook both their hands.

Rain walked a complete circle around the truck while Stratton talked with the boy. She wasn't wild about the cracked windshield or the camouflage paint job.

"You two are welcomed to give it a spin. It's dependable as hell," Loyal Turner promised. "I'm just a bit short on cash at the moment. My brother's letting me camp out in his backyard until I can get back on my feet."

Stratton nodded vaguely, motioned for Rain to slide in behind the steering wheel. She did, the heat of the leather seat stinging her thighs.

"Now, this is kind of a classic you've got your hands on, ma'am. This is a 1980 Ford F-100. Last year they made this vehicle. Engine heavy as an airplane."

He was at her window now, smiling. She could see that he thought himself good looking, despite the dirt and stink. He wasn't entirely wrong.

"Where's the key?" she asked.

"Oh, sorry about that."

He fished out a wooden-handled screwdriver with a metal slot specially welded in.

"You're kidding me."

"Now don't worry about that. It works fine. I never had the key myself but this works just fine. Here, let me show you."

He leaned across her, jammed the end into the ignition fitting and twisted. The engine churned and caught.

"Rev her up. You'll see."

She angled her foot down. The truck made a sound like something afflicted.

"You sure about this, Loyal Turner?"

She didn't know why, but he seemed like the kind of man you should call by both names.

"She's fine. Go ahead and give her a whirl."

Rain eased down on the shift and the truck lurched and rolled forward as she took to the dirt drive and then circled back to the hardtop road. When she braked they lurched, the suspension rocking.

"Well, at least the brakes are good," Stratton observed.

She turned out left and brought the speed up, watched for oncoming traffic by leaning toward the center line to see around the foot-long windshield crack. Stratton tinkered with the radio knobs, rolled past static and AM talk. Tried the air and the heat. Hot air, but that was it.

"Well, he's priced it right."

"How much?" she asked.

"Seven hundred. But I'll bet he'll take six."

She pulled into the parking lot of an auto parts store, said she imagined it wouldn't be her last trip to such a place if they were to buy it. Stratton agreed. They drove back.

"What did you think?" Loyal Turner greeted them as he wiped some nameless gunk from between his hands with a torn rag. "She's the genuine thing."

"She's something, all right," Stratton said. "We need to think about it a day before we decide something, though."

"Well, I guess she'll still be here. Hope so. You want me to give you a call if somebody else makes an offer?"

Stratton looked at Rain, hesitated a moment before he said, "Yeah, let me write my number down for you." He went over to the Honda to get a piece of paper and a pen. Loyal Turner stood a bit closer to Rain while Stratton was occupied, though he tried to make it as casual as he could.

"You ever drove a truck before?" he asked.

"Once or twice. Any tips?"

"Naw, not really. Just keep it between the lines and you should be fine."

"I imagine I can handle that."

He stood there a further minute. She found she didn't mind his presence at all.

"You all aren't going to buy the truck, are you?"

"No," she said. "Probably not."

"Well, that's just the way it works. Still, if you ever want to talk or something, you've got my number. My brother's number, anyhow. I'll be around for a while. Might want to get a hamburger or something sometime and you'll think, now that Loyal Turner, I bet he'd be a good old boy to get a hamburger with."

His smile was like a pretty favor.

"I'll keep that in mind, Loyal Turner," she told him.

Stratton came back, handed over his phone number, said to take care. When they drove away Rain waved goodbye. Loyal Turner grinned like it earned him money.

HIS BROTHER was sitting at the table, turning pages in a *Shooter's Bible* and drinking a cup of coffee. The television across the room had a couple of sportscasters hollering at each other. Each time one of them scored a rhetorical victory their running point meter ticked up.

"What say, bud? You manage to unload the beast?"

Loyal went into the kitchen, opened the refrigerator door, looked inside for a minute, then closed it without taking anything out.

"Not a snowball's chance, I'm afraid. It was worth what I was able to set my eyes on, though."

"Lord God."

"What?" Loyal asked, though he was already smiling.

"If you're talking like that then it means there's a woman involved. Haven't you learned enough from that already? It ain't a accident you're so damn broke you're camping in big brother's back lot."

"Yeah, well. Life is supposed to be interesting. Anyhow, nothing might come of it. I did get her number so I can reach out and touch her if I take the notion though."

Under his breath his brother said, "Dumb little peckerhead."

Loyal sprawled out on the couch, tried to watch the TV, though he didn't give a damn for professional sports or the men in suits who made money yelling and giggling about them.

"How much money you pay for this Direct TV bullshit?" he asked.

"Plenty. Why? You wanting to kick in a little rent money to soothe your freeloading guilt?"

"Just curious."

"Well, curious, why don't you get a bit more curious about these help wanted ads," he said, tapped his finger at the loose sheet he'd set out. "Man's charity can only be extended so far before it injures the love between two brothers."

"Why is it you talk like the Bible whenever you get to riding my ass?"

"That's just the gospel of common sense you're hearing."

Just then the baby woke up and started fussing. His brother let his book fall shut and went back to the bedroom to fetch him. A minute later he came back with a ball of kicking arms and legs.

"That was a hell of a nap there, boy," his brother said.

The baby punched the air and farted.

"Stop cussing at the young'un. It's indecent."

"You're the authority on decency now? Well, that's good. Nothing wrong with a little strong language around the child. Teaches him the power of a well-tuned sentence. You still going to be able to look after him for me tonight?"

"Yeah, I told you I would."

"Don't sound so excited about it. Would have thought you'd have enjoyed a little bit of time to bond with your only nephew."

"No, you're right. I'm looking forward to it. We can talk about the fact he's still crawling around on his hands and knees and his daddy's already running around with another woman about to make him a half-brother."

"His mama and I had problems long before he ever came along. Besides, Georgia's a good girl. She's smart too. It's a nice change of pace to be around somebody like that."

Loyal let the insult go untouched.

"Here, hand me that boy."

His brother did so and the child immediately calmed.

"The hell you do that?"

"Just got the touch, I imagine. You better run off and make yourself presentable. Let old uncle take care of things from here on out."

His brother didn't offer a disagreement, went off to the back of the trailer to shower and shave.

It was just getting dark when his brother was leaving on his date. He stood there at the door, jangling his keys like they had the power to weigh the worth of his decision.

"Now don't go getting drunk on me. If anything happens, you're supposed to be the responsible one. You know that, don't you?"

"Shut the door. You're letting the mosquitoes in."

"Loyal, you hear me, don't you?"

"Yeah, I hear you. Time I don't have to though. Get on."

He propped his nephew up on one hip and took him to the window to watch his daddy get in his car and drive off.

"Look at that, boy. Your old man is just crazy for a woman, ain't he?"

The baby gurgled. His head nodded and shook under its enormous weight.

"Come here, fellow," Loyal said, steadied the child's neck with his hand. "Understand, it's not a criticism. It seems to be a problem that runs in the family. Man is born to certain weaknesses, I'm afraid."

The baby moaned. Loyal went to the fridge and stuck a bottle of formula in its bird mouth. The child suckled with profound contentment.

"See, that's exactly what I mean."

14

STRATTON HAD Rain drive the CR-V the first couple of weeks of school while he put the used Bronco through its paces. It had been a good buy and he'd immediately handed the cash across the hood to the old man who seemed bereaved at the sudden loss of the vehicle. A good sign, he'd decided.

"You make sure this young lady takes care of this," the old man had told him, unable to part without a note of reprimand.

Stratton's last class the next day ran late despite his trying to shave off a few minutes to get on the road before traffic got bad. He had a student who was worried about a grade. Said he'd tried his best and wanted to know if there was anything he could do to bump up his average through some extra credit. He was a Marine Corps vet, an older man who had insisted on being called his service nickname of "Monster," though Stratton had steadily refused, referring to him by his Christian name of Harold instead. It had caused tension throughout the semester.

"I'm just not getting it," Monster told him, tugged at the bill of his trucker's hat with its eagle, globe, and anchor insignia. It seemed that he had no other clothes than those which advertised his military history.

"I need you to be more specific than that."

"I can't be!" Monster said, swung his camouflage backpack out to his side like it was the object of his frustration. "I just try to sit down and read the text, but it doesn't stick. Can't you do something?"

He felt bad for the man. He could see that he did try, that he probably spent hours poring over the terms, trying to mash the reading inside his head the same way he packed a rucksack. Pushing hard against every shape of information until it slid into place.

"Here, let me see that test."

He went through the sheet, noted where the answers had been left blank. He wrote in a few page numbers in the text where the answers could be found.

"Take a look at my markings. You get back to me with some corrections by the beginning of next class, and we'll see what we can do, okay?"

"Okay, professor. Thank you."

"Don't worry about it. Beginning of next class, okay?"

"Yessir," Monster said, marched out.

Once he was able to get clear of the building he drove over to I-81 and opened the truck up, let the speedometer nudge and hover at eighty before he felt the slight tremor of strain coming up from the chassis. He eased it back to seventy-five to keep even with southbound traffic. A good performance for a twenty-year-old truck. Older even than the driver it was meant for.

He took it into Newport for a tune-up, handed the keys over and sat in the air-conditioned waiting room with its racks of *Field and Stream* and *Outdoor Life*, scorched coffee with powdered creamer, Dr. Phil on the TV. He tried reading the magazines but the volume was too loud. He couldn't get all that nasal pop psychology out of his head; he told the mechanic he was going to take a walk around the corner to the diner and to call his cell phone when the truck was ready.

The restaurant was a white clapboard building set just off the road called The Lunch House. A meat and three with a reputation for spicy fried chicken that wasn't to be refused if on special. Stratton thought he'd chance it, get a coffee and slice of coconut pie if nothing else. At the very least the place should provide the comfort of shade and quiet.

It was still early for supper so most of the counter was just short of empty. Save one seat. As soon as Stratton recognized who it was he nearly backed out.

"Now if it ain't the wayfaring stranger," Buck Wiley crowed as he swung around on his stool. "I've been worried that you've gone on and quit me."

"Hey, Buck."

No way to avoid him. He sat one stool over, pulled a plastic menu from the clamps of a condiment stand. Ordered coffee only. No reason to prolong bad company more than he needed to.

"You haven't gone teetotaler on me, I hope?" Wiley asked.

"No, I've just been busy. School's started back up, so I don't have the time I did."

Wiley sawed a piece of meatloaf with a butter knife, popped it in his mouth. He had a way of eating that made it seem like he was getting back at the food. Like it had wronged him somewhere along the line and had to pay.

"That's right. I forget you actually have to work part of the year. That's a hard row, sounds like."

Stratton had nothing to say to that.

"So I've been hearing a few things about you."

"Something tells me you're anxious to share."

Wiley smiled, motioned for a refill of his iced tea.

"Sugar, can you get me some more lemon too? Doctor told me I need to get extra citrus in my diet."

"Sure thing, Buck," the waitress said, went away to fetch what he'd asked for.

"You having issues with scurvy?" Stratton asked.

"What's that? Oh, the lemon. I get it. That's clever. That must be why you get to call yourself professor. Quite clever. But seriously, what is that I've heard about you having some young girl living at the house out there with you? If I didn't know you to be a distinguished citizen of Cocke County I'm afraid I'd have to arrive at a number of indecent conclusions."

Stratton picked up his coffee, sipped, briefly considered spitting it in Wiley's eye before he swallowed.

"You must be talking about my niece, Rain. My sister's kid."

"Sister, huh?"

"Yeah, that's right. Families. Most people have them."

"I've heard that. Damndest thing, ain't it?"

Stratton lifted his hand to get the waitress to bring him the check.

"Going so soon? You just sat down."

"Yeah, I've got to get the car from the mechanic. Plus, something's made my stomach go bad."

"I hate to hear that. I hope it's not too serious."

"The car or the stomach?"

Wiley grinned, made that expression that reminded Stratton so well of a close-range target. "Either one," he said. "Or both. Hope you don't ail too bad. We miss you down at the bar. Customers like you help me keep the lights on."

He paid and left, walked back and stood in the full sun until the Bronco was ready. The mechanic came around and told him it was good for another ten thousand miles. Stratton paid him with his debit card, took the receipt, folded it once and put it in the glove box. On the way home he stopped at the convenience store for a six pack of beer and a sleeve of beef jerky, passed a trio of men at an overpass waving Confederate battle flags. A little towheaded boy standing with them had a sign that said OBAMA, THE GREAT RENEGER. Stratton rolled down the window, gave them the finger and drove on.

He sat down on the porch steps and cracked open one of the beer cans and began to drink and eat the jerky. It was a pleasant kind of day, the first forecast of cool air coming in with the hard September sky. A good time of year when the heavy yield of late summer began to thin, to go to earth. The seasons didn't bother with what men made of their time. For that, at least, he was grateful.

EASTERDAY CAME out to gather Liza's photographs that weekend. He crunched up the drive in a pickup pulling a rented U-Haul trailer, turned around in the dirt flat and backed close to the front steps. Rain had gone off with some friends from school so it was only the two of them who were there to load. Stratton met him on the porch with a cup of coffee, then they walked up into the empti- ness of the trailer's storage. They talked a while before they finally went back into the house to pull out what he'd come to collect.

It was slow work. Stratton had wanted to leave everything on the walls for as long as he could. Easterday was in no rush either. Before he would take a picture down he would study it a long time and make a note of it in a small ledger then lower it into a packing box, pad it against damage.

"I didn't think there would be so many," Easterday said. "I've not seen a lot of these."

"She didn't show all of her work," Stratton told him. "She held back. Said it was better for her career."

Easterday nodded. They continued to take the pictures down. Morning was consumed by their work. By the middle of the day it had grown warm and clear. They took a simple lunch of turkey sandwiches and sat on the front steps in the sun. A period to gaze after the mounting wall of boxes pressed to the back of the trailer, to contemplate the arrangement of what was ready to be taken away.

"I've wondered something about her attitude toward her sub- jects," he said after a time. "Many people think Liza was cruel to the people in her photos. That she deprived them of dignity. But I've never been able to decide. Did she hate what she was showing the viewer? Was she ridiculing it?"

Stratton turned the coffee cup on its saucer, thought it felt like a kind of last supper sitting here with this man talking about his dead wife. When the words *dead wife* hit him it was as though the individ- ual letters had lost their symbolic authority, that they were only an arbitrary arrangement of shapes that could have easily spelled out *tree* or *stone*. He sipped the coffee once more.

"I don't know what she thought," he said after a time. "I hated some of her pictures. They came out of a place I couldn't ever un- derstand. You see how ugly she could make something. How is a man supposed to feel about that? Something that his wife creates."

Easterday was silent. Stratton had noticed when they'd met that he wore a wedding band. Stratton wondered what kind of wife he had, how he may have lived in a marriage of contentment or despair.

"I think, Mister Bryant, that she was saying something very dear. And I think she would be grateful to you for making sure others can hear her."

As Stratton walked him out to his vehicle, Easterday said that he would be regularly in contact with details about the installation and the premiere of the exhibit, likely sometime in late January or early February. He had to get the university publicity lined up, make sure the debut was as heralded as it merited. Stratton thanked him, shook his hand, and watched as he drove away. He stayed in the yard for a while, found ways to kill time for much of the afternoon in an effort to delay going back into the emptied house. When there was no way to avoid it he went in and gazed at the voided walls, at the spaces where people were supposed to be looking back at him. He lay his hand against the expressionless wall as though his hand might read what his eyes couldn't. But it was just skin against paint—two illusions indifferent to one another.

15

SHE DROVE out early Saturday morning to pick up Wendy and the other girls from school. It was the first day Stratton had turned the Bronco over to her, and she was a bit slow grinding through the gears before she got the particular feel for shifting. It wasn't the first time she'd handled a standard transmission, but it had been a while and she knew that finding the right touch required patience, an agreement between muscle and metal. A way to teach the hand how to hold the tool.

Wendy met her in front of her apartment building, already wearing a two-piece swimsuit with a long net covering that covered little.

"Hey, Sweet Pea. You ready to get your toes wet?"

"Sure thing. You need help with anything?"

"Naw, let's get on down the road and fetch those other chickadees."

She swung her canvas tote into the back and climbed up.

They were picking up two other girls from their math class, Harper and Stacey, a pair of nursing students who were already struggling to keep up with the coursework even though school had only been in session for two weeks. Still, they were both sweet, and smart in their own way. Good and easy company for an empty day.

Both girls were standing at the end of the gravel road where they lived together, their bags and a couple of soft pack coolers piled between them. Each wore a black bathing suit with neon stripes.

Harper looked better in hers. Stacey's had a baggy skirt attached. On their feet were dollar store flip-flops.

"Hidy, sexpots!" Wendy sang. "Haul your bones up here and let's get while the getting's good."

They wrestled themselves around the seats until they were in. Rain turned out for the Carolina state line, took things easy at first until the road tempted her. Then her foot fed the gas by steady increments until the engine roared and the women howled. She turned up the radio so that they could listen to some shitkicker tunes tumbling half broken by static out of Knoxville. It seemed not to matter what words were being sung, only that they came free and unmeasured, made a wild twist in the air around their heads.

It was still early when they came in to Hot Springs and had to slow for the town speed traps as they bounced across the railroad tracks, eased past the spa with its corny plyboard sign with a cartoon man and woman coiled together in a hot tub. Soon they were across the bridge and the other side of town, running up then down a long green grade. Wendy told Rain to slow down and pull off where the road dead-ended. They parked in an unmarked lot next to a closed coffee shop overlooking a small clean river with a sign that said Big Laurel.

"Come on, young'uns. Let's get in there before it gets crowded."

Wendy slung her bag and led them down a narrow dirt track paralleling the river. As it neared the water and leveled the path turned stony and wide. Its softer parts were cut up by boot and dog prints, but the tree branches were low and thick overhead, so that there was a sense of passing through a place of rarity, shaded and slowed.

As they rounded the first big corner they saw a blue heron fishing along the opposite bank. At the sound of their voices it lifted soundlessly and fled upstream. Rain watched it fly, registered a moment of quiet respect before going on along with the others.

They passed a couple of fly fishermen standing on shoals, the water lapping their waists. Their bright floating lines bellied out with the movement of current until the length had reached its extreme limit. Then they would recast with that smooth drawing up and away of the rod tip, the light flick and roll at the shoulder. Rain thought the men might be writing questions in the air with those fishing lines when they cast. Perhaps their answers were hidden beneath the surface of the water.

Wendy took them on a little farther until they saw a crown of dry rocks above a surge of white water. The river there sang a fullthroated song and spray was thrown high enough that Rain could feel it prick her shins as she went to the edge and looked down. Harper and Stacey appeared hesitant.

"You sure about this, Wendy?" Stacey asked, pinched her fingers across her bangs, a tic of hers. "That current looks awful strong."

"Sure thing, honey. I've done it a million times. You don't have nothing to worry about. Hey, Rain, can you get some of this suntan lotion on my back? I can't reach."

Wendy spread her towel and shed her covering, lay flat on her stomach. Rain spread the coconut-scented oil between her freckled shoulders and down to the backside of her waist. Harper and Stacey took turns rubbing thick cream into each other's pale backs, then edged down a stair step of smaller rocks that encircled the rapid until they could slip into the water where it calmed and pooled in a smooth black nest.

"Those girls are something else," Wendy said. "I'm pretty sure they'd shit their britches at the sight of their own shadows. Come on, girl, last one in is a skinny sonofabitch!"

Wendy sprang to her feet and leapt from the rock's edge into the boiling rapid, her head going under, then sleekly popping back up downstream. She whooped and hollered, splashed. Rain got up to pick her spot, then jumped.

The water was warm and Rain took to it immediately, made a slow swimmer's crawl against the eddy and let herself drift in the circling current. She could see her legs hanging limply beneath her in the sun-brazened stream and it felt good to kick and sense the strength there. She saw that Harper and Stacey had come into the river as far as their kneecaps, though they seemed in no hurry to go further.

"Come on, girls," she called.

They waved and smiled but stood where they were, rinsing their backs and shoulders with dripping handfuls of water. Rain held her breath and went under, let the current shuttle her downstream, floated without resistance to where it moved her. As her breath grew tight she came back to the surface and reached for the edge of a stone, anchored there while the river continued to tear down the length of her body. Wendy swam a few strokes until she could stand on a shoal. She reached back and wrung her ponytail.

"Lord, girl. My hair is going to be as matted up as yours by the time we get back to the house. How long you let yours go that way, get all dreaded up, I mean?"

"Three years, maybe," Rain told her. "You should try it. Make a proper hippie out of you."

"Shit, it'll take more than that, I think. Plus, I don't think old Wes would hold any truck with it. He likes to keep things traditional. Hey, I want to ask you a question."

"I'm listening."

She leaned in, made an obvious display of her secrecy.

"What do you think of them two gals?"

"What do you mean?"

"I mean, don't you think they seem awful attached to one another?"

Rain glanced over, saw Stacey and Harper drawn up on the dry rocks now, talking and sharing water from a Nalgene bottle.

"What, you mean lesbians?"

"It don't bother me. I was just curious is all. Them living together and not showing any inclination to menfolk. Not that I should hold that against them. Hell, that's just good sense, really."

Rain smiled, said, "What about this Wes I keep hearing about. Seems like you're pretty hung up on him."

"Shit. Wes is a door prize at a charity event. He's what happens when you realize you've got better memories than you do daydreams. Still, he's pretty good in his own way. By the by, he said he wants to go out this evening when we get back, go dancing. You got any pretty little boy you might want to bring along? It'll be a time."

"I don't know," Rain said. "Maybe."

"All right, maybe. Why don't we swim on back there and grab a couple of beers. Show them girls how they need to act."

She said that was a good idea, said it would be just about the right kind of wrong and raced her back to the rocks.

RAIN CALLED Loyal Turner's number from Wendy's apartment, talked to his brother, who said he'd go out to the yard and get him. In the time it took him to come to the phone she thought of hanging up three times.

"This is Loyal," he answered in a tight voice that sounded like it might be stretched by a smile. Must not get too many calls from women, she decided. Or maybe he did. She couldn't tell which would be worse.

She told him her name and that she'd thought it a good idea to give him a call after all, though not about the truck.

"No? And why's that? You calling to tell me about how you got a better deal somewhere else and I'm just sitting here without hamburger money?"

"No, not just that, though I did get a better deal. Not cheaper but better."

She waited for his easy laugh, but it was only silence on the other end.

She asked him then if he was free to come out that evening, to meet her and some friends at a dance hall just a bit shy of Gatlinburg. He asked her if she could hold on a minute and before she could answer he covered up the phone and said something she couldn't hear, likely talking to his brother.

"Yeah, I might be able to get down there and shake a leg," he told her. "What's the name of this fine establishment?"

"I think it's called The Doorstop. Is that right, Wendy?"

"Yeah, honey," she called from the living room, at work on her toenails with paint the color of war. "It's just off the highway. Big as Dallas."

"I know the place," Loyal Turner said. "When will I see you all down there?"

"Seven?"

"Seven it is."

"See you."

She flipped her phone shut, counted a few beats to settle herself before she went out to sit with Wendy.

"Looks like he's coming."

"Well, hot damn, girl. What you going to wear?"

"What I've got on my back."

"Jesus, honey. You might be pretty, but you ain't pretty enough to go out like that. Those jeans are okay, I guess, but I'll let you borrow a top. Some shoes too. You want to grab a shower?"

"I guess I could."

"I think that would be a good idea. There's plenty of soap, so knock yourself out. You can help yourself to one of those razors too. I'm going to give you something sleeveless and you don't want to go out looking like you're half monkey."

Wendy took her back to the apartment's single bathroom, pulled out a clean towel and made sure she was completely accessorized before leaving her to her hygiene. Rain closed the door and undressed, hung her jeans carefully across the towel rack and put everything else on the floor. She turned the shower on and stood beneath a spray so hot that it stung.

Wendy knocked on the door when the shower went off twenty minutes later, handed through the blouse and a pair of straw mules.

"These aren't too high in the heel," she said. "Don't want you to go out there and bust your ass."

Rain closed the door back and slipped the top over her head. It was a soft and pale pink with a light decoration of gold filament. She thought it pretty. In the mirror she saw a version of herself that appeared to be a form of normal. She put her hair over her shoulder, picked up her dirty clothes, and went out to the living room.

"Not bad, girl. Good thing you've got them twenty-year-old tits, 'cause I don't have a bra that'll fit you. Don't imagine any of the boys will be complaining, though."

"They usually don't," Rain said, and they both laughed.

Wendy went to her purse, picked out a couple of prescription bottles and tossed back a couple of pills. She saw Rain watching her.

"Don't worry, it's on the up and up."

Rain shook her head, said it was none of her business.

"Well, let's pretend it is, honey. It's just something I have to take sometimes or I can't crawl out of bed. I've been on them for about five years now. It ruins some things and helps others. Still, let's me hold a job, keep my ass in school, so that's something, ain't it?"

"I guess it is."

"All right then. Let's get on. My dancing shoes are starting to itch."

THEY MET Loyal Turner at The Doorstop after they'd gone by to get Wes and the Corolla so they would have two cars in case somebody decided they needed to quit the fun prematurely. Loyal was standing right at the front door next to the bouncer, dressed out in full duds—tight Levis and a blue pearl-button snap shirt that looked like it was half a size too large. He swung a black Stetson in his hand that was as big around as a basketball hoop.

"What do you think?" he asked, gave off that easy smile of his.

"That's a pretty good gitty-up, partner," Wendy commented. "Though you might have missed it a hair on your boots."

They all glanced down at his Timberland steel toes.

"Yeah, they're my brother's. I borrowed all this stuff from him. I asked him about cowboy boots but he said he was afraid I'd bust my ass trying to dance with the heel."

Rain saw Wendy give her a twisted grin, but she said nothing. Everyone introduced themselves, shook hands.

"How about we get something to drink and shake our asses," Wendy prompted, pulled her ID out for the bouncer. They fell in line and followed her in. When he asked to see Rain's license, Wendy cut in and said he didn't need to worry about it, that she was chaperoned well enough. After the exchange of a ten-dollar bill and a quick wink, he said that it appeared she was indeed and let her through without a problem.

The dance hall was wide and loud and strung with tiers of small white Christmas lights. On the wall were black-and-white portraits of old country music singers, many of them signed by people who had long been dead. At the far end a house band was on stage, but they were still tuning up. It seemed everybody was in a line at the bar or else standing in their own small circles of loud and laughing conversation waiting for when the air would rip loose with the sound of a slide guitar and a wailing voice.

Loyal Turner leaned into her shoulder.

"You gonna let me buy you a beer?"

"I thought you were short of hamburger money?"

"Well, I'll skip a couple of meals. Wait right here, will you?"

She said that she would. As soon as he'd gone, Wendy came up, laid a hand on her shoulder.

"You got yourself a pretty one, all right. Does he have a daddy?"

Wes shook his head, smiled tolerantly.

"You want a rum and coke?" he asked.

"Please and thank you," she answered, lit a brief kiss on his cheek.

"He's sweet," Rain told her. "He's awful good at putting up with your mess."

"Yeah, he'll do in a pinch, I guess. I've got him broke in at this point anyhow, so I might as well keep him around."

The band started up before the men got back from the bar, had played through Johnny and June Carter Cash's "Jackson" and had started in on some Hank Williams by the time they had their drinks. They toasted each other and watched the few couples that had already taken to the floor, mostly still just goofs and show-offs this early in the evening.

"I wish they'd dim down the lights a little bit and I'd get out there. I feel like I'm being wheeled in for gallbladder surgery in here," Wendy complained. As if on cue, the lights went down to a faint whistling applause throughout the hall. "Well, hell. I guess I've got to go and keep my word now. Come on, Wes, or I'll never live it down. Here, you two hold our drinks for a minute."

Wes led her out to the floor, held her hand like it was an expensive piece of glasswork, fragile and surpassing estimable value. He did not pull her to his tall frame as much as guide her there by the arrangement of his long limbs, an open and elegant embrace that seemed as natural to him as the gray in his mustache hairs. Wendy placed herself against his chest and the next song began, Sturgill Simpson's "The Promise."

"How long have you been friends?" Loyal Turner asked, a little louder and closer than he needed to.

"Not long. We're in school together."

"That right? I didn't know I was out with college women. I better be careful not to get above my raising."

She shook her head, more embarrassed than she thought she could be with him.

"Just community college is all. I don't even know what I want to major in."

"Still, though. That's a big step. I tried college a couple of years ago. Didn't work out so hot. You seem to me like you'd be cut out for it."

"Is that right?"

"It is. Hey, I can hold two drinks and dance at the same time. Can you?"

"I don't know. Should we try it?"

"As long as I don't get held accountable for any broken hips or busted beer bottles."

"I can't promise that," she said, inclining her head toward the dance floor.

They stood facing each other and shuffled with deliberate clumsiness through the rest of the song, giggling at missteps and the threat of spilled drinks. Despite the show he was making, Rain could tell that Loyal was quick on his feet, and he matched his movements to hers without conscious effort. She liked his simple grace. She liked too that he wasn't proud of it.

At the end of the song Wes and Wendy swept in and took their drinks back so that Rain and Loyal each had a free hand. The band started in with a song that was a bit slower than what had come up to that point with lyrics that didn't make much sense. Loyal tugged a long swallow from his beer while he reached out his hand toward her. She took it and moved a touch closer, let his easy stride match her own.

They danced together through two more songs, drank their beers. Then they found their friends pinned up against the wall watching everybody out on the floor. They seemed to be enjoying themselves, content to watch and share each other's company, at ease in their familiarity. Wes asked Loyal if he'd help him bring back a second round of drinks, to which he readily complied. Wendy asked Rain to run to the ladies' room with her while they were gone. When they all met back up they saw that the men had brought back a tray of tequila shots. From then on, things started to tear loose.

They swapped out dancing partners and sang into each other's ears, sometimes in keeping with the tune being played but often not. As it grew later the dance hall became an engine of sound coming from all quarters. The music on stage, yes, but also the stamping of feet and the free voices sprung from throats that howled and warbled. They held to friendly bodies like stones amid violent winds, bowed up and strange looking to any sober eye, though it would have been an achievement to find one there. By midnight the crowd had been beaten back to the edges, so many booze-weary couples taking refuge in the corners of the vast space, some even gone outside to stand weaving on their toes in the gravel lot while they stared down at the ground smoking cigarettes.

Last call was announced and before they knew they were left standing together, Wes and Rain saw that their dates had made one final sally for the bar.

"Damn, I had enough a hour ago," Wes lamented, found a pair of chairs for them near an empty dartboard. "Might as well see it to its end, I guess."

She took the other chair, thanked him.

"Hey, you mind if I ask a question?" Rain asked, aware of the effort it took to match her tongue to the syllables she intended.

"Shoot."

"Why is it you two haven't moved in together yet? You aren't planning on letting her get away, I hope."

She could tell the tequila had given her a rush of moral courage.

Wes laughed, said, "You're blunt enough to drive a railroad spike."

"Answer the question," she said, tried to stake him in place with her look. By his grin it seemed not to have much effect.

"Okay, I'll tell you a secret. I've tried to get her to move in with me for the last three years. Hell, I even asked her to marry me."

"Bullshit," she said, belched with what she thought was discretion.

"Ask her then. No, it's not for lack of trying. I love her to pieces and she knows it. I don't know what it is. What is it that makes people take up house with one another? I think maybe she's afraid of what she would give up, remind her too much of what things were like when she was married."

"Wendy, married?"

"Yeah. I guess you didn't know she had a little girl too. One that would be just a couple of years shy of your age now. Except she hasn't seen her in almost ten years. Not since she left her with her daddy."

His eyes had gone hard in a way that made Rain uncomfortable.

"Anyhow, sometimes you just have to find a way to accept the conditions you have to if you care about someone. I don't guess there's such a thing as a perfect love, a perfect way of showing that love. So you grab on to the things that seem to make the day hold onto its sunlight, keeps you from seeing all the shadows the middle of the night can throw across your brain. There's a difference between finding something to just attach yourself to and loving. I think there is, anyway."

They sat without saying anything more for a while. It seemed to be taking all night for the others to come back with the drinks.

"What is her name?" Rain then asked.

"What? Whose name?"

"Her daughter's. What is her daughter's name?"

"Hell, I don't know," he said, shook his head. "She never told me."

Loyal and Wendy came back with beers in plastic cups for carrying outside. They drank without saying much, the tide of the evening having already slipped out from underneath them. The house lights brightened, the band played out on "There's a Tear in My Beer" and everyone began to find their way out into what might still be a wilder night.

Wendy took Rain off to the side and asked if she was all right on her own and if so that she would leave her to whatever that handsome boy had in mind for her. She said she was fine, to go on. Wendy gave her and Loyal big hugs and said she was dead on her feet and was ready to be trucked home. Wes put his hand around her waist and led her out under the spread of sodium lights, his free hand flipping a brief salute goodnight.

"You aren't itching to go yet, I hope," Loyal said.

She answered by taking his arm and walking out to the edge of the lot and up toward a ridge of ground just within the quiet woods. They sat on a wind-felled pine and looked over the busy rumble of men and women finding their way to the cars and driving off. It was as good as watching TV, he said. She agreed, seeing the small dramas enacting themselves there at the peak of the evening.

"I like your friends," he told her. "They seem like decent people."

"What about you?"

"Excuse me?"

"Are you decent people?"

"I'd like to think so."

"I'd like to think that too."

She put her hand on the back of his neck as he kissed her and the night popped brightly behind her eyelids like the afterimage from gazing into something for too long. They lost time like that for a while, not talking, but feeling themselves grow past their physical shapes into something mutual and dream-like.

Gradually they separated, held hands. She had the desire to tell him about what had happened to her before she'd met him, make him understand the route that had brought her here, but there was no way to give it words. Especially not to him. Especially not now. Even when she repeated the things to herself that she'd had to do to survive while she was on the road they sounded like horrors that befell someone else. So much distance already between here and there. She stood, told him they should head back to their cars and get home. He reluctantly stood and followed her down.

They said goodnight at their cars, Loyal staying to make sure she was on the road headed home before he cranked the truck and turned back the other way. She stopped at an all-night gas station off the interstate and drank a sugared and creamed coffee sitting in the lot to clear her head. Thought she saw a couple of meteors scratch lightly against the sky, though she couldn't swear to it.

She killed the headlights as soon as she turned up the drive. She didn't know the exact time but she was sure that Stratton would have gone on to bed and she wanted to keep from waking him. The stilled engine ticked in the dark and she listened to it amid the unseasonable coolness. She could have made use of a sweater, but she didn't want to move from where she was. Adrift, thinking.

A sound then, tuneless and pained. She opened her eyes, lowered her window. As dead a silence as could be imagined before the wail again started low and unwound with profound sadness. A chill settled around her. She reached into the glovebox for the small plastic flashlight there.

The beam was weak as she came around the side of the house, heard the sound once more. Without definite source. She crawled the light back and forth across the hedges, the flowers, but there was nothing more for many minutes, and she began to think it had passed on but then the yowl repeated from under the house itself. She bent and shone the beam onto a pair of red eyes, saw the switching of the cat's tail.

"Hey, boy. Come on out, will you?"

Though the cat didn't move she heard something else shift its weight there in the crawl space. She moved the light across until she saw the gray coiled haunches of a coyote. It had backed the cat into its corner, ready to snap its neck.

"Get out of there, you sonofabitch," she growled, smacked the dirt with the haft of the flashlight. The coyote remained fixed, a whine coming from deep within its throat. Damn Cat hissed.

She cast around for something to flush it out, found only a piece of broken brick. The lob fell short but the coyote spooked, snapped at the air before circling in closer to the cat.

She went quickly up the stairs and to the hall closet. Picked up the shotgun she'd seen Stratton place there, unzipped it from its case. In her hands it registered heavier than she'd expected. He had told her it was loaded for pests in case she encountered problems working the garden.

Neither of the creatures had moved by the time she got back. She got down on her stomach and aligned the light with the shotgun barrel, yanked the trigger. The butt of the gun punched back, jolted from her hands. On her knees, she reached for the flashlight, patted the earth until she sensed its shape. A dark flowing movement surged past her. She swept the light in search of the coyote, but it had fled, leaving a thin cursive of blood on the ground. She turned the light back beneath the house. Damn Cat gazed at her and slowly blinked.

Above, she heard the thump of footsteps. She came back around to the front and called up, "It's okay, it's just me."

The light on the second floor came on then and Stratton poked his head out of the window. She shone the flashlight on the shotgun so he could see.

"Coyote," she said. "Was trying to get the cat."

As if to verify, Damn Cat strolled out, circled her once and gazed up at Stratton with an accusatory meow.

"Come in. Both of you," he called down, shut off the light.

She reached down and scooped Damn Cat up, carried him to the front hall where Stratton waited. She handed him the tabby and went to put the shotgun away. When she turned back he had the cat held up across his chest, their heads butting softly against one another in a mutual claim of ownership.

"How'd you know?" he asked.

"Just heard him is all. I would have got you but didn't know how much time he had."

He went to the kitchen, still holding the cat, and poured out a small saucer of milk. He sat them both on the kitchen table and stroked him behind the ears as he lapped and purred.

"Thank you," he said. "It means a lot that you did that."

"Of course."

She went back to her room and softly closed the door, undressed, and got under the crisp sheets of her bed. Sleep would not come when she closed her eyes because of the strange hour of night and because of so much else too. She heard Stratton carry Damn Cat with him upstairs, heard him speaking to the animal in affectionate tones. She wondered why he hadn't questioned her about being out so late. She wasn't his to protect, but still there was a quality of belonging here now, an attachment that had become common.

She tried to sleep but soon realized it had slipped past her, that she was chasing down a receding horizon and would be left in the quiet but tense hold of these sheltering hours. Still, she didn't switch on the light because there was a protection in the darkness when it was something she decided for herself. There was a new kind of peace in such wakefulness.

Part III

16

HIS TIME in Carolina had been hard.

After he'd lost the girl, the one that was like his own blood, the one who was a cure to his old screaming hurt, he'd sworn to himself that he would not forfeit Winter as well. By nightfall of the day Rain had deserted them they had reached the North Carolina state line and made camp in a flat stretch at the back end of a rest stop. He sent Winter over to stand just beyond the security lights to see what interest she might effect, but the evening was thinned of travelers and she elicited no paying invitations. She went on into the women's toilet and washed her face with liquid soap before coming back. He handed her a metal bowl of boiled noodles.

"Folks must be looking for something a bit more tender in years," he told her, not bothering to look up.

"Must be," she replied.

He slapped her lightly against the hip, said he was only messing with her. She sat and ate the noodles by hand.

Earlier that afternoon she had proposed where they were now headed. Her sister and her husband's place over in Candler, just west of Asheville. A little over thirty miles up I-40. They were big Christians, she said. They believed in helping people. He had made no effort to conceal his scowl when she told him this, but he had no better option to offer. That night he slept through a course of bad dreams and woke to a midnight fear without name. To guard himself from it he put his body close to Winter and enveloped her, made deep comfort of her physical presence, though it was not only her that he thought of. She stirred, turned her head into his chest, and he felt her hand move against his thigh, but nothing in him responded. In time, she succumbed to the half-sleep that lured her and he stared into the blankness above him, dared to whisper the lost name.

Early the next morning they had their first luck in days. An elderly man driving a Winnebago stopped at the grounds to walk his German shepherd and happened upon their campsite. He was unguarded and convivial in that way the old and lonely often are, and it was easy to see that he enjoyed a break from many hours of silent travel. Before they could ask for a ride he offered, even telling them he would be happy to wait while they struck camp and secured all that they'd brought.

The old man let them off at the interstate exit. The air was cooler at this elevation and the poor night's rest still provided relief enough to make their way more tolerable. Within an hour they had come to the edge of the place where Winter's sister lived. She told him to wait there just at the edge of the property line under the pine trees while she had a chance to go on and talk with her family, secure the invitation they needed. He didn't like being tied up like her pet, but he knew no valid protest. He went where she told him, waited like some charity case to answer her beck.

The day lengthened and he saw no signs from the house. He rolled a joint and smoked it, watched the traffic and the soft prickling breeze in the tree limbs. At the sensation of a foreign body attached under his arm he plucked out a blood-pampered tick and held it to the cherried end of the joint. He dropped it with a curse when he burned his fingertips. In Winter's pack he found a tube of salve and dabbed it on, then rooted around for signs of a protein bar he might have overlooked but found nothing.

By twilight irritation had given way to fury. More than five hours she'd been up there without sending word. Conspiracies mounted in his brain. Had she misled him and only pretended this was the home of her sister, slipped out of sight and deserted him there? Or was she holed up inside with no intention of finding a place for him? He sat pounding the earth with his fists as if he could knock loose the force that held him in place.

He had no sense of the hour when finally she came to him, his name a trouble on her lips. The last several days had exhausted him beyond his ability to bear, and he despised the weakness he felt as he rose and went toward her with gratitude. Hope, he recognized, had made him a coward.

"It's all right," she said. "You can come up now. They've agreed to meet you, let you stay the night."

"The night?"

"Just come up and talk with them, okay? That's all."

He followed her up in the shifting dimensions of new moonlight, crossed the dirt drive and stepped through the springy turf of manicured grass. A tall man wearing a golf shirt and khaki trousers stood waiting for them on the covered deck. The light overhead shone down on his head, gave strict shape to the precisely combed and gelled hair. The man held his hand out and as he took it he became aware of the unselfconscious strength. At close distance the man's staring blue eyes seemed capable of seeing straight through to the back of his head.

"Ellen here has told me your name. Pretty unusual, isn't it?"

"Yes."

The man expressed a version of a smile.

"I'm David. My wife's Ava. She's gone to bed already, but you'll meet her in the morning. She's sharing our room with Ellen here for tonight. Do you understand?"

He said that he did.

"Good. That's very good. Ellen, you should go ahead now. I'll show him where he'll be tonight."

She went inside, said nothing as she left him there with her brother-in-law.

"Stay here," David told him. "I'll be back in a moment."

The door eased quietly shut while he stood there, pinned in place by the harsh circle of artificial light. David was true to his promise, returning shortly with a black flashlight, though in his powerful hand it resembled a cudgel.

"Come around here then," he said as he stepped down the side of the deck and took the stairs along the back of the house. The beam gored the dark as they trod through the yard past a plastic outbuilding and a bass boat under a drum-snug tarp. They moved toward a wall of scrub and a small white camper that threw back a garish reflection of the flashlight. A pair of cinder blocks served as steps. Each wobbled as they took weight.

"No power tonight, I'm afraid," David explained rather than apologized. "The toilet's not hooked up, so if you need to take a call of nature you'll have to come outside. Bed's got a sleeping bag on it." He vaguely pointed the flashlight toward the far end of the camper where a bedroll was coiled atop a thin mattress. "You look beat, so I'll leave you to it. Breakfast is at seven. Think you can manage to wake up on your own or you want me to get you?"

He said that he'd be fine on his own.

"All right. Glad to hear it. Here, you can keep this with you," he said as he handed over the flashlight and went back toward the house in the smoothed-over dark, his shape lost almost instantly to the color of night.

He settled the backpacks under the dining niche table and sat on the camper's floor facing out the open door, his feet propped on the unsettled cinder blocks. He could just make out the presence of the house across the sprawling yard, more felt than seen. Perhaps that was what compelled him to look on and cast his mind out there in the invisible air in search of the slightest dream of content. To imagine himself closer to the solidity of what the house kept behind its walls.

He held the flashlight between his knees with the beam aimed under his chin, switched the halogen bulb on and off in a regular rhythm so that the light made blinking parentheses of his face. He did not care if he was seen.

DAYBREAK WOKE him. It was good to get free of the bed. The softness of it was something that would require adjustment. He turned on the kitchen faucet but it was dry, unconnected. He went up to the rear of the house and turned the garden hose on, washed his face and drank from it. He'd not recalled water ever tasting so clean and necessary.

He waited for some time at the front door before David answered. Already shaved, dressed for work in a button-up Oxford shirt and tie. He led him to the kitchen and had him sit. Neither Winter nor her sister was present.

"We've changed some plans. Ellen and my wife left early. They won't be back until this afternoon. Do you understand?"

He said that he did.

"Good," David said and paused before continuing. "I want this to be pleasant. To avoid unpleasantness. I think that's important."

He had nothing to add, retained his mask of patience.

"I've talked with Ellen. We both have. And we're very grateful that she's sought us out in this time of spiritual need. She has obviously faced tests to her faith. Having spent so much time on the road with so little."

"We always found a way to get by."

"Well, maybe so, but things need to change. She needs to change. She's said as much."

"Is that right? Mind if I ask her that to her face?"

"I've told you she isn't here right now."

"That's right. You did tell me that."

The room's silence was a third person penned up there with them.

"Now, I understand you and Ellen care for one another. And that's why I'm willing to offer this chance to you. This chance for both of you to have a fresh start, make yourselves clean again. Do you understand what I mean?"

"Well, you're probably not just talking about a shower."

That stone smile of David's. "No, not just a shower. I'm willing to let you stay here, let both of you stay here until you get on your feet. As long as you follow certain rules. Man's nothing if he can't keep to his own civil contract. I expect you to work and I expect you to start living clean right off the bat. That means you stay out there in the camper. You can see Ellen here in the house, but that's it. You aren't sleeping in the same bed, not until you're joined by the church. You need to work too. You can work for me down at the restaurant. I always need somebody back in the kitchen. Have you ever done kitchen work?"

He said that he hadn't.

"Well, that's okay. It's nothing you can't pick up if you set your mind to it. You keep a job and you stay in the camper rent free. You don't have a job, you don't have a place to lay your head."

"What else?"

"I want you to come to the church with the family. I want you to start walking the path. Tomorrow's Wednesday, so we'll be headed out there tomorrow evening. We can run down to the Kmart and get you some proper trousers, a polo shirt. You'll need to wash and cut your hair. We can do that here. Save the money. That's all I'm asking. That's all the Lord asks any of us, to do the best we can do from one day till the next. Why don't you give it a little time? Give it until the afternoon and let me know what you've decided. You want a cup of coffee? It's fresh brewed."

"Yeah, I'll take a cup. Black."

David set it there in front of him but took nothing for himself. Watched him take his sips as though they might be costing him his conscience. He thanked David when he was finished and said he'd talk to him about his decision by suppertime. He went back out to the camper and closed the door, pulled the rucksack out, shoved his hands to the bottom until he felt the cool gun barrel and pulled it out, unwrapped it from a soiled T-shirt. He aimed the pistol out the window at the main house, thumbed back the hammer and lightly tested the trigger tension before he eased it down. Then he went to work on a panel at the head of the bunk with one of the spare steak knives lying in the sink, pried at the softened wall until the pocket of soft insulation just showed. There, the pistol went in, vanished like something foreign into a wound's seam.

THE NEXT day he emerged from the camper without hair on his face or skull, wore the khaki trousers and white shirt that David had given him. As before, they alone sat in the kitchen and talked over coffee. The women remained gone, but he did not ask about them.

"Come down with me today," David told him. "We'll start you in for the lunch rush."

He rode down to David's restaurant, a brick rectangle with a big glass front that had pictures of a dancing chicken and a trio of crosses stenciled across. HIS GRACE COUNTRY RESTAURANT. He was given a red T-shirt and a stained apron and told to change in the employee restroom, a small closet with a toilet that could only be accessed from outside with a key kept on a chock of wood. He went back into the humid kitchen, where David pointed him to a light-skinned black man with a tattoo of a tiger on his forearm and a paper hat on his head.

"This is Melvin. He'll teach you. Listen to Melvin. He'll tell you when you're done."

Melvin made no offer to shake hands, merely pointed at the stainless-steel sink with a long spray hose. The top fitting of the hose looped over an iron ring above the garbage disposal, bent over the slurry of food waste like a neck in prayer.

"You wash and I'll rack the plates. Everything on the tray. Then open the washer. Here. I'll show you."

He reached for a silver lever and wrenched the side of the washer open, slid a tray of silverware inside, then slammed it shut. The machine whirred and snorted steam.

"You got it?"

"Yeah."

"You sure?"

"Sure."

He started in on the gunked bowls and plates left over from breakfast, shot more hot water on himself than the dishes before he got used to the spray. But it wasn't long before he discovered the rhythm of the work, made a system of what kinds of dishes and glasses to group together. The body took over for the mind and it was an act of spectating then, the boom of the washer slamming shut, the procession of plates. Melvin walked the emptied wash racks back and watched him for a minute with his hands on his hips. Satisfied, he told him when he finished with the last load to come out back while he smoked a cigarette.

It had grown warm but that side of the building was in shade. They looked out over a field of tall weeds and beyond that the green side of a mountain with big second homes stuck to the higher ridges.

"You see them houses up there?" Melvin asked, waved his hand in the air so that the cigarette made a drifting scrawl. "They look like advertisements, don't they?"

"Advertisements?"

"Yeah, advertisements for someplace you ain't never gonna be. It's like a piece of movie-star ass. Like that Scarlett Johansson. Shit they even put her in those superhero movies, get all the little boys all wound up and horny, thinking that's what they got coming to them if they work hard and do what they're told to do. That's some sick shit, you ask me. I busted my tail and I ain't never put my dick in Scarlett Johansson. Have you?"

"I don't care about money," he said.

"You don't care about it, huh? That's good. That's mighty Christian of you. I bet that sits with Ole Dave just fine, don't it? Well, I care about money. I care about it enough to know it's all that keeps me from sleeping on a side of cardboard under a overpass. I've got the feeling that there's something more at stake with you and Dave, though. Something about this itches my ass."

"I don't know what to tell you. I'm just doing what I was told to."

Melvin laughed so hard he choked on his smoke.

"Okay, it doesn't matter to me one way or the other. Let me show you what else you need to know how to do, Dave's boy. I like the ring of that, don't you? Dave's boy. That sounds like something that might just have legs."

THAT EVENING was the first time since they had come to Carolina that he saw Winter. She and David's wife Ava were sitting together in the living room talking when he and David came in from the restaurant. Ava was tall and coldly beautiful. Cool brown hair styled to her chin. A stinginess of makeup that served to accent her magazine good looks rather than conceal them. Jewelry thin as monofilament. When she stood to be introduced he became aware of the stink of the kitchen in his clothes, became aware too how she shared more of the easy superior sense of her husband than the features of her sister, who sat awkwardly on the couch in a long denim skirt that hid the scrollwork of her tattoos.

Ava took his hand in hers, pressed it dryly. He considered what it would be like to hear the bones in her fingers give way under pressure, what sound might escape her throat.

"We still have some time before we have to leave for church," she said with a hollow decorum. "Perhaps you'd like to freshen up with some clean clothes? David, tell me that you got more than just what our guest has on his back?"

"Yes, we'll take care of it."

David showed him the bathroom at the end of the hall, handed him a plastic bag full of identical shirts and trousers. He pulled them out and looked at them, held the articles in front of his naked body as he stood in front of the mirror. Copies of copies, rendering him from one inferior precedent to the next. He heard the others waiting in the living room speaking in low tones. He stepped under the spray of the shower to make himself over into their idea of acceptable.

Winter and Ava rode together in the backseat while he was in the passenger's seat next to David. There was not much room for talk because of the CD of a man preaching about the correlation between material accruement and God's blessings. The sermon had just ended by the time they pulled into the church complex with its overflow parking, its electric billboard. The church itself had no steeple or decoration of tradition that he could tell. Instead, it was a network of tall brick walls surrounding a domed auditorium. Inside, they walked shoulder to shoulder with a gathering crowd along the hushed hallways of plush carpeting, past a Starbuck's stall, past a cafeteria with Coke fountain machines capable of combining experimental flavors. On the walls were still shots of the preacher from one of his commercials that ran before the feature presentation at the local movie theaters. His smile was gorgeous.

They found four seats together in the upper tier of the auditorium. Over the main stage an enormous television screen was suspended. It transmitted a duplicate of the scene beneath it, magnified the tiny figures into intimidating shapes that were somehow both intimate and austere. A blonde teenager in a long cotton dress was singing into a microphone about the men who'd died in the service of country and Jesus. When she was done the crowd lightly clapped.

The lights went down, touching off a tense thrill in the crowd. The house orchestra seeped in, a shivering of cymbals before the full bawling play of the brass and the vocals. Then the preacher entered, both hands raised in benediction to the crowd. As he took the stage the congregation stood. He wore a microphone set clasped to the side of his head. His shirt was untucked over pressed designer jeans. Tony Lama cowboy boots stuck out from the denim break.

"Peace and light be to you," he said.

"And peace and light be to you," the congregation answered.

ONCE THE habit of work and devotion was established, time lost its edge. Within the week Winter was moved into her own room. At night she would go to bed early and turn off the lamp but then turn it on again once David and Ava were asleep to let him know that it was safe to approach. He did so reluctantly, part of him wanting to punish her for her complicity in isolating him. But he could only keep away for so long before he was drawn across the yard to her window where he would tap lightly and she would kill the light before sliding the pane open.

"Hey," she whispered.

"So it speaks."

"Don't, all right? I'm doing what I can."

"Yeah, me too, Ellen."

He put his hand through the window, felt her breast beneath her nightgown. A spasm of desire and loathing overtook him and he tried to encircle her waist but she pulled away.

"Don't, they'll hear."

"Damn them. Come here."

She stayed beyond his reach.

"Just so you know. I'm not staying here forever," he told her.

"I don't expect you to."

"Does that mean you won't come with me?"

She answered after a pause, "I don't know what it means."

"Well," he said. "You better find out soon."

EARLY MORNINGS became the time that was set aside for him and David to have devotions. They sat together over a copy of a New International Version of the Bible. Memorized passages from the gospels and the Psalms, read commandments and curses from the Pentateuch. He liked the practice of committing the text to memory. Absorbing the scripture was the only way he could tolerate it. He took it in like some measure of poison that might immunize him against affliction.

Work at the restaurant was an intermission in his newfound faith, a chance to work through the hours as he approached the moment of action. He had never felt as relieved of burden as when he let the time slide by knowing that he had crossed a point of decision. He saw the wisdom in becoming a viewer in his own life rather than a participant. He didn't even mind Melvin's jibes about his name, about his incompetence, about his bald skull.

At night he waited for Winter to come to him, to see him in the broken-down camper. But she never did. She remained content to leave him to the bad end of chance. Even when she was permitted to speak to him, she rarely did. How quickly she melded her life to theirs. How easily she became one of them. How truly she could betray.

And then he began to see the profoundness of his hatred take shape and where he might most sharply inflict it. No need to force the details because they had put taproots down in his brain in the shuffling course of weeks. He exercised patience, even as September cooled and the leaves of October reddened. He felt the heightened pulse of the landscape lend credence to his own quickened senses, his need to manifest what he held back, but he recognized too the virtue of waiting for that which presented itself for use.

In making the house ready for a gathering of church friends, David told him to stay behind from the restaurant for the day so that he could help Ava clean out one of the spare rooms and carry what wasn't needed for storage in the attic. Winter was out buying groceries, so only the two of them were left to make everything tidy. It was easy work, required little more than waiting for direction, then lifting a few odd items that were too heavy for Ava alone. When she had nothing left for him to do she had him disassemble a large oak desk that was too wide to fit through the doorway and then seemed to forget about him altogether, wandered off on one of her many domestic projects. He finished detaching the heavy wooden legs without much trouble and sat there without anything in his mind for a while before he decided to walk back and look into the empty bedrooms.

Winter's room was much as he expected it to be. Plain, transient. A single Ikea chest of drawers and a double bed with floral cotton sheets. A couple of framed pieces of scripture on the wall. One beneath a picture of the cross at sunset. The other beside footprints on a white beach.

He stepped out, stood in the hallway a while to determine if he heard Ava nearby before he went into her and David's bedroom. There he saw that the bed was large and soft and had too many pillows to count. Gauze curtains that scalloped whitely in a light breeze. Framed pictures of Ava and David through the last several years. On beaches, in mountains. Vacation snapshots taken by some invisible fellow tourist they'd flagged down and coerced with their rhetorical smiles. Strange that they were childless. Perhaps, like Abraham's Sarah, she was barren.

He looked into the closet and saw everything hung with precision. A bicameral arrangement with David's clothes to the left and Ava's to the right. He let his hands drag across the long elegant hems of her dresses, let them linger where the natural divisions of material would have closed and fastened her naked body from sight. The persistent tease of the hook latched within the eye.

In her bureau he found the small cedar box unlocked. In it the jewelry folded and nested. He lifted the thin necklaces and draped them over his hands, saw how they festooned once the slack was drawn out. A wonder to see it like this and know how it might decorate the slender architecture of bones it was intended to.

It was not a voice that startled him, but a certain settling of weight in the room told him he was no longer alone. He turned, saw Ava watching him. He walked toward her, and though she did not move or cry out, he could tell that fear had taken her whole.

"You put those back," she said in a voice tight with control. "You put those back and I won't say anything."

His gaze fell to the jewelry as he circled around and got between the door and her.

"No, I don't think I will."

"I'll scream."

"Is that right?" he said. "I'd be disappointed if you didn't."

And then he was on her, his hand around her throat, tightening even as they struck the floor and her nails raked at his eyes. He was shocked at the strength of her fight and when he loosened his grip to get at her shorts she wrenched away and gained enough space to land a hard kick to his stomach. It pitched him against the drywall and he felt the surface soften and give way. She tried for the door then, but he stepped forward and tripped her, got on her back then and twisted the length of her hair into his fist until she cried out.

He jerked her shorts and underwear down and was trying to unfold himself when he heard the sound of steps. Then felt the blow of something heavy taking the side of his head.

HE WOKE hogtied with extension cord and electrical tape. The pain in his skull was so complete that it felt like he had been cut in two and nailed back together. He could smell his own blood, taste it too. His memory was hurt as well. He could recall what he'd been doing to Ava, what he'd meant to achieve, but how he arrived there wasn't in a pattern he could recognize. To bring himself back he focused on the few details in his immediate surroundings. A few feet away he saw one of the desk's legs left in the middle of the bedroom. That had been what had put this ache on him. That, among other things.

He stilled when he heard voices coming from another room. Women only, he determined. Winter then. It must have been she who came back and found him and Ava as they were. There might

be enough time left for him to get clear if he could slip the restraints. He rolled his wrists against the binding, made the tape flex
and give way by the smallest of degrees. Within ten minutes he had
one free hand. Within twenty he was free.

He slipped out the window and crossed the yard to get what he
still had in the camper. Already the sun was masked in the treetops
and David would have to be home soon by now. The women were
sure to have phoned him. He flung the camper door open, grabbed
his ruck, went back to where he'd stashed the pistol, but when he
reached inside the wall he could feel only the soft guts of insulation.
He jerked out handfuls of the padded mess but was forced to go on
without the weapon.

The road was a threat, so he struck through the back wooded
property to make distance. The buffer proved to be thinner than
he'd guessed and he was soon tramping through the backyards of
several connected houses in a development. Men in their garages
and women on their porches stood transfixed as he passed. Some
few muttered vague curses and demands that he get off their land
before they called the law. He merely waved and continued through
in search of woodlands to harbor him, but the houses continued to
rise up in all directions.

Only at night did he feel safe enough to pause and settle. Once
he did and once he had let his mind free itself from the immediate
concern of his survival, he knew how final his act had been, how
it was the end of so many things and how little he grieved this fact.
But the time there had not been wasted. He had learned certain
things about himself. He had grown toward something precise and
dangerous, and for this he knew he owed David and Ava a significant
debt. If only he had the pistol he would have been able to properly
repay them.

17

THE WEEK of midterms Stratton received a curious voicemail. It was from a man named Connor McElmurray who said he worked with the Appalachian Mountain Project, an anti-mountaintop removal nonprofit in Whitesburg, Kentucky. He said that he'd heard about the photography exhibit that was being planned for Liza's photographs in a few months and he had some more work that the curator might want to include, some pictures Liza had taken when she was covering the work of the nonprofit shortly before she was killed. When Stratton returned the call it went unanswered. He left his own voicemail stating that he'd like to talk about the pictures, but several days passed and he heard nothing more. With the increasing busyness of the semester the issue faded from his immediate attention, but it was strange and something about it bothered him, though not terribly. It had the feel of something unfinished, something pent.

The last week of October McElmurray resurfaced, this time in the form of an email sent to Stratton's work address. In it he said that he absolutely had to meet with him face-to-face, that he would deliver the photographs because Stratton was the only one who could decide how the images should be used. There was an air of desperation to it. But there also appeared to be a quality of resolve, an underlying concern for doing what his conscience dictated that made Stratton nervous. He had learned many times over that a man convinced he was doing the right thing was someone at his most dangerous. Still, he had to meet this man, see what he had of Liza's.

They arranged to meet the following Saturday afternoon, the day before Halloween. There was a truck stop in Jellico, on the border of Tennessee and Kentucky, where they could sit down. It split the distance for both of them. Stratton told Rain he should be back in time for supper but not to wait for him in case she and Loyal got hungry.

He stopped at the gas station for some burned coffee, thought about tossing the stuff out but nursed it as he drove until it was all gone and his nerves were tight as piano wires. He counted Jesus signs stuck on the side of the road once he got out into the country, crosses on hillsides, some as big as water towers. The Holy Word writ large across the surface of the earth—an ancient page that didn't care.

It was windy when he got into Jellico, enough to take a man's ball cap. He clapped his hand over his head as he made his way to the diner's side entrance. He passed a pair of uncoupled truck cabs that were parked near the door. One of the drivers leaned out, pointed at Stratton's Braves hat and asked if he ever got tired of having his heart broken. Stratton said that the heart, like other muscles, could become numb, and the man laughed.

He sat at a booth near the door and asked the waitress if they had something to drink without caffeine. She brought him a Sprite.

Within a quarter of an hour a young man with a military haircut came in through the front, scanned the booths before he gave Stratton a nod and approached.

"Mister Bryant," he said, offered his hand. Stratton took it and waved for him to sit down. When he did he picked up a menu, studied it without interest, and ordered a black coffee. While they waited they each made stumbling efforts at small talk. McElmurray had the nervous habit of brushing the short bristles at the side of his head with his palms. It seemed to get worse the longer they sat together.

"So you mentioned that you worked with Liza while she was working on the mountaintop removal series," Stratton finally prompted.

"Yes. That's right. She attended several rallies, took many photos. She was well-liked. Within the organization, at least. Not sure the miners cared too much for her. She didn't really try to hold to journalistic objectivity, though."

"No, that wasn't much her style."

McElmurray clearly desired to say something more, but remained incapable, stopped somewhere short of whatever reason had driven him thus far. Such boyishness in him, as if he'd just been discovered in some wrongdoing but was unable to admit it.

"You see, there's something different about these pictures," he continued, haltingly. "They're not of the rallies or any of that. These are more private."

Stratton realized then. He realized who it was that sat across from him. He put his hands under the table, tried to strangle the rising anger out of himself.

"I think I'm beginning to understand," he said.

McElmurray only nodded.

After a couple of minutes of not saying anything, McElmurray stood up and asked if he wanted to go out and see the prints. Stratton answered by dropping a creased five-dollar bill on the table and mutely following. In his hands he felt a force that grew more tense as they crossed the wind-blasted parking lot and came to McElmurray's Subaru. The hatch popped and opened. The pictures were framed and buffered by soft sheets of white foam. Before McElmurray could reach in, Stratton twisted his collar so that he was brought up on his toes. He did not resist, but looked at him through his pale young eyes.

"I recognize you," Stratton hissed, though in a voice that made little sound amid so much wind. It was a foolish act in a humiliating play, and he felt these clumsy lines coming out of his mouth, knew that they were a discredit to him and the young man he said them to.

"I've seen the picture she took of you," he choked out.

McElmurray would say nothing. Would not fight back at all. His weight was in Stratton's hands with complete and maddening submission. Stratton shook him once as though it might stir some animal resistance, but McElmurray wouldn't come to life. Stratton threw a punch at the point of his jaw. They both went sprawling into the dirt. He kneeled over him, breathed in dust and saw that his fist had whitened. Red eyes bled along his knuckles, though he felt little but the electric buzz in his muscles, his bones.

He helped McElmurray up. The younger man's jaw was beginning to swell but he was otherwise unhurt. Once they regained their breath they began to transfer the prints from the back of the Subaru to Stratton's vehicle. What had been between them was done.

"Is that all?" Stratton asked.

"Yes, that's everything. You have my number then?"

There was a strange note of hope in McElmurray's voice.

"I'll let you know if there's anything I need."

McElmurray backed away a few paces but did not yet return to his car, waited to make sure that Stratton was set to travel back and had no final words for him. Then he got out of the mean wind, wedged himself under the dumb compass of his steering wheel and drove back to Kentucky.

STRATTON CHECKED in briefly with Rain and Loyal, who were building a fire in the living room, and said he'd be out to sit with them as soon as he finished putting a few things away. Rain was immediately curious, but she didn't ask what he meant, only if he needed any help. He said that he was fine, to get the fire tall and the whiskey poured, then carried all the pictures up to his bedroom. There were twelve in total. He'd looked at only a few of them, but they appeared to be mostly color. Unusual.

He went down to find Loyal and Rain with chairs drawn close to the fire. On the mantel a jack-o'-lantern grinned. A faceted glass of bourbon was already set out on the side table. They toasted and drank.

"A good holiday homecoming," he said.

"We thought you'd appreciate it," she said, gave Loyal a light shoulder squeeze. "By the way, another agent called this afternoon while you were out, asked if they could show the house tomorrow afternoon."

"Hmm? Oh, sure. I guess we'll have to clear out for a bit then. Do you two have anywhere you might be able to kill a couple of hours?"

She and Loyal traded what was supposed to be a furtive look. An allusion to some kind of carnal mischief, no doubt. Stratton preferred not to dwell on it. When had he become such a prude, he wondered. Probably just lechery living under another name and putting on a clean suit. But goddamned if it didn't make him feel like dry bones in a box. Worn down by his own disinterest.

A fist rapped against the front door.

"Who in the hell is that?" Stratton demanded.

"Can't you figure it out?" Rain said, crossed to the side room on her way out front. "It's the Saturday before Halloween."

"I've never heard trick or treaters this far out."

"Not until I signed you up on the rural Halloween route at the plant nursery, you didn't. Your real estate agent was happy to hear about it, though."

He leaned from where he was sitting, saw the church bus at the end of the drive, as well as a steady train of macabre children wielding scythes, fangs, and bone-crossed plastic sacks. He shook his head, grinned at the small army of gruesomes.

"You better be glad you've got me hanging around or you'd be headed for some bloodthirsty trick or treaters for sure," she told him.

She opened the door and complimented the children's costumes, rattled her hand through a plastic bowl of candies, handed them out to a thin ripple of thank-yous, then closed the door. A simple and happily domestic moment, Stratton thought. Familiar yet intimate. Perhaps this was what one remembered over the span of a full life. These small rituals that dug into the great wall of years, the common moments that gain a certain mass of significance over time.

He went into the adjoining room and settled in front of the old piano, began to play a variation on Nils Frahm. A basic but powerful piece of music that rendered the quiet truth of a life lived in solitude. When he'd first heard it played, Stratton thought it profoundly sad, but in time he had learned the slight but rich emotion beneath. The rush of associations made more powerful because of their passage through understated melody.

He loved to play, he truly did, but having it be a habit of the home had always been enough for him. This was what he had never been able to adequately explain to Liza. She had understood his music as an ambition, as an object of pursuit. Maybe she desired to be jealous of it, to have to face it down in order to retain his affection. She needed the competition. It had always driven her in her own work. But for Stratton music was a voice that spoke in a way that nothing else could. If it came from him, from whatever skills he might develop, that was fine. But the deep meaning behind it did not depend on belonging to him. There was no ownership in his passion.

He finished his drink and told Rain and Loyal goodnight, said to stay up as long as they liked. Upstairs, he closed his bedroom door and began to unstack the prints and place them against the wall so that he could view them all at once. He had been right before. They were all in color, with the single exception of the *Adultery* picture, the one that she'd cared so much about that she'd brought back a copy for herself. But there was another trait about them too. Something so extraordinary that it caused a physical hurt. Liza was the subject. Posed and framed but still an essential part of each composition. She danced alone on a dance floor, a Pabst Blue Ribbon in hand. She dove from rocks into a lake. She stood with arms linked with fellow protestors against a mountaintop removal dozer. That picture was the best. Unflinching and beautiful in how it arrested a specific instance of dynamic movement. He leaned closer to read the title. *In the House of Wilderness.*

After he had spent much of an hour studying the pictures, he put them carefully away in their original protective stack-work. He felt loneliness overtake him, as if seeing her as she had been in those photographs touched a new reserve of grief. He wanted to talk to someone, to have another person to share this immensity with him, but there was no one, no one who could hear him as he needed to be heard.

18

RAIN LEFT while it was still morning dark for her Sunday morning shift at the Waffle House. She had not slept well, up late texting with Loyal once he'd got back to Sevierville just before midnight. And even when they had both said goodnight, she had turned over what she had meant to tell Stratton the evening before. As soon as he'd come home from his meeting with that man from Kentucky, she knew that would be impossible. Stratton's mind was heavy with something and she didn't want to contribute any more to whatever it was that weighed on him.

Loyal was disappointed that she hadn't talked to him. There had been no mistaking his irritability after Stratton had gone up to his bedroom. They'd sat there in front of the fire and whispered about what it would be like to soon live together under the same roof, how they'd be rich with happiness despite their poverty, but there was a desperation about it all, a sense that they were enacting old roles that would have benefited from a wiser hand's revision. Part of her was afraid of telling Stratton of their plan because she understood the haste of it, the recklessness. Maybe Loyal had guessed this, why he had doubled down, pressed her to start looking for an apartment they could afford on her part-time restaurant work and his new job stocking groceries overnight at the Food City. She hoped it would work, hoped Stratton wouldn't say anything. She didn't think she could stand his disappointment.

The restaurant was a twenty-four-hour place. A couple of girls on the outgoing shift were standing around back smoking cigarettes where the employees had to park. She told them good morning and they nodded at her through the smoke, said they were glad she was coming on and not them.

Inside, the cook Lou was wiping down the grill, boomed hello in his radio announcer voice. Otherwise it was empty except for Old Man Falls, who was a five a.m. regular, weekday or weekend. He was a small, nearsighted man with what might have been a Cherokee's face. His back was bent into a hook so deep he looked like something you could pick up and hang on a clothes rack. He took his time when he ate, said it was because he liked to flirt, said Rain reminded him of Dolly Parton. He wasn't a day shy of eighty.

Once she'd checked to see that all her booths were stocked up and squared away she went behind the counter, got the freshest pot of coffee that she could turn up, and went down to top off the old man's cup. He looked up through his wrinkled face and smiled.

"Thanks, sugar."

She went back to the kitchen to see if there was anything that needed catching up, but everything was as cleaned and stacked as if it were awaiting military inspection. She hated it. The best thing about her job was the way time disappeared in a rush of order and fulfillment. Busyness ate through the hours, but when it was like this she could only chat with Lou and one of the other girls for so long before the crush of thoughts would get to her, worry her down to something ready to be cast off. Little more than a husk, a spent breath.

"Dammit, you run everybody off, Lou?" she asked.

He grinned, swiped his enormous palm across the waxy dome of his head.

"Been like this all night. Relax, people always have to eat. It's the law of the hungry belly. Ain't never had it let me down."

She shook her head, got herself a cup of coffee and waited for several minutes at a booth, but no one other than the other waitress coming on shift walked in. She told Lou that she had to run out to the car for something and she'd be back in a minute. He told her not to bust her ass. Old Man Falls laughed and tried not to spit his coffee.

Behind the front seat of the truck, she went through her tote and picked out her Social Problems text, a composition book for notes, and hurried back inside. She found her solitary booth and began to skim the reading, recording the ideas that seemed important: education and poverty rates, rural demographics and historical influences, single motherhood, cycles of economic inferiority, sexually transmitted diseases. She shut it to give herself a break. It was like hearing a lecture about her growing up with her mother. This wasn't something that required study. She wanted to forget about what life had been then, not turn it over like a smoldering log on a fire.

She flipped a few pages in the composition book and wrote the words WHO I AM with a vivid underline. Her pen tapped the page for a long while before she began to write other words in a column. First, WOMAN, and later, HIPPIE, WAITRESS, PROSTITUTE, COLLEGE STUDENT, and finally MOTHER? She scratched and looped over the final entry until all traces were covered up by a rough bramble of blue ink. She knew she was late, but perhaps she was jumping to conclusions. Her cycle had always been erratic, especially after the miscarriage she'd had with Wolf the winter before. She hadn't mentioned the possibility to Loyal, of course. There would be no sense in adding more complication to his desire to live together. No sense in involving him when it was unclear what that would really mean.

She was spared idleness when a couple of tables filled with customers. She put her study materials behind the counter and was glad to be on her feet and occupied by the rhythm of work. It continued steadily through the rest of her shift, and by the afternoon she'd picked up sixty dollars in tips. A good Sunday, but she wasn't sorry to see it gone.

Stratton was in his office listening to music when she got home, so she went on to the shower to get the stink of grease out of her skin. She toweled off and put on a sweatshirt and jeans. Studied in her room for a while before she got hungry and came out to make a peanut butter sandwich. On her way to the kitchen she saw that Stratton had come into the living room and was sitting on the floor brushing out long swatches of loose hair from Damn Cat. There appeared to be enough hair to compose a second animal.

"I've read about this for school," she said. "It's called asexual reproduction."

He laughed. "I think you might be right about that. Hey, would you mind bringing the garbage can in here."

She did and sat next to him on the floor stroking the tom between his ears. Her hand lightly vibrated from the crackle of his purr.

"Work okay?"

"Hmm? Yeah, fine."

"Not getting in the way of school, I hope?"

"No, no, that's been fine."

"What about other . . . distractions?"

She smiled, knew how poor he was at beating around the bush.

"Everything's in check, Dad."

He nodded, continued brushing out the cat.

"Hey, I need your opinion on something. Do you have a minute?"

She told him she did.

"I'd like you to look at these new pictures. The ones I just picked up."

They went upstairs, and he led her into his room where he already had the pictures propped up against the wall, as if they were prepped for installation. She counted them. Eleven in total. Every one in color. She took her time, walked her way through the entirety of the display.

"These are Liza, aren't they?"

"Yes. These are all her."

"Who took them?"

He shrugged, looked at something else in the room.

"These have to be part of the exhibit. You know that, don't you?"

She didn't hear if he answered as she kneeled in front of the picture of Liza dancing, saw the form of that living body now gone. She stared at it and blinked, as though she could take a picture that way herself, to know this unknown woman. It seemed important that she try.

"Will you call the man from the university to come out and get them?"

"No," he said. "I'll take them myself."

"I'd like to come, if that would be okay."

He considered it a moment.

"Sure, all right. I'll let you know when we do it."

She smiled, kissed him on the cheek, and went back downstairs.

THEY HEADED for Knoxville straight from the Walters State campus as soon as Rain's Wednesday afternoon sociology class had ended. It had grown cool and windy and some of the early turning leaves had been stripped from their branches. This was how time was best measured, Rain thought. This cycle of years without months. One turn to the next. The way it carves us down, makes us live within its pace. She cracked her window to hear the boring speech of the road with its asphalt and engines and then the higher pitch of the wind itself. There was something to be gained by listening to the repetition for long periods of time apart from the human distractions of conversation and radio. Something to be understood about how one moves through it.

They met Easterday just as most of the staff was closing offices and going home for the day. He had a dolly they could take down on the elevator to trundle the photographs out to the building where they would be hung. After they'd loaded everything up and ground the dolly across several rough parking lots, she held the big swinging doors as they bounced over the metal thresholds trying not to damage the glass panes. They entered a gray room relieved by periodic capsules of soft light. The walls had been bared so that they were like looking into a face without expression.

"Is this where they will hang?" she asked.

"Yes," Easterday answered. "This is the main exhibit hall. They'll be here for a time and then they will be archived. Held in special collections."

"What does that mean?"

"It means they'll be put away then," Stratton answered. "For good."

"You mean people won't be able to see them?"

"That's not exactly true," Easterday cut in. "Here, wait a minute." He went ahead and unlocked a steel framed door by punching in a numeric key. They eased the dolly inside where other framed photographs and paintings were stored on pallets, protected in soft gauze and identified by soft brush metal tags on the frames' edges.

"It's not that people won't be able to see them," Easterday continued. "The images will be recorded for our database and then the original will be kept safe in an area specially designed to do so. Available if researchers and scholars have the need to confirm something not available in the digital copies. It's the only responsible thing to do. Light will kill a photograph over a period of time."

Though she remained bothered, Rain said nothing more as they put Liza's work away, left it in the muted and blind room.

Easterday tried to take them to dinner downtown, but Stratton insisted that they had to get back home. Though disappointed, Easterday said he understood. They shook hands and promised to see each other in January when the show would debut.

They rode back in silence for several minutes. Rain watched the blurring movement of tree line at the interstate's edge, the incessant run of the white line bordering the shoulder. A chore finished. A piece of work disposed. As if it were as dead as the one who had created it.

"Doesn't it bother you?" she asked, at last.

"Does what bother me?"

"Giving her pictures up like that. Just to have them shut up somewhere. Kept out of sight."

"That's not how I see it."

"No? Then how do you? I want to know."

He shrugged, looked down the endless spool of road ahead.

"Her pictures are already out there. They've done what they're going to do. She only got to see them go so far while she was alive. Now, it's up to me to see that the work is respected, put in context. It's not pretty, necessarily, but this is one way that it gets done. Everything has to go to sleep eventually. It's time."

She leaned her head to the passenger window, sensed the stiff resistance of the road and the place beneath that held it.

"Maybe they shouldn't be let go yet," she said. "Maybe they're still doing things that matter to people."

SHE WAS on the way to school after having eaten an apple and a piece of cinnamon toast. She was late and her head was still in a fog from having wakened in the middle of the night with too many ideas taking root in her brain. While she was driving, a sudden violence came up through her and she had just time enough to pull to the side of the road and vomit onto the hardtop. She swore, wiped her mouth with some Kleenex from the glovebox, and then drove on.

In class she couldn't concentrate, didn't understand a problem when the math instructor called on her directly. She tried to answer something, but the words turned to something hard and painful in her throat and she swept her book into her bag, walked out ten minutes before dismissal. Wendy chased her.

"Hey, what's the damage, Sister?"

"It's nothing," she answered, didn't break stride as they left the building and crossed the parking lot.

"Bullshit it is. That's not like you. Spill it."

"I told you, nothing. Goddammit, take a fucking hint."

She didn't wait to see how her words had taken hold. She got in the Bronco and put as much distance as possible between her and everyone else. She drove back toward the house but was afraid Stratton might be home, so she continued east until she entered the national park, went on until she found a trailhead where only a few tourists were parked at the pull-off. She killed the engine and stepped into the woods.

Normally, as soon as she felt dirt and stone beneath her feet, ferns brushing her ankles, her anxiety eased. But even as she covered a mile or more, striding out along the damp and cool trails roofed over with rhododendron, she felt an awful weight centered in her stomach. The pure and dread certainty of it. The inescapability. There had been a time when she desired to have a child with Wolf, but that was before she had seen the opportunity for something else. For a life lived rather than merely endured. And while she had strong feelings for Loyal, she was certain that he was unprepared to take care of a child, to provide for it. Nor would she want to ask him to. He was a beautiful boy, yes, but he was still a boy. Strange how much older she had come to feel in the last few months living with Stratton. Strange how a life could take such a turn. Strange and terrible but perfect too, somehow.

She came to a creek and sat on its banks, shed her shoes. The water ran over clear sand, flecks of undisturbed mica. She eased her feet in and pressed them into the sand until the grit softened and filled the cracks between her toes. It was good to feel so small there. To have a place to reckon the way of her singular world.

When she was little she had decided, like so many other little girls, that she would one day become a marine biologist. She wanted to know underwater life and what it held from an existence above the surface. Perhaps it had been a curiosity about secret spaces, their mystic oddity. But a part of her had also believed that she belonged to an experience apart, a place refracted and weightless. She closed her eyes to imagine herself as one of the creatures who lived in the shallows of the stream. It would be like being put into a dimension of paradise, she decided, living within the lyric of quietly running water.

She carried her shoes as she walked up the streamside path. The water widened and deepened where it circled among the strong white boulders. She saw the shadow-flitting shapes of fish there, their tails gently whisking against the current. Just as small and waiting as what was inside her now. A shade of a life that wasn't ready for the outer world. She took a handful of gravel from the edge of the trail and pitched it across the surface of the water, watched the fish scurry for greater depths until she couldn't see a single one. She went up the trail to make herself as small amid the timber as she could.

19

HE SPENT a few nights under a downtown bridge, not wanting to chance being seen at one of the shelters. It had been cold there just above the river, but the concrete V had provided a windbreak. The train occasionally came through with its prehistoric bellow, waking him, and he would sit up and listen to the murmur of the city, think of how he could find a way to call it home.

He ate to the bottom of the ruck within three days despite close rationing. He scouted dumpsters behind the nearby barbeque place, the line of beer joints, but most of them were padlocked and those that weren't held only cardboard and glass. He would need money.

Asheville was a tourist town, so he learned quickly where the out-of-towners came. He went to Pack Square, asked any stranger for bus fare. The more elaborate the backstory the better. The tourists would rather give him money to shut him up than be forced to hear the story to its conclusion. He stood in the shadow of the stone obelisk and watched the sun clock around while he begged.

"The fuck you doing?" shouted a man wearing torn jeans and a thrift store sheepskin coat. His vast black beard reeked of cigarette smoke.

"Fuck off," he said, watching for any new mark, not interested in a challenge to territory.

"Shit, that the way you talk to a man trying to do you a favor? Look, you lunatic, the cops will have your ass out here. This is for performers, get it?"

He lifted his arm to show a violin case clutched there.

"What's your name, partner?"

He gave it to him. The man stroked his chin whiskers with concern.

"Well," he said. "That's not exactly gonna work. Not if you want to make a go of it with me. I'll tell you what, from now on your stage name is Jesco, like that hick from *The Dancing Outlaw*. How about that? Jesco is about as hickified as you can get."

"What the hell are you talking about?"

"I'm talking about a business partnership, dumbass. Look, I can tear it out on this fiddle, but there's about a half-dozen other buskers around here that are every bit as good as I am. Hell, I'll be honest with you. They're considerably better. Competition is killing me. But what I need is something to set me apart. I need a clogger. That'll spit enough cornpone in your eye to make you shit or go blind. What do you say? You want to be my clogger?"

"I don't know how to."

"Shit, you think that makes a difference? Hell, try to help a man. Tell me something. What size shoe do you wear?"

"Ten. Ten and a half maybe."

"Well, we can invest in some tap shoes. They're good to turn up at one of the Goodwill stores. But let's give her a run in bare feet. Hell, that might even be better, now that I think about it. Folks will pay top dollar to see a hillbilly dance barefoot, especially this time of year."

"What's your name?"

"Well, that's a serious question, ain't it? Now I could tell you the truth or I could give you a fiction you'd be none the wiser to, but I'll tell you straight. My name is Clementine."

"You're full of bullshit."

"The hell I am. How could a man be born into this world with a handle like that and not earn his dollar by a trade of the street? It's the God's honest. I'm built to render the delights of the modern minstrel. I have come to gift the truth of gossip and horseflies."

He shook his head at Clementine's persisting babble even as he snatched the shoes from his feet and stuffed them inside his rucksack. The pavement shocked his feet with its coldness, but he stamped them a few times until the blood enflamed his soles as he tried a few quick steps. Clementine grinned madly from between the coarse thicket of his beard, quickly peeled the fiddle from its case and hit a few long and lonesome licks. And then it became a weird tangle of sound and movement, the dance steps coming from some wild notion deep within memory and sprung out in a kind of wobbling repudiation of the world at large. He danced and circled, or did what was at best an earnest pantomime of dance, though it appeared to most who came to gawk with their dollar-clenched fists as a thrashing of limbs and joints—reckless, naive, and simian. He closed his eyes to the spectators as he felt the circulation of his furious energy rising and rising, like some terrible attack of the body against the soul. His head tipped back and his mouth swung open as he tongued a shriek aimed at breaking open the sky. The fiddle quickened and cried. He stamped ever harder.

"Godamighty, take a breather there, Jesco, my boy," Clementine shouted, pointed at the open fiddle case greened over with hand-worn bills. He realized then that the music had stopped, had been silent for some time, while he had continued to dance.

CLEMENTINE LET him stay on his couch in a basement apartment he rented on the east side of Asheville, over in the Oakley district. It was stuck back in a neighborhood of midcentury brick ranches with older residents. Retirees mostly, or those on the verge. He had to sneak in the side entrance after dark because the landlord lived upstairs and would have hiked the rent if he knew his tenant had taken in someone new. It was a small and warm hole in the ground: a room of whitewashed particle board walls and a peeling laminate floor. The ceiling was cross-worked with upstairs plumbing, but nothing dripped. The small attached bathroom was the sole source of natural light. The window there was high on the wall, perhaps a foot or so above ground level. A dead wolf spider was flattened against the outside pane.

They ate from whatever could be heated in Clementine's micro-wave, an artifact that used a dial timer. Mostly Jimmy Dean sausage biscuits and Hot Pockets. Sometimes, a store brand chicken pot pie. He said little, mostly listened to Clementine declaim about his musical ambitions, his designs on touring abroad. Perhaps as far as Europe. Take their hillbilly show to their Continental roots, fling it at the Old World like a fist to the jaw.

For two days it rained so hard they decided it was not worth leaving the room to chance what little they might be able to earn. That, and there was the risk of catching cold, which was of particular concern for Clementine. He said that an ill dancer wouldn't play well, wouldn't convey the true delight of a man following his natu-ral talent.

"We could always find a roof to stand under," he had said, not wanting to be caged up with Clementine's mouth for that long, but even he had not been committed to facing the wet and cold. It irritated him to think that he might be going soft.

By the third morning it had gotten to be too much. So many hours of aimless talk had pushed him to the point of action. The rain had stopped but it had grown blustery outside. An ugly wind had invaded. He could see it twitch the lifeless legs of the wolf spi-der. But he demanded they go out. Clementine reluctantly yielded.

They took the bus downtown and tried a spot on Lexington Av-enue. The sidewalk was too slick for him to dance so they hunted around until they found an empty cardboard box set aside in one of the alleys and broke it down flat to use as a platform. Clementine struck up with a tune and he began to go through a few warming steps, but the slapping of his feet was changed by the cardboard, diminished in a way that each of them sensed. The passersby also seemed to notice. Few stopped. Those who did left little more than change.

In the afternoon they moved over a few streets to Pritchard Park, where some homeless men played chess on the all-weather boards. The sidewalks had dried and when he began to dance, he could tell an immediate change. The resounding snap and return of skin against concrete. But still, few took notice. Only a couple of old men at one of the boards who clapped and brandished their teeth. He became more emphatic in his movement, as though he was trying to jar his feet loose, to be shed of himself. He quickly tired but kept on, pleased to have this physical suffering to clutch to.

"Cut it out," Clementine finally told him. "No one's paying us a lick of attention. We're burning daylight on a short wick. Let's go on back to the house."

On the bus ride back they didn't speak. He felt a hardness settle into his chest, a presence there that was like being filled with something dark and permanently resident. He watched trees nod and sway. A crow flapped against the wind to hold its place in the sky. It saddened him, and he was glad when the bus had gone on and he didn't have to see it anymore.

When they got out at the head of their road it was still not quite dark, so they walked over to the convenience store to buy some beer to take back to the apartment. He waited outside smoking a cigarette while Clementine went in. For some time he watched the cars at the gas pumps without registering details, merely gazing on the coming and going vehicles with the slow eyes of someone utterly spent. But then, like a dream cracking open when he woke, he realized a police car had parked in the distant corner of the lot and the cop seated inside it was staring. Awareness snapped inside him like a switch. He pinched the cigarette butt tightly between his lips, ready to be gone.

Within a few minutes Clementine swung out of the store with a brown paper bag under one arm, passed it along for him to carry. They cut out the side lot with its blown plastic bags and pools of spilled motor oil and jogged across the street. He got a bit ahead and led the way to a trail that wound through a narrow patch of pine woods.

"You got something against sidewalk?" Clementine asked.

"It's quicker this way," he said, did not turn his head when he spoke.

"Whatever you say, Jesco."

"That's not my name," he said.

Clementine snorted, said, "That has nothing to do with nothing."

THE NEXT morning was a Saturday, and though still cool the wind had calmed. The tourists were more disposed to stand and watch for a while, to see the patterns he made with his feet on the pavement and how they translated to the waves of motion that traveled through his body like strange currents. A man wearing a fishing shirt and a panama hat folded a ten-dollar bill and dropped it into the fiddle case. Then a woman with a stroller holding a baby with a vast and tightly veined forehead dropped in another five. It kept coming like that. On and on, the money growing there like a small paper animal.

They ate lunch at a small noodle shop on the square. The waitress brought them waters and slivers of sliced potatoes. From behind the heavy red curtains they looked out on the midday pedestrians.

"I like this town," Clementine said.

He nodded but said nothing.

"I said I like this town."

"I heard you."

"You have anything to add?"

He considered, shook his head.

"Not particularly."

Clementine folded his noodles elaborately over his chopsticks and slurped. Broth speckled his beard, the tablecloth.

"You're awfully odd, Jesco. You know that? I've never met someone who seemed as completely disinterested in the world as you. I wonder why that is? What the story might be?"

He offered nothing, concerned himself solely with his meal.

That afternoon they played and danced at the corner of the square nearest the courthouse. The tourists clapped and snapped pictures, but the money was thin, scattered, their attention largely distracted by the specialty coffee and chocolate shops, the greening statues, the cobblestones. With one exception. A police car had parked beside the city fountain. He saw that the man inside was the same one who had watched him the previous day. The cop spoke into the radio receiver clipped to his shoulder and looked on.

He told Clementine that he wasn't feeling well, that the lunch had disagreed with him, and that they needed to move on. His partner was easy to convince. He settled his instrument into the case and they stepped around the corner to wait for the bus. From the corner of his eye he saw the cruiser start and ease along behind them.

"Hey there," the cop called from behind his lowered window. "I'll give you a ride."

Clementine put his hand up, waved. "That's all right. We're good to walk."

"I wasn't talking to you, hillbilly Jack. I was talking to your dancing friend there."

"No, I'm fine," he said, kept pace with Clementine.

"It wasn't a question, asshole. Get in the back of the car."

Knowing that he had no choice, he walked around, got in.

"The fuck is this?" Clementine shouted. "He's my partner, for chrissake!"

But the cruiser was in motion by then, the window raised. He felt himself press against the backseat with gathering speed. They came out of the narrow back streets and within minutes swept down toward Biltmore Village before turning out along the river, running so fast that the engine was something felt rather than heard. He buckled his seat belt.

"Not reading me my rights, I guess?"

The cop glanced at him in the rearview mirror.

"No, I don't think we'll be doing that."

He noticed the use of the plural but saw no reason to comment. They came to the interstate ramp and then the multilane. Competing traffic slunk back as they merged and headed west. It was getting harder to breathe.

When the cop exited the highway a few minutes later, he called in to the dispatcher to report himself out at lunch at a Bojangles fried chicken restaurant, though they passed it and kept driving deeper into the country. It was back roads shortly thereafter, a confusion of turns and a close winding hug to the gravel embankments. He saw a creek and then a laurel hell, leaves like small and tight fingers in the cold. The water below made a sound like something ensnared. They turned up a steep drive with a plastic mailbox and

began to climb. Rocks spat back and ticked against the chassis as the
tires slogged and fought their way up the mountain.

At the top there was no home, not yet anyhow. Instead, merely
a foundation. A building site frozen in its early stage. The earth
graded, the pyramids of sawhorses holding beams of uncut lumber.
It was a plan for something lacking execution, a puncture out there
in the woods.

"Get out," the cop told him.

"That's okay. I'm fine back here."

The automatic lock snapped open.

"No, you're not."

He got out when the door swung open and went to the edge of
the building site. From there he could see where a basement had
been dug and within it shallow trenches that must have been for
piping not yet laid.

"You sit over there," the cop told him, waved toward a small pile
of unmortared cinder blocks.

They waited across from one another, though he was unsure
what it was they waited for. The cop stood and paced while he tried
to empty himself of anything at all as he watched the twilight come
in soft increments. Perhaps this would be the last of what he saw
in this world, this gradual rendering of the earth in a different and
more profoundly meditative light. He had witnessed so many hours
like this, had held them close. If nothing else could be said of him,
he knew that he was a man who understood the cycles of the place
that gave him being. He belonged to it, this time between extremes.
Above were the first stars of the evening. They hung over him like
something intestate, possessions inherited by happenstance.

He heard the crunching of rocks at the base of the mountain,
and then, not long after, the labor of an automobile engine. The
livid flash of headlights paled the trees as the car topped the rise
and settled. He was transfixed by the bulging rush of light. He
raised his hand to guard his eyes, but the cop told him to move
not an inch as he unholstered his sidearm and let it hang along his
trouser seam. The vehicle hummed for a while before it stopped
like a weary voice. The lights doused.

"It must have come hell or high water," the familiar voice called from the darkness. "Because that is the man we've been hunting."

David came forward. He was still only a blur there, though his voice seemed all the sharper for the occlusion of his figure.

"You got anything to say for yourself?" David asked as he pulled on a pair of leather gloves.

"No, no, I don't guess I do. You go ahead and do what you're going to."

He felt the concussive force of the blow before the pain caught up. Fists on him in a steady and workmanlike rhythm. David mostly, but the cop too. When he went to the ground he tried to cover up, but that did little against the aimed kicks to his solar plexus and then his kidneys. His pants leg went warm from his bladder emptying. After a few minutes they paused to catch their breath before they came back and started again. They were careful to stay away from his head. Didn't want to grant him the luxury of unconsciousness, David told him.

In a while the moon was up and breeze moved over the ridgeline. The trees jostled in the weird light. He rolled over on his back and looked at it through his good eye. He spread his arms and legs, left himself fully exposed to their violence.

"No, it's not going to be like that," David said. He squatted down by his head, put an aluminum cup of water to his lips. "I never meant to kill you. If I had I would have used your own gun, made it look like you'd had enough and finished things yourself. Of course, I'm sure you've wondered what happened to it. Found it in about five minutes."

And then the pistol appeared at his head. A vacuum opened up in the small space between the muzzle and his temple. He expected the fraction of time to open as if split by thunder, but David did not fire. Instead, the heavy metal struck him, sent him into a profounder darkness still.

SOMETIME LATER he crawled his way up toward a slash of light with great effort, to realize that movement was an illusion, and he had only opened his eyes. He lay staring at the night sky and the moon now bearing down on him with its fixed and glaring stare. There seemed such little distance in the composition of object and orbit. A child's mirage, but still an attractive one. That he might simply climb to the tops of the whiskered pines and grab hold of the lucent hole in the sky to discover what sphere of bright nothing it held.

But then his body demanded its tax. He had to breathe, and when he did the complete pain of his injuries broke something loose inside him, and he began to sob. Everything felt swollen, ruptured, and degraded. Once unconscious the men must have continued to beat him because there were things that felt different now, felt changed permanently.

So he learned to breathe with great care, managed, after some time, to allay the worst of the pain. He remained like that for the rest of the night despite the cold. He merely survived, recognized the grim victory in that, and waited for first light.

20

SHE HAD told Stratton about the pregnancy without meaning to. Maybe it was the habit of sitting with him in the evenings that made it easy to tell him the truth when she'd been unable to do so with Loyal. They had been sitting by the fire listening to the evening TV news, the wickedness of the world coming to them with its weary and cyclical talk, and then it had just come out of her mouth, not confessional but merely as a problem that weighed, another pain that must be felt.

"How far along are you?" he asked.

"I don't know. Maybe eight or nine weeks."

He nodded, went to the fire to poke at the middle log until it broke apart with air and a sudden gust of flame. From behind he looked like an old man come to tend the fire of something permanently lost.

"And you're not interested in keeping it?" he asked over his shoulder.

"No. For several reasons, no."

"Guess it wouldn't be a problem to have a drink, then?"

"You go ahead. I'm fine."

He went to the kitchen and poured a bourbon over ice, came back and sat with her. His hands were bathed in the amber light of the drink he was holding.

"You know, I'm the wrong man to come to for advice. You know that, don't you?"

"I don't know that that's true at all."

"Loyal doesn't know?"

She shook her head.

"And from what I gather, you don't intend to tell him, is that right?"

She said yes.

"I can help you. I can get you the money . . ."

"No, I've got the money," she quickly put in, not wanting him to misunderstand. "I've been saving from my work. I just want someone to be with me when I go. Make sure I . . . everything's okay, you know?"

He could have asked her if Wendy or one of the other girls from school was better suited, but he didn't do that. He simply sat there by the fire, took her by the hand, and told her he'd do whatever it was she needed him to do.

That night she went to bed early, but she could hear that Stratton stayed up late burning wood in the fireplace. It comforted her to know that he was still up. She felt it take a bit of her own loneliness away and she was able to rest without bad dreams.

He drove her over to the Planned Parenthood clinic in Knoxville at the end of the week. She'd already answered the pre-op screening questionnaire and had fasted since eight o'clock the evening before. He went in with her and sat while they waited for her to be called back. Time seemed stuck in place, as if it would never properly lapse, as if she'd never be able to be free of the many cutting seconds. He sensed the worry on her, squeezed her knee.

"Look at that," he said, pointed at an enormous bowl of complimentary condoms, "They must have known I was coming."

She laughed at his stupid pun, grateful for it and for him. Things would be hard now but it would be all right after this. She had a place where she could go when everything was done. She had somewhere where she was loved.

HE MET her at the side entrance with the car when they signed her out and took her to the curb in a wheelchair. She was wobbly on her feet, but between Stratton and the nurse, they managed to get her in safely, if not gracefully. As she came out of the anesthesia she began to feel a chill and she asked if there was a blanket in the back. There wasn't, but he gave her his jacket, which helped.

The roadside was somewhat of a drunken swell given the speed Stratton was driving and Rain's still drugged senses. When she tried to talk words followed, but they sounded dislocated and out of true time. She wanted to listen to the radio, but she was talking of the birds alighted on the overhead power lines and it was impossible to bring her intended subject into the strange speech sounds she was making. Finally, she pointed, tapped the dial until he understood what she wanted. The music tumbled in, wrapped her up, and she was glad not to have the problem of her own voice any longer.

They stopped at the pharmacy on the edge of town to pick up her prescriptions for pain and shrinking her insides back in place. While they waited in the drive-thru line, a few flakes of snow came down and melted into brittle threads of water on the windshield. How clean that water seemed to her, and how perfectly cold. She would have liked to have water like that running through her body now, some strong and cleansing element to cut through the veil of dullness the sedative draped across her hurt.

She closed her eyes but couldn't sleep. When the woman at the window handed across a small clipboard to her, she sat up and signed without reading what the form signified. She kept her eyes closed then for the rest of the ride home. Stratton drove slowly and made sure to take easy turns. Perhaps he was afraid to wake her, though she guessed he knew she couldn't sleep. Instead, it was something rare and significant, this awareness of how much space he took up in the world. How the mindfulness of his actions mattered.

Once home he tried to help her out and up the stairs but she wanted to try on her own. Though a touch unsteadily, she was able to go up the steps and make it to the couch in the living room. She lay there under an electric blanket he settled over her and switched on. Damn Cat leapt up and installed himself next to her in the cocoon of warmth. She stroked his head and he answered with a consumptive purr.

"You all right in here by yourself for a minute?" Stratton asked.

"Yeah. I'm good. Do whatever you need to do."

He went outside and began to gather pieces of dry wood from under the tarp at the side of the house. They seemed to weigh only slightly on him as he came inside and settled them next to the fireplace, began to lay the foundation on the grate. The fire had given him something to do with his hands. That must have been it. That must have been how he managed to carry on with this natural ease.

"You're a good man, Stratton," she told him.

He showed his face briefly over his shoulder before turning back to the business of building the flames.

"The hell you say," he said.

She smiled, but didn't push the moment. She knew he would shrug and deflect whatever she might say because that was how he had learned to deal with exchanges of intimacy with her. She wondered what kind of father he would have made for someone, if he had ever considered it seriously himself. He seemed so practiced at standing in and doing what was needed. When her eyes closed she could still hear him there in the room with her, which was all she desired.

SHE MISSED only a couple of days at school before she went back. She'd emailed her professors in order to stay as caught up as she could. A couple of cold replies and a couple of kind ones. She was sure none of them believed her excuse of a family emergency, but her grades were good enough that she didn't expect any real problems. She might not have been the quickest, but she wasn't the slowest either.

Sitting in classes was harder than she'd anticipated, though. The drone of the instructors' talk, the intensity of overhead lights. It was the little things that touched something off inside her, prodded what she'd meant to keep hidden. The stray tear, the agitation, the disquieting stares. She was embarrassed that her private life could overstep its place and have her mood announce itself so that others asked her if she was okay, if there was something they could do. Her Social Problems professor had gone so far as to ask her to stay after class one afternoon so they could talk. After the other students filed out she went through the regular battery of concerned questions. If everything was all right at home. If she might like to see a counselor. Confidentially, of course. Rain had said she was fine, that it was just end-of-the-term stress, that she would pull it all together when it mattered. Everything she knew the woman wanted to hear.

But the worst was seeing Wendy again. She maintained a punitive silence, didn't stop to help her when she'd gotten up from her desk and knocked her papers into a disordered mess within Wendy's reach. That hurt her as much as anything. She crammed everything into her pack, tearing several sheets but not caring.

Later that week as she was heading to her truck she saw Wendy standing by herself smoking a cigarette. It was getting late and the evening security lights were beginning to wobble on. There were only a few more students coming out from the building on their way home. In another five minutes she'd be alone.

"Hey," Rain said.

"Hey," Wendy answered, waved her hand through the curlicues of smoke.

"You waiting on somebody?"

"Well, I thought I was. Those girls, Stacey and Harper, they said they would pick me up after class. Looks like that was worth about as much as a fart in a handbag. I told Wes not to worry about it, but now my damn phone's dead and I can't get a decent cuss at a one of them."

"Come on with me. I'm running your way anyhow."

"You sure, hon? I know I've been an asshole to you lately. But dammit, you hurt my feelings, you know?"

"Yeah. It's okay. I'm from a long line of assholes myself. Come on."

They caught the highway back, covered the miles just as it had gotten fully dark with that clear and hard autumn sky capped over everything, infinitely clear. Those frightful distances above that pointed to the ones here. When they came into the apartment building's parking lot Wendy asked if she wanted to come up and smoke a joint. Rain parked and followed her in.

"Sorry about the mess, doll. Brace yourself."

She flipped on the overhead lights on a disheveled scene. Laundry and magazines. The husks of microwaved dinners. A battered carton of tin roof ice cream. The smell of something not meant to be shared.

"Jesus, Wendy."

"Yeah. It's bad, I know. I had one of my spells. Tried going off my meds. Didn't turn out so hot. Here, let me clean the couch and we can sit down."

Once she'd sprayed the upholstery, Rain found one corner where there wasn't too much that needed to be shoved aside, made herself small and mute while Wendy busied through, raking great handfuls of discard into a black garbage sack. The clutter made sad, hollow sounds in the bag as she carried everything back to the bedroom and closed the door on it.

"You want something to drink? I've got some Cokes in there."

"No, no I'm fine. Are you sure you're okay? I can go on home if you need me to."

"No, it's all good. It's good to have somebody to just sit with for a little bit."

Even in the darkness of the room, Wendy's eyes were bright, as if on the verge of catching fire. Rain wanted to hold her hand and tell her everything was fine, though she couldn't do that, no more than Wendy could do the same for her. So she sat and listened to Wendy chatter on as she rolled the joint and smoked as the night continued its steady invasion. Because that was what she could do for her friend. She could close her eyes and listen.

She and Wes had argued and she'd said things she regretted. It was nothing new, Wendy told her, but it felt different this time, as if after all the years the fighting had taken something essential from both of them, something that made apologies feel weak and selfish. So they hadn't talked for a week and she had gone cold turkey on the pills, and now there was this cancer in her heart that made their life together feel empty and wrong. As if their love had been slowly bled across the years and nothing remained but the cold bodies of that love.

"Can I ask you something?" Rain said after they'd sat silent for a while.

"Of course, honey. I wouldn't be spilling my stinking guts to you if you couldn't."

Still, she hesitated before she spoke.

"I wanted to know about your daughter, about what became of her."

"Wes told you, huh?"

"He did, but don't be upset with him. He was just talking."

She cracked open a Coke, tipped it back and swallowed long.

"She doesn't talk to me," she said finally. "I don't blame her. There was no way in hell I'd've forgiven me if I was in her shoes. But that doesn't change that I had to do it, see? I was dying with her daddy, and while he was a shit husband I knew he was a good father. It's possible for both of those things to be true, isn't it? I tell myself it is, anyhow. Anyhow, yeah, I left her. I left her to grow up without a mama. That's something I'll never be able to get away from. Not as long as I live."

"What's her name?"

"It was a family name. Frances Loraine. She hated it so she told everybody to call her Frankie L. Like she was an infielder for the Braves or some such shit. But I always thought it was so pretty. She was a real pretty girl too. Tall and redheaded. Freckles on her face like somebody had sprayed them on. But that name fit her to a T. Seemed old-fashioned but remade by her having it somehow too. Why do you want to know, hon?"

Rain shook her head, smiled.

"I don't know," she said. "Just seems like something I ought to know about a friend."

"Well, there's a lot to know about anyone, I imagine. A great big heap of what we don't turn loose of too easy."

21

STRATTON SUGGESTED the idea of Thanksgiving dinner at the house before he'd considered what that might mean for himself, and others too. He had been busy at work, a mercy considering how empty time had a way of putting its heavy hand over him. But his classes had been good, attended by students who were curious and attentive. A few of them even gifted. He'd had to write half a dozen recommendation letters for the University of Tennessee, one for Vanderbilt. Now with the Thanksgiving break the semester was largely complete. Only grades to be submitted and then the gulf of jobless December to cross.

His friend Josh Callum turned up at about nine Thanksgiving morning with a brace of Irish whiskey bottles and half-cranky demands that he be served. Stratton put on a second pot of coffee and began to whip the cream and sugar until it was the texture of soft candy. He liked working in the kitchen. Serving those who visited. He'd learned the habit from his mother, this standing by and anticipating what might content someone, perhaps even before they had realized the desire themselves. He poured the whiskey and then the coffee over it, topped it all with the whipped cream and a small spoon tilted at the rim.

"By God, the best Irish coffee in Christendom," Josh said before he had yet put it to his lips. "Compliments to the chef."

Stratton wiped his hands on the oven towel and sat down, tested his own coffee.

"Where's the barbarian princess?" Josh asked, leaned back in his chair to shoot a glance down the back hall. Was satisfied that Rain couldn't have heard him, that he was safe for the time being.

"She ran out to the store to get a few things. Might have sent her out for Advil if I would have known you were coming this early."

"Aww hell. You're happy to see me. Need some friction in your holiday. Besides, I already told my sister I wasn't coming up. I'm here for the turkey and the football. I hope the company won't disagree too much."

"I imagine it'll meet your standards."

They drank the coffee, just sat and visited for a while.

"You heard anything about selling the house?"

"Not a peep. You interested?"

"Naw. I'm thinking of running away to join the circus. I'm afraid I'm too much of a flight risk. Bankers can see that on you. You need a hand with any of the cooking? I can boil a mean pan of water."

"No, that's all right. You're our designated drinker for the day."

"I can handle that."

Rain came in the front door with four plastic sacks of groceries hanging from her arms. Josh all but broke his legs trying to get there to help her.

"Hold on there, girl. I'm on the way," he said.

But she had crossed the hall and flung everything onto the kitchen counter before he could relieve her.

"I see you're living with one of those independent women," Josh said to Stratton.

"Yeah, looks that way," he said.

Rain frowned, shook her head, began pulling out the vegetables and cans of mushroom soup.

"You two drunk already? I should have known not to have left you alone for long."

"Just a cup of holiday cheer," Josh said. "I would have thunk to have fixed you one as well. I do love to take a drink in mixed company. I'd even go so far as to call it civilizing."

"Well," she said. "Go ahead and pour me one, then. If there's anything around here we need it's a bit of civilizing."

Stratton got up and assembled the drink, placed it next to her on the counter where she chopped onions on the cutting board for dressing. She cut down in short aggressive strokes, as if from a desire to commit some crime in haste. He worried she might hurt herself but knew not to say anything. She had been short with him when she'd found out that he had invited Loyal to dinner. They still saw each other, he knew, though not like they had before. He had meant to be kind only, but she had seen it as a piece of interference.

"Hey, bud. You up for a little bit of manual labor?" Stratton asked Josh. "I've got a load of wood out there we could split and get this fire snapping before the company shows up. Rain can take over in the kitchen for a while, can't you?"

She said that she could, didn't bother to look up when she answered.

"Well, I could do with a spell of exercise," Josh said, rose and swallowed what was left of his coffee. "Come on, Jeremiah Johnson. Show me this woodpile of yours."

They walked out into the cold in their shirtsleeves, each with an axe from the end of the porch, and began to split dried logs that had been stacked along the side of the house where the old garden had been. The work quickly warmed them and their motions became easy and repetitive; the wood halves steadily mounted.

"You and your girl get into a lover's spat?" Josh asked as he drove the head into a block of persimmon that broke and clattered.

"I wish you'd cut that shit out," Stratton told him as he tossed a couple of pieces into the pile. "She's got a boyfriend for chrissake."

"Hell, I'm just paying attention. That girl's peeved at you about something. Usually that comes down to what's swinging between your legs."

Stratton paused, said, "You know, for somebody who's educated, you might be the biggest philistine I've ever met."

"Thank you."

"That wasn't a compliment."

"Thank you just the same."

As they finished chopping the wood a battered silver sedan fumbled up the drive and pulled into the front yard. Wendy, sequined, hair-sprayed, and rolling on some oily swell of pharmaceuticals, tumbled out from the passenger's side.

"There's the man himself," she called to Stratton. A cigarette juddered from between her lips when she talked.

"Lord God," he said under his breath.

Josh reached a hand across and squeezed him by the shoulder blade so hard it hurt.

"I think this is what the intellectuals like to call Appalachian Gothic," he said from behind his pained smile.

They went up to say hello. Stratton introduced Josh to Wendy first, then Wes. They talked a little, then Wes handed over a twelve pack of Bud Light, said he was glad to be invited, glad to have a chance to see the old farmhouse he'd heard so much about.

"Hell, come on then. Let's give you the full tour," Stratton said. He told Josh, "You won't mind toting the wood in and getting the fire started, will you, bud? Hospitality calls and all that."

"You go on. I see how it is. Takes a real man to perform the necessary duties. You run off and play Martha Stewart."

"I appreciate it."

"I bet you do."

"Y'all don't mind him. He's just upset because he knows he's going have to watch the Cowboys lose later."

"I thought you were the one from Texas?" Wendy said.

"Yeah, that's right. Losing's in the blood for me."

They went up the front steps with Wes steadying Wendy. Stratton was unsure if she was aware of the hand there at her elbow. Once they were inside, she gazed around at the front room with eyes as big as noon.

"Real pretty," she said. It took her a moment to realize Rain had come up, was standing in front of her, expecting to be hugged.

"Hey, darling. I'm sorry. I'm just running a loop today. Don't mind me. This place is beautiful, though. Really something else to behold."

Wes tried to hide his awkwardness over Wendy's behavior, asked if he could take the beer to the fridge. Stratton said he'd go on and show him where it was.

Stratton poured Wes one of his signature coffees and then led him around the back rooms and after that upstairs, showed him the full run of the place. All of it presented to its best advantage, the furnishings arranged now not so much with the idea of selling the house as to reflect the life it sheltered. He enjoyed pointing out his home's particularities—the troubled floorboards, the solid oak door frame slightly out of square, the gentle heaving warp of the master bedroom wall. Not imperfections exactly, but distinctions. The broken lines that gave it shape. The small ways he was touched by something that was supposed to be limited to cold geometry.

"I remember driving past this place when I was a little boy," Wes told him. "My grandparents, they lived up the road and we'd come through. I thought it was about the best kind of perfect I could get my head around. If I can tell you the truth, I think you're crazy for wanting to let it go."

"You think so, huh?"

"I do. This house has roots. It's permanently part of something. It's good to take hold of that."

By the time they had gone back downstairs, Rain had gotten Wendy to come to the kitchen to help her with the side dishes and Josh was kneeling by the fireplace with a newly charged tumbler of whiskey, a couple of fat chips of ice floating at the top.

"We ready to turn this sucker loose?" he asked.

"By all means," Stratton said, handed him a lighter as he went to the side table to pour out a couple more glasses of brown liquor. They all drank and quietly watched the fire twist into something more.

SHE HAD steadied Wendy with a cup of black coffee and now had her mashing a bowl of potatoes. The activity alone might have been enough to bring her back from the floating world she occupied, but Rain made sure to have her talking too, even if it was about nothing of consequence, because even then there would be the as-surance of hearing a human voice, the compulsion of finding a trail of words that held meaning. Anything to fill that absence the medicine carved into her.

"How long you been taking this new stuff?" Rain asked after a while.

"Hmmm? Oh, the pills? I don't know. A week or so. It levels me out quite a bit. I've been keeping the house up, though. It's not like it was when you came over. Wes, he's been helping me out when he can, you know."

"You two look like you've made up pretty well."

"Yeah, it looks that way, don't it? Hell, I'm happy to be dragged through this life however I can get to the end in one piece."

Rain heard the front door open and the men welcoming Loyal in. The sound of his voice was like something catching in her own throat.

"You got this for a minute?" she asked Wendy, who said everything was fine, to go on and see her man. She dried her hands and went out.

"There you are, stranger," Loyal said, came forward and hugged her tight to him as he placed a chaste kiss against her cheek. "I've started to forget what you looked like."

"It's just been busy, Loyal. I've told you that."

"Yeah, yeah, that's what I've been hearing. You need any help in the kitchen?"

"We'll get to visit after dinner, okay? Why don't you watch football out here with Stratton and his friend?"

"Well, can I get a beer at least?"

"Just go on out there and I'll bring you one."

He dragged his boots heavily as he went on to the side room where they had pulled the TV out, the announcer talking about how the Dallas Cowboys were still America's team and how it was sure to be another holiday classic. He sunk down into the armchair as heavily as if his skeleton were cut from concrete. Just like a scolded child, she thought.

She carried out three Budweisers to where the men sat, then headed back to the kitchen without a word. Wendy was there bent over in front of the oven, peeking at the bagged turkey.

"What the hell is wrong with men?" Rain asked her and nobody at all.

"That's the question of the ages, honey," she said, shut the oven door. "You want to talk about it or drink about it?"

And before she could answer, Wendy had reached into the refrigerator, got them both a beer. When Rain drank it was so cold that it was like freezing her mind shut, so she saw no reason to stop.

LOYAL TURNED the beer bottle in his fingers and looked out the window while the other men hooted at the football game. He'd rather be out there walking the woods, maybe kicking up a rabbit or some quail. Take Rain along with him. Maybe she'd even enjoy it. Lord knows that's all he wanted to do for her, to make her feel like life could hold a little basic pleasure, though everything had seemed to sour in the past few weeks. He couldn't put his finger on why, though he'd started to suspect something was off about how she was with Stratton. It was like one of those funny pictures that you'd see in a personality test. There was one picture that was clear as day when you first looked at it, but when you realized the image was just negative space for another picture—an old woman's hooked nose swapped out for a beautiful woman's cheek, or a candlestick where a pair of facing lovers were supposed to be—there was no way to keep looking at it without the feeling that you had been deliberately tricked. After a while all you could see was the trick and that put a feeling in your stomach that was all mixed up with sickness and anger.

"Loyal, you okay on that beer?" Stratton asked.

"Yeah, I'm peachy."

Stratton kept his eyes on him a minute. Loyal was about to tell him to get his goddamn face out of his just as he turned and went into the kitchen to bring some snacks back for everybody else who wanted them.

"You alright there, Loyal?" Callum asked.

Both he and Wes were watching him. His scalp started to prickle, embarrassed.

"I think I need to move on," he said, set the half-full beer on the window ledge, touched his fingers to his temples and massaged small circles there. "Something's gone wrong with my head. I might need to just lay down for a bit."

"I'm sure there's somewhere upstairs they could put you."

"No, no. That's fine. You all have a good Thanksgiving."

He didn't tell Stratton or Rain goodbye. When he was back on the road he was happy to put as much distance behind him as quickly as he could.

22

HE SPENT the large part of a month on the road, tenanting in for-gotten smokehouses and boatsheds, even the occasional chicken house surrounded by time-torn wire. The property was often con-signed to the lower elevations, so it was dank and beyond the scope of the sun. But these retreats were disregarded and safe, separate from the landowners' immediate concerns. That was how he found the time to heal, to let his body and mind assume their former in-tegrity as well as they could, though there were certain damages that produced a difference in how he walked and even how he spoke.

He let his hair grow, and by the bad half of December it was long enough to comb, though he lacked any tools for grooming, so it stuck up in stiff dirty tufts that crowned his head like fur. He was aware of the indecency of his appearance, so he kept to the woods during hours of daylight. At night he foraged, stole up to the edge of the country houses and picked over what was left in outdoor garbage bins. A stew of discarded vegetables and meats that he collected and combined in shallow aluminum plates and ate under cold skies.

Though he was not conscious of it at the time, there was a pat-tern to his progress, moving eastward and through the mountain pass, down toward the promise of Tennessee.

He came into Cocke County where the French Broad River flowed, and stayed for a day behind a green farmhouse that kept roaming chickens. He watched them hungrily through much of an afternoon, beckoned them toward him in his mind, though they refused his psychic invitation. At twilight an old fat woman in a flowered housecoat and a collie dog at heel came out and shooed the fowl into a small pen just at the rear of the house. He waited for half an hour and early dark to come on before he slipped from his concealment and came up around the back end of the enclosure. He squatted there for a minute and listened for any signs of alarm, heard only the eerie muttering of the hens at roost. He crept forward to lift the latch.

As soon as he seized the nearest hen every other bird clamored and beat its wings to war. In the evening light he was quickly turned around and could not find the way he had come in. He tucked his captive tightly under one arm while he guided his free hand over the chicken wire to discover the gate. House lights flooded at his back.

"Come on, goddammit."

Finally he found the opening, jammed it forward against a ledge of packed leaves and stepped, but his shoe skated over the smoothed cake of chicken shit, and he leveled in the air before he struck the ground with the flat of his back. He rolled out clear of the pen and stumbled to his feet, tried to gather his direction before he sprinted for the wood line because now the back door had swung wide and the old woman's figure was caught up in the coffin-shaped back-lighting, holding what appeared to be a shotgun broken open at the breech.

"You better run, you sonofabitch," the woman called out against the barking of her dog. As punctuation to this advice, a blast tore overhead, the shot losing itself into the indistinct woods he was running toward.

"Merry Christmas, motherfucker!" she shouted, slammed the house door shut.

HE WALKED deep into the woods with the dead chicken under his arm before he began to collect wood for a fire. Once he had enough to serve his purpose his hunger was so great he doubted he'd be able to wait until the meat was cooked, but he knew the night would grow hypothermic if he didn't have a way to stay warm in the open air, so he disciplined himself as he turned the breast above the flames. When finally he ate there was no savor to it, only the abeyance of belly pain.

A light snow began to fall in the middle of the night and by first light had stacked enough to silence the woods. He gathered wood once more and revived the fire in case the weather worsened, but by midday the sun appeared and tree limbs ticked and dribbled with melt. He stamped the fire and covered it and walked the ridgeline that overlooked the French Broad, followed it as it flowed into the valley country.

By evening he'd begun to come into the outskirts of Newport, though he was still out of sight from the road save for the closest inspection. He could see the bulk of warehouses by the waterfront, heard the tight passage of street traffic. Along the main street the telephone poles were decorated with red and white lights. At their peaks they wore green tinsel meant to signify Christmas trees and wreaths.

A wind began to blow hard; he knew that he needed to find cover somewhere at the edge of town, so he stepped down from the woods. He saw a bar, a place without windows along the front that settled next to the river. It had a painted beer sign affixed next to the door and didn't look like it would cost much money. He gleaned a five-dollar bill, half a dozen singles, and a few quarters from his pocket and went in.

Inside the lights were lowered but still bright enough to pick out the ugliness of the place, all plyboard and bad carpet. A slate with drink prices in chalk, and at the head, the name WILEY'S LOUNGE. A retired couple two-stepped to some new country tune he couldn't name on what purported to be a dance floor. The music came from small speakers attached to a CD player on a side table. Every few seconds it would skip and stutter before catching the correct train of lyrics. He sat at the dimmest end of the bar and ordered a glass of PBR. The bartender, a man who had eyes that seemed to look at more than one place at a time, brought the beer to him and went back down to the other customers without saying anything, not even to ask for money. He thought it strange, but didn't make a comment. Drank the flat beer, listened to the music and waited. In half an hour he raised his empty glass to draw the bartender's attention. The man slowly walked over, bent his head forward in an imitation of deference. Even in the bad light he could see a strangely shaped birthmark above the bartender's jaw.

"Nother one?" the bartender asked.

"Yeah, I believe I will."

"You paying with money or bullshit?"

"Excuse me?"

"You heard what I wanted to know. I'm a Christian, so I'm happy to serve any man on the eve of our Lord's birth. But this ain't a soup kitchen, shitbird."

"I got money," he said.

"Well, I'm glad to hear it, because I've got beer. But let's see it this time. Two-fifty a pop, so that's five bucks."

He shoved the bill across the bar.

"Bring me another beer, asshole."

The bartender took the money, stuck it in his pocket, and smiled before turning around to pull the tap. He set the full pint glass on top of a cocktail napkin in front of him.

"No tip?" the bartender asked.

He reached into his pocket, found a penny and pushed it toward him. The bartender smiled again, put that in his pocket before he left him alone with his drink.

A few more people came in as the night developed, crowded into their familiar clusters. Mostly rednecks getting off from shift work, a few of them leaning in against bored wives and girlfriends, drinking rail whiskey and saying God's blessings while arguing they wouldn't say "happy holidays" when everyone knew good and god-damn well it was meant to be "merry Christmas." After a while they toasted one another's health. In the confusion of bodies, he slipped away to the men's room.

It was as small as he'd expected, with only a toilet and a single urinal, but as in the main room there was a drop ceiling of the same plyboard that comprised the wall and, he suspected, the carpeted floor. He lowered the toilet seat and balanced there so that he could lift up on the panel directly overhead. It gave under pressure, slid from its place with a soft sense of being unburdened. He hung briefly by the board to test its strength before he clambered up and slid the panel back so that he was concealed in the attic space.

He waited for his eyes to become accustomed to the darkness before he eased out along the ceiling support beams where the horizontal slashes of ventilation showed the blue night. The sounds of music and voices from below thumped up through the soles of his feet, jarred him, but he was grateful for the indoor heat, so he relaxed into this new shelter as best he could. Pulled off his shoes and rolled his Army cargo coat into a pillow, lay there looking up through the dust at the narrow view of the sky until his mind grew heavy and stupid with tedium.

The shifted light of the moon woke him some time later. Hours it seemed. The chemical weight of deep sleep was on his body, though he could remember no dreams. He was hungry but had nothing with him. He thought of going down to check what might have been behind the bar, but he could still hear water running through the pipes. Cleaning up before shutting everything down, he supposed. He settled in to wait as long as he needed to.

He thought of when, as a boy, he had found shelter in a treehouse much like this. Windowless and closed up by plyboard. It had been his secret, though a secret he shared with his grandfather, a man who loved the woods as much as he did. The old man had moved in with his family after his stroke and roomed in the converted garage for less than a week before he dragged out a heavy general-purpose military tent that had been boxed and forgotten for more than a decade. It had belonged to the old man at one time, had been what he erected when he had taken his children, both his sons, fishing and turkey hunting for weeklong trips in the Bankhead National Forest. But he had preferred even that, ancient and begrimed from disuse as it had become, to sleeping another day under his son's suburban roof.

Still, the tent had not given the old man the autonomy he needed. The family knew the old man and his son had been cut from different pieces altogether. The son had made his money sitting inside climate control, moving paper across a desk. The old man had built his world through the action of his own hands. Money had not come easily, but still it had come in sufficient measure to feed and house his sons and wife. The son had never been able to forgive the father for this providence.

Yet, the grandson loved his grandfather, inherited his affinity for the natural world. He had hammered in the stakes with a sledge-hammer until the tent stretched and held, sat with him by the Coleman lantern and played endless hands of gin, even on school nights when he had to sneak from his bedroom window or risk his father's punishments. So he had required no convincing to agree to a plan of building a place farther back in the woods with pieces of scrap and salvage. The treehouse was a conspiracy, a way for him and the old man to devise a world apart from the family house with its predictably arranged symmetries. The roughness of his and the old man's design had given them something worthy to hold.

After the old man died, he had spent most of his afternoons and evenings in the treehouse. While other boys his age began to date girls and drive cars, he read books about the Cherokee and mountain people, how to devise fish traps in streams, how to build lodges from deadfall and mud. Though he did poorly in school, he taught himself Eliot Wigginton's *Foxfire* books and all they had to say about folk knowledge. Most importantly, he learned how he needed to grow toward the truth of his manhood alone.

So it had been natural for him to run away one morning when his parents had already driven off to their separate workplaces in opposite ends of the city. He simply packed his oversized gym bag with a change of clothes, some emergency cash he knew his father kept hidden in his chest of drawers, and walked straight into the woods behind his house until he came to the highway, where he hitchhiked with the first person willing to take him as far as the Appalachian Trail. He left no note.

He now heard the front door close and the lock slide home. From the ventilation opening he could see the bartender, uneasy on his legs, lurch and tumble into an old Lincoln and stab a key into the ignition. A moment later the engine caught and the car fishtailed across the gravel lot and was gone into the otherwise quiet night. He waited a few minutes more, listening for any sound at all before he climbed down.

The lights in the barroom had all been doused except for a neon Miller sign near a pool table that glowed under the steady pulse of green into red. The scattered billiard balls appeared to advance and recede by the changing cast of light, so that they moved by shaded degrees, small and lurid worlds. He palmed the cue ball and rolled it toward the far rail, where it rebounded with a deadened thump and came back at a bad angle. The balls clacked loosely but none found a pocket.

He ate stale pretzels and peanuts from the bottom of a big plastic container behind the bar. Broke into a perforated box of Hershey's plain chocolate bars and ate two while he sipped from a glass of PBR draft. Somehow, the emptiness of it all filled him and he then began to search for signs of a key to the cash register. He saw no evidence of a safe.

Within fifteen minutes, he found a ring of keys hanging from a nail in the back office. He tried all of them, but the drawer remained sealed. No doubt it would yield under sufficient force, but he considered other values the bar might hold. Returning to the office with its desk overburdened with ledgers and pornography, he tried the keys in each of the drawers. Mostly small cash, but also a Smith and Wesson snub-nosed .38, nickel plated, loaded, and clean. He considered taking it, but thought perhaps he already had something more important at hand. At the back door the first key entered the lock and turned the deadbolt. He stood there on the small iron stairway with the key pinched between his fingers and listened to the river for a long time. He worked the single key free then and returned the key ring to its place, left everything as undisturbed as he could before he locked the door and walked down to the river as it began to silver with daybreak.

23

STRATTON SAW little of Rain over the Christmas holidays. She seemed to be working at the restaurant as much as possible, so her hours were often at odds with his and the little time they did have together was over a quick meal before she hurried off. He found himself lonely in the house when she wasn't there, and he tried to play the piano and listen to his music to enliven the empty rooms, but that often made it worse. After a few days of this he decided he needed to get out on his own. With his best winter jacket, duck boots, and a full thermos of coffee, he put himself on the road without a specific destination in mind.

Within an hour he was in Johnson City and decided to press on for Elizabethton where the Watauga River came alive after its dam release. He had taken Liza there a couple of times to fish when they'd first moved to the Tennessee house. The dam wall made an impression on her he'd not anticipated. She'd asked him if it was safe to be there and when he'd assured her that it was she gave him a look that lacked all confidence. When half an hour later the five-minute warning horn sounded, she lost no time in beating her way back to the car, convinced that the event would be cataclysm rather than the modest churning and rise of the waterline it was.

Past Hampton, he came into Roan Mountain State Park, where the road swiftly climbed and took him past the cabins and car

camping and into the mountain itself. Driving here always felt like
he was being gathered in by the belly of the mountain. The ground
had to digest him. The road tightened and he accelerated into it,
drew all the slack from his hands and arms so that the winding
pressure of staying within his lane was tuned as sharply as possible
to his touch. He had to grab hold of speed itself.

He slowed at Carvers Gap, nosed in along all the other hikers'
trucks and cars parked along the shoulder of winter grass. As he
stepped out the wind reminded him of the change in altitude, the
temperature close to twenty degrees colder than it had been at the
house. After a sip of the coffee, he set across the road and mounted
the trail, nodding hello to the few others who were coming back
down from the top of the mountain.

He walked quickly up through the tunneled shade of rhododendron until he felt his face redden and his breathing catch. Badly
out of shape, he knew. He slowed, having no desire to court cardiac
disaster when he might be farther from medical help that he would
have liked. Strange how that happened, how one day you woke up
with a body that didn't seem completely familiar. Of course, the
body wasn't all that changed. For a couple of years after turning
forty he'd fallen into an odd version of a midlife crisis where he
developed a fear that he was incrementally losing who he was each
time he would sleep through the night. It had gotten so bad that
he began to believe that it was true, that he could actually *feel* a
significant part of him erode between one day and the next, as if
he were something washed so thin that he verged on dissolving.
He tried sleeping pills for a while, hoping the deep tumble into the
back nowhere of his shut-down mind could keep the animal part
of who he was intact. But that was slowness he couldn't keep for
long. Perhaps it had been around that time when Liza had become
a stranger to him, just as he had become a stranger to himself.

He came to the ridge crest where the tan landscape rolled away
on all sides, the sun and cloud shadows vying across the range for
a sense of geographic depth. He cut away from the main trail for a
small copse of trees encircling a scorched fire pit. Several piles of
flat stones had been dragged up for seating. He settled his weight

on the most stable looking of these and poured the thermos cap full, drank as he watched a distant hawk buoy up on coursing thermals, the country beneath him distant and unreal.

The hawk's flight reminded him of a piece of music he deeply admired—Max Richter's recomposition of Vivaldi's *Four Seasons*. The violin from Summer 2. A sure and solitary movement that was not so much a reworking of Vivaldi as a distillation of what the beauty of the world could be when it was left on its own, a sphere apart from human interference.

For a time he had been a recreational environmentalist. Sorted recyclables, volunteered for river cleanups, attended Earth Day festivals. Anything reasonably easy and suburban. Liza had been the enthusiast in that regard, after all, wholly impassioned. But it seemed to him that things had changed. He wasn't exactly sure when it had happened, but a spirit of resignation had settled over those who had once been so ardent to defend the integrity of the natural world. Perhaps it was simply a reaction to the sustained indifference, both political and personal. Regardless of cause or the many lost possibilities for creating a different future, he had no doubt now that the world was dying, though it was the human world, not the earth, that would suffer and disappear. It shouldn't have been allowed to happen, but that had no bearing on the fact that it had. Strange how something still in the future could seem as though it had been written long ago on tablets of stone and then lost. He remembered a line from Edward Abbey's *Desert Solitaire*, as profound a comfort as he'd ever had:

Men come and go, cities rise and fall, whole civilizations appear and disappear—the earth remains. . . . I sometimes choose to think, no doubt perversely, that man is a dream, thought an illusion, and only rock is real. Rock and sun.

What would that mean for who was left? Would that mean that they were only the dreams of rocks?

Late that afternoon he went back down to his car and drove home, arrived half an hour after dark. He had not left lights on inside and the light switch in the front hall wouldn't work. The emptiness as he stood there was its own kind of immensity, so he allowed it to stay with him for a while. He would have gone to bed with it left like that but he didn't want Rain to have to come in from work without a way to see. Turning on the standing lamp, he mounted the stairs.

HE SLEPT late the next morning, roused by daylight rather than the normal hard nosing of the cat. He stood at the window to see a frost had set in overnight. The thin grass was wearing a jacket of cold. He was awake for several minutes before he became concerned.

He went back to Rain's room and tapped lightly to see if she was awake, but there was no answer. He cracked the door, saw her still sleeping, but the cat wasn't there. The cat bed in the den was empty and the bowl of kibble appeared to be untouched since before he'd left for the mountain. He stood on the front porch and called for five minutes before he turned back inside and began to search the house.

The cat was under one corner of a pile of blankets at the dark end of a closet in one of the spare bedrooms. He lifted his head only slightly, gazed into a distance without definition. Stratton placed his hands beneath the flanks that were damp with urine and carried him into the front room. The weight was slack and alien. Once he settled him on the couch the cat's only movement was the slow collapse of his breath. He sat and petted him until this too stopped.

He wrapped the cat in one of Liza's scarves and carried it outside to place on the ground next to where he would bury it in the soft soil of the old garden. The spade tip went in deep and the soil broke and popped when he twisted. The frozen ground around it appeared hard, but the plot opened up with an easiness beyond anything Stratton could have expected. As he lay the cat in the bottom of the hole and covered it, the wind began to blow, the trees rustle.

With the grave closed, he had expected something to come, some grief to articulate, either in tears or that deep body ache of having lost something important out of his private world. Instead, there was only the fact of having finished what had been required. He put the shovel away and squatted there for a long time, decided to find a good stone for a marker and to make sure the body was guarded from scavengers. There was a piece of river rock under the front steps, rounded and heavy. He carried it over and set it to the ground. And it was then, with the perfection of the rock put to its right place that it all broke loose and he wept as he never had, not for Liza or anything else that had been ripped from his life, because for so long he thought he had been beyond any further grief, that losing her had been the completion of what could inflict hurt. But now he realized that the loss would go on and on, that he had no protection from it, that each new loss would always be a magnification of losing her.

24

RAIN CAME up the back stairs of Loyal's apartment. She knocked at the door and called his name. She looked down at the cracks between crosspieces in the decking. More daylight showed through than looked safe. She was glad to be off of it when he hurried to the door and hustled her in.

"Hey, baby," he said, took her in his arms.

She waited for him to let her go, then went on to the kitchen where she set down the bottle of wine she'd brought from the grocery store.

"You got any glasses?"

"Yeah, reach us out a couple in the cupboard."

She saw only a coffee mug and a few plastic soda cups. She pulled out one from McDonald's and another from the Weigel's gas station, filled them both halfway. She feared she might need it if she was going to go on and tell him what she'd planned to.

"You ready for the grand tour?" he asked.

"The what?"

"The apartment. Don't you want to see how I've got it all set up?"

"Yeah, sure. Go ahead."

There was little that she couldn't already see. The small front room with its plaid loveseat and oversized television, the short hall that led to the bedroom with its box springs and mattress flat on the tan carpet. Nothing on the walls but a car parts calendar. On the coffee table a copy of *Guns and Ammo* and *Maxim*. Still, she told him that it looked nice, that she could tell he'd put some work into making it comfortable.

"Yeah, it's coming together. I really think it is. Are you hungry yet? I can go ahead and put the pizza in the oven."

She told him to go ahead, that she'd find them something to watch on TV. She flipped through the channels, settled on something with figure skaters dressed up in holiday costumes. They danced and flounced to show tunes while the crowd faintly applauded. He came out and plopped beside her with the grace of a dropped sack. She knew what would come then, had braced herself for it as soon as she had entered. He pulled her tight to him and breathed across the back of her neck, tried to make himself a piece of her, something made of instinct and sharp smell. She told him to stop, that she wanted to talk first, but he laughed and ignored her, made his body inhabit as much space as he could. His hand went around her back and snaked up to her breast, pinched through her dress at her nipple.

"Jesus, hold on a minute, will you?"

"Well, goddamn. Excuse the fuck out of me."

A hard look then, as if she had denied him something already owed. He turned up his wine, then went back into the kitchen to bring the bottle out.

"I want you to explain something to me," he said, drank. "I want you to explain why this is how you come over and treat me."

"How I treat you?"

"That's right."

"I'm starting to see this was a bad idea."

She started to stand but his hand clenched her by the wrist. Her eyes went there and stayed until he realized how hard he had taken hold. Gradually, he released his grip. Her whitened skin resumed its color.

"Look, I'm sorry. Please, just wait a minute," he told her. "I thought this could be something nice. Hell, I've busted my ass to get enough money saved back to get this place. A place for both of us. Don't you want to get out of that old house, with that fucking guy? I know good and damn well he isn't your uncle. Do you think I'm stupid, that we all are? It's not my business to know what all was going on there, but Jesus, he must be fifty years old."

"This isn't about him."

"No? Boy, it sure seems it is, though. Why don't you explain the whole of it then, huh? Why don't you tell the whole fucking story?"

"I'm leaving, Loyal. And you better not put your hands on me again. Do you understand?"

"Yeah, I understand real well."

She put on her coat and was out the door, not turning when he called her name in the hammering wind.

SHE PARALLEL parked on the downtown street and went into the dollar store to kill some time. Inside, she found many remnants of Christmas strewn in the deep wooden bins—ornaments, tinsel, hard peppermint candies, all under bright discount signs that stood like flags. She absently placed her hand over the individual pieces, raked through them as she would a segment of torn earth in a desire to find some root or seed worth salvaging. It was a kind of pleasant trance, a removal from the moment.

She had wanted to break it off with Loyal as directly as she could, but her anger had ignited and overwhelmed her. Now, it remained this indeterminate thing, this shade that hung about her with a sense of incompletion. It was beyond her how she couldn't simply find the words, the specific conveyance of what she needed to find herself, to become who she was in a way that had never been allowed to happen. How could she expect Loyal to understand something like that when she felt incapable of rounding out its true phrasing? He wanted her to become part of his world, to cede herself to his idea of what would make him happy. In every way, he was the opposite end of what life she had made with Stratton.

She walked to the back of the store amid the dense clothes racks. Mostly blouses and skirts that were too thinly spun and loudly styled. She pulled a few and went back to where the girl stood at the check-in for the small changing room. She took a number on a small plastic tag and closed herself inside for a quarter of an hour. The new clothes hung on the peg, untried. Instead, she watched herself in the mirror, wondered what to make of the face that gazed back at her.

"Thank you," she said to the girl on the way back out, handed what she'd checked. "Nothing fits."

She had intended to leave then, to go home and close herself up in her room, but something caught her eye in the men's department. A wool sports jacket with darkened elbow patches. She lifted it from the rack and held it out at arm's length to get a sense of the size, pondered her idea of Stratton's frame, guessed that it was just about the right fit. At the front counter she counted out the cost in singles from last week's tips, and headed home with a lighter feeling, a feeling of having discovered something fundamental and specific.

She arrived at the house to find Stratton in the side yard in the dark under the floodlight where he'd buried the cat. He held a small paint brush and bucket. He waved when she pulled up.

"What you doing?" she asked, pulling her arms tight to her body to keep out the evening cold. Her eyes went down to the stone that was the grave marker. It had been painted a new and smooth white.

"Just freshening things up a bit."

"You going to put his name?"

"No. I like this better. Just the clean slate for the old fellow. I think he would have appreciated it. What's in the bag?"

"A surprise. Come inside and I'll show you."

He wiped his hands against the dry grass and followed her inside to the living room. She drew the coat from the sack and told him to turn around. He did, extending his arms so that the jacket fell into place like it had been slotted for him.

"You shouldn't have spent the money," he told her, though she thought his voice sounded pleased.

"Does it fit?"

"Like a good hat."

"Good. I thought you could wear it to Liza's exhibition. Be every inch the professor while you're out and about."

"I will. Thank you."

A discoloration at the edge of one cuff caught his eye. He flipped his wrist over.

"Oh, Goddammit."

"What?"

He frowned.

"It's paint. I've got some paint on the material. Jesus Christ."

"It's okay. Don't get upset. Just wait here a sec."

She went into the kitchen and dampened a washcloth, came back and took his hand in hers, turned it so that she could blot the stain. He seemed to relax somewhat in her grip and the awareness of this warmed something along the skin of her arms and chest.

"I thought you were going to see Loyal," he said.

"I did. I did see him. Now I'm back."

"And now you're back."

She was expecting him to lean toward her, to kiss her perhaps, but he didn't. Instead, he held her in that close gaze.

"Please don't do something stupid," she asked.

He placed his free hand on her shoulder.

"I won't. Have you eaten?"

"I'm not really hungry."

"Well, I am. Keep me company?"

She nodded, released his wrist.

One of the overhead lightbulbs in the kitchen had gone out, so as they sat at the table they looked across at one another across a kindness of half-light. He ate heated leftovers that he scraped straight from the container. Even so, there was an elegance about how he did so. The fork a slim and strong extension of the hand holding it. A certain detailed sense of knowing the most elegant way to accomplish a task.

"Who taught you to eat like that?"

He glanced up, laughed.

"No one. My father hated it. Said I used a knife and fork like some men loved a woman. I guess maybe he was right. Even when I was a boy I wanted to make sure I did things so that others wouldn't feel uncomfortable. I wanted to be able to do it so that no one would want to correct me. I hated the attention. Maybe that's why I so rarely got in trouble."

"I can't imagine you having ever really been bad."

"No? I guess I can't either, really. It always seemed like so much effort went into being disobedient. I wonder if I was right, though."

"I don't think you missed out on anything," she said and smiled. "Bad boys are overrated."

"I take it this is wisdom gained from experience?"

She shrugged. "Take it however," she said. "It's the truth. But what about bad girls? Do you think that might have been what attracted you to Liza? She didn't play by the rules at all, it seems to me."

"No, I guess that's right."

He seemed unwilling to discuss it any further. That gentle tease of the past. So often it was a chance to see into a part of him that he denied, but these opportunities quickly passed, closed up like nets being drawn tight at the lightest touch, catching nothing.

Once he had finished his meal she collected the few things that needed to be washed and rinsed them and a few dirty plates remaining from earlier in the day. He told her to leave them but she said that she liked the hot water running over her hands. He stood there for a while watching her. She could feel his eyes on her, though neither of them said anything. He then went out to the main room and sat down to the piano and began to play. The music moved like a warm wind through everything.

25

RAIN DID not recognize him as she strode briskly past on the narrow sidewalk. How strange that was, that she might pass within an arm's length and still not sense his nearness. Of course, his appearance had changed, his long hair and beard docked, but his shape and presence must have remained essential. How could she have let go of him so thoroughly as to mistake him for someone irrelevant? He turned and watched her step into the small truck. A tall man in jeans and a leather jacket appeared from a back-alley staircase, called her name and cursed. She ignored him and knocked the engine to life, then roared up the main street without regard for the stop sign or competing traffic.

He shrugged within his hooded sweatshirt and stepped into the alcove of a closed barber shop to escape the wind, watched the man who stood looking after her with his hands on his hips and furious words in his mouth. Within a minute or less the cold proved too much and the man headed back up the stairs, slammed the door.

He checked the mailbox at the base of the stairs to impress the memory of where the man lived, then went on toward the edge of town. Twilight came and deepened swiftly into a dark hour beyond that. The mountains went to sleep in that gloom and still he was alone as he footed along the side of the road with little stellar light to guide him. It seemed as though all destinations, save his, had been reached by those who had desired them.

When finally he came into the parking lot for Wiley's Lounge the way was nearly blocked by cars lined along the shoulder and double parked in front of the building itself. A curled script of blinking red lights loosed itself along the roof trim, with the accidental abbreviation HPPY NW YER lit on either side of the burnt vowel lights. The front door was crowded with bodies. Under the front light, their faces were scalded by drink and the cold.

He pushed through toward the bar and ordered a beer from the backup bartender, turned so that the owner, the man who'd served him before, wouldn't recognize him. He watched the rolls of holiday cash amass in the drawer of the register as he gently sipped. On the television the New York faces talked about all the deaths and movies and political mischief of the past year and what mutations of the same the American public could expect in the months ahead.

He waited after the crowd had counted down to the new morning and the bar lights had flickered before he quietly paid his tab and left by the front door. Around the back he found a squat gathering of rhododendron where he could conceal himself with a good view of the lounge. The revelers began to shuffle out within a few minutes, last beer swallows on their breaths and in their blurred voices, their drugged and drunken legs taking them out in floating patterns. Cars hummed and bucked and made soft but not catastrophic impacts as they jockeyed free of the parking lot glut. Screams of joy and farewell glanced off the glass fragile night.

Cold now once again. The hug of indoor heat had dissipated and he began to shiver as he watched the silhouettes of the bartender and owner cross the window as they cleaned the bar debris. He had little to distract him from the creeping minutes, and this lack amplified every second into a lapsing of time far beyond any static measurement until he thought he would have to move along the riverside for the sake of jarring his blood. Just then the interior lights cut and the two men exited, went to their separate vehicles and diverged into some distant emptiness.

He went up the rear stairs where the river laughed beneath, the key in the palm of his hand—cold, immaculate, silver. It entered the lock, and like a spell cast, the door submitted. He stepped across the threshold and shut the door behind, stood for a while in the darkened hall to confirm his solitude, then went on to the bar to pour himself a drink since there would be no need to hurry now.

He drank the best whiskey he could find and soon any thought of the cold was gone. He slipped the framing hammer from where he'd kept it hidden in the waistband of his jeans and jammed the claw into the opening of the cash register drawer. Simple leverage broke the spring and the drawer rolled open.

Unlike the scruffy upkeep of the bar, the cash was neatly organized and stowed in the bill slots. He set everything out on the bar surface and began to count. He had been right to wait for this night. In the drawer alone was more than fifteen hundred. Under the sink in a black cabinet he found an envelope to serve as temporary wallet. He stuffed the cash inside, tucked it into his waistline, and went back to the office.

The pistol was still in its place. There was a little more cash as well, which he added to the envelope without counting. He tucked the whiskey bottle under his arm and then set out on foot for the motel a quarter of a mile up the highway. As he left, he did not bother to shut the door. He did, however, leave the key on top of the bar, and beside it a single penny.

HIS MOTEL room was small, with carpet that held a peculiar funk and a mattress more topographic than was strictly comfortable. But the heat from the wall unit was steady and curative. He placed his hands over the vents until his frozen fingers loosened and pain returned. Afterward, he took a steaming shower. Because his clothes were filthy and the room warm, he didn't dress but sat in the single chair wrapped in a towel.

As he sipped the whiskey he rolled through the different cable channels but found nothing that wasn't an advertisement for some version of a life he despised. He shut it off so that he wouldn't slam the bedside lamp through the screen. Sleep would have been the solution then and he tried to force it by bottoming the whiskey, but it wouldn't be bought even as he lay in the bed and stared at the dark ceiling. He swung his legs over the side of the bed and snapped the light back on, pulled the Gideon Bible from its drawer. He found the verses he'd memorized with David those devotional mornings. Once he found them he carefully removed each page from the volume so that no shredded edge remained bound, as if the sections had been extracted rather than roughly torn. He lay each of the pages out on the bed and placed the Bible back in the drawer. He pulled the empty wastebasket closer, removed its plastic bag. Standing on the bed, he pried the smoke detector open, unfixed the battery from its wires. Then he struck a match and touched the spitting flame to the first leaf of the pages, letting it burn, blacken, and wither until dropping the remnants in the metal bin. He struck a second match and repeated the gesture. Each new sheet was a clean and meditative disposal of what had been expected of him. The disintegration was as pleasant a spectacle as anything he could remember.

The next morning found him waking later than he'd expected, nearly nine. He rolled out of the bed and went through the pasteboard furniture looking for a copy of the Yellow Pages, but the drawers were empty. He called down to the office to see if they could give him the information, but the voice told him it was a motel not a directory, that if he wanted to look something up he was in possession of two legs and could follow the neon sign spelling O-F-F-I-C-E. The line cut.

He put the phone down and dressed.

A woman with iron-colored hair and wearing a pair of bright glasses sat with a shih tzu on her lap behind the office front desk. She drank a cup of black coffee and smoked a long cigarette while she watched the *Today* show on a small television stuck into a nook in the wall. The shih tzu yapped when he came in the door and the cattle bell clonked. She popped it once with the flat of her hand and it hushed. She looked up at him through those glasses that looked more like a toy or some hastily donned prop than serviceable eyewear.

"You the one down in nine?"

He said that he was.

"Here, here's the book," she said, hauled out a directory from behind the counter. When he turned the pages they threatened to come apart.

"You know a used car lot here in town?"

She didn't turn her head from watching the morning show when she answered him.

"Yeah, there's a couple. Lemons mostly, though I guess that goes with the territory. There's a place called Hooper's out on the other side of the interstate. Too far to walk, if that's what you've got in mind."

He dialed a cab and dropped the key in the deposit box, decided to wait outside in the cold rather than share another minute with the present company. A quarter of an hour later a hungover cabbie driving a minivan pulled up and wordlessly took him on to the car lot. He paid the fare with a twenty, which was ten too much. When he asked for his change the cabbie patted his pockets vainly and told him he had nothing on him at the moment. He was sure that the cabbie was lying but told him that it was fine, that he should drive on.

He walked around for a few minutes, looked at a couple of old sedans with prices marked in white grease pencil. Several, though, were without a price. He would have to talk to someone to see what he could afford. The car lot office was up in a singlewide that lacked an underpinning. He could see lights on inside but no one came to the door when he knocked. He knocked again, much harder, until he heard booming footsteps.

A fat man in a burgundy blazer swung the door open, invited him in, showed his fondest Rotary Club smile.

"Sorry about that," the man told him. "Dozed off for a bit. Didn't expect anyone in this early of the morning. Can I get you a cup of coffee?"

He accepted the offer for the promise of warmth alone. He took the small Styrofoam cup in both of his hands and drank, felt that desired warmth, though little more. Dark water, strained and heated.

"So, do you have an idea of what you're looking for?"

He unfolded and counted out a thousand dollars in cash on the desk.

"Something that falls in a fixed budget," he said.

The car salesman's face darkened with the briefest fog of conscience before he overcame it with a shiteating grin.

"I've got a couple of things that might interest you. It's not much, of course, but it being the holidays and cash being already on the barrel, I imagine we can find something that suits you."

The selection, however, was no more satisfactory than the coffee. A two-tone Cutlass with a peeling vinyl roof, a decrepit LeBaron, two cheerless Fiestas. They walked and he listened to the salesman talk, a babble that was as empty of content as the gusting wind. He was beginning to think the effort useless before he saw a black Crown Victoria parked at the back.

"What about that one?" he asked, pointed.

The salesman wrung his hands a bit, made a big show of turning over the possibility that he actually wanted to let him consider that particular car. The whole theatrical playbill of an experienced huckster. Then he told them that yes, he could see it, that he'd get the key even though he'd be losing money on the deal, he'd still go ahead and let him take a look, because it was the holidays and every man deserved the modern independence an automobile could afford.

The car was about ten years old and had a bad dent on the driver's side so that you couldn't enter there but had to get in on the passenger's side and slide across. But it had a remarkable engine. It was a retired police interceptor, so it had power coiled there that the appearance belied. He test-drove it down to the Gatlinburg interstate exit at ninety, wheeled around at the defunct gas station there, and had already decided he would take it by the time they got back.

After he'd signed the few tax and tag papers back at the office, he coasted back to Newport looking for a place to pick up a few necessities, but most everything was closed for the holiday except for the Dollar General. He went in and filled a buggy with a couple of polyester blankets, some assorted cans of food, a big bottle of Coke. When he paid he had a little over fifty dollars left in his pocket. Enough to get him through what he intended.

He drove back to the street where he'd seen Rain and the man who had sworn at her. There was an open space at the corner where he could see the entrance to his building, so he parked and sat, nursed the Coke down while he waited in the cold car for as long as he could stand until he cranked the engine for the benefit of the heater. A bit of snow began to drift and stick. By nightfall he knew he would have to move on and he did, driving the quiet streets back out of town.

He had expected the place by the river to be empty and it was. He pulled in behind a screen of freeze-tightened rhododendron where it would have been hard to see him from the road. There was scant deadfall in the immediate area, but he gathered what he could and built a poor campfire that did little more than knock out the ambient chill in the pork and beans he heated on the edge of the foundation log and ate straight from the can.

He could see stars still. A miraculous thing with the snow coming as thick as it was, growing around him with its weight of silence. His grandfather had told him once that no matter how long and terrible the night might seem, it would always justify suffering by the scattered sight of distant worlds overhead, as stark and trim as this one. Even sitting here marooned on the banks of a strange river, he felt he glimpsed something of great meaning in that black sky and what lay behind it. He spoke to his grandfather then, as he hadn't in many years. They shared a conversation in the dark that opened a portal across many lost days. When they had finished, he remained for a long time in silence and decision, the vestiges of firelight on his face like a chain of floating runes.

He slept in the car under both blankets, waking when it had become so cold that he couldn't endure it, when he would crank the engine and let the heat run until he began to sweat. At daybreak he left, drove back to town.

More faces in the cold the next morning. A few proprietors appeared at the sidewalks to shovel the fronts of their businesses, motions as stiff and eager as starlings. Nothing from the building where the man lived. Not for many hours.

He appeared only when noon sun had made the thaw into something you could hear running in the streets and down the gutters. All motion and caught light and then him, stepping suddenly from the alley entrance, his face wrinkled up at the sun as he struck a match and lit a cigarette. A proud and oblivious act. An act that made him want to open the man's chest with his teeth.

The man walked half a block to an old pickup truck and got in. As the man merged into traffic headed the opposite direction, he wheeled around and followed, giving several car lengths' interval.

They drove across the interstate overpass and out into the snow-dappled country, passed a few scratch motels and franchised eateries, then got away from the familiar and contrived as they turned down another rural road with the mountains in front of them. So large and imminent. He realized then where the man was going, where Rain had made her home since leaving him.

"The bitch. The goddamn whoring bitch."

He stopped at the end of the road beside a cluster of scrub oak and watched as the man turned up the winding drive to the old farmhouse. The man, the boy really, seemed to be at ease. He walked in and the door closed behind, enclosed him there as naturally as if he were a piece of the house's furniture.

He got out of the car but remained concealed in the cage-like shadow of the oak. Some men had doors and others trees and thickets. The recesses that matched their own best prospects. Rain had once understood this, about him and herself as well. That was why they had revealed themselves to one another, true and at peace in the woodlands. Or he thought they had. He had pledged marriage under the unmatched sky because she had claimed the open world as her passion, and that was why he had given her the name Rain. She had the power to move across the face of the earth, to make it feel the impact of her difference.

But he had a name too. A name that drove deep into the center of his mind. A name that had the power to break rocks and bleed flesh. To exact obedience and loyalty, to remind others of what had been promised.

He got back in the car and pulled the pistol from the glove box, set it in his lap, waited there a while before he steered the Crown Vic back toward town, tires popping and scrubbing dust as they met the hardtop.

26

ANOTHER SNOWSTORM came a week later, threatening the exhibit's opening at the university, but too much had already been undertaken on the part of the museum to justify a last-minute cancellation. For prudence's sake, though, Stratton agreed to take the Bronco instead of his car, trusting in the rugged mechanical advantage of the machine if not entirely convinced that Rain knew how to handle the bad weather. He knew not to suggest that he drive. That would have distanced and upset her, and he needed her to be with him this night.

He waited out front while she was getting dressed. He had on the blazer she'd bought him. It was a bit old-fashioned for his taste, but he was glad that it pleased her, glad that he had the power to do so by so simple a gesture.

"I'm almost ready," she called from down the hall. "Another minute."

"We've got time. World enough too."

He smiled to himself, watched through the window the snow falling.

A short time later she appeared in a modest black dress, her hair tucked neatly over her left shoulder. She wore no makeup. A child really, so direct and attractive in her enthusiasm.

"Come on, dear niece," he said, lifted the royal blue winter coat he'd already gathered and slipped it over her shoulders.

He put on his own peacoat, buttoned it, and tugged on his gloves.

"Ready?"

"Yes."

The roads were white with snow for the first country miles but as soon as they met the interstate they were able to go a bit faster, riding the right lane where snow trucks had salted. Still, the weather was largely sideways and it cost something to maintain the concentration to stay at a safe distance from the other travelers. He could see that she was worried about the road conditions and whether she was equal to them, though she didn't want to say anything.

"How about some tunes?" he offered, snapped a silence that had grown tense.

"Yeah, it's a ways out yet, but give her a shot."

He switched on the radio and spun the manual dial. All of FM was an incoherent wash. Only AM was strong enough to come through, and it was nothing but Baptists and local politics. Neither one suited his idea of a way to pass a peaceable segment of time. He turned it off.

"Well, hell. I guess we're trapped with each other's company."

She smiled, flexed her hands on the steering wheel.

"Don't piss me off, then," she said, chanced a brief glance away from the road and toward him. "Hell of a time and place to decide this bus can run solo."

"That would suit me fine. Save me from having to actually show up there tonight. Besides, I've got good thick skin. Winter skin."

"I thought you were excited to see it all, to see that others got to see it too."

A car passed them too fast on the left, tossed up a fan of slush as it went on and became a vivid blush of taillights until it succumbed to invisible distance.

"Stratton? You in there?"

"Yeah, sorry. It's fine. I'm just not sure what I'm supposed to say or do. I've always walked around with my hands in my pockets at these things. I guess that's how it's meant to be, but it doesn't make it any easier. I never really liked being seen when Liza had a show. It was too much of a contradiction, too much performance. People always had an idea of what she was and inferred what I must be as her husband, but it never fit. People don't work that way. They aren't just what they produce, what they leave as a footprint. I always felt like I was a disappointment, that she was too."

She drove a while before she spoke.

"I need to tell you something."

The strain in her voice was odd, like something newfound. He told her to go ahead.

"I have one of her pictures, one that I took when we . . . did that to your house," she said, steadied herself before continuing. "When we robbed you. When I did. There was a picture, one she took of a girl who looked a lot like me. I don't know why I did it. It felt wrong, more wrong that just taking something that could be replaced with money. But I felt something because of it. And I've kept it, even though I don't have any right to. It's helped me. It's helped me understand you and myself and maybe a little bit of her too. I know that sounds ridiculous to you, but I think it's true, that it matters. That what you're doing tonight matters in ways that might not be as clear as you would like them to be."

He placed his hand on her hers, squeezed it once then let it go.

"I appreciate you saying it," he said. "I've wanted to tell you a little about her since I know you've been curious. About who she was outside of the photos, about her as a person."

"I'd like that," she said.

He told her then of a story Liza had told him after they'd left her dying father in a nursing home, something he'd not been able to fully understand at the time because he could only be struck by what he believed to be the cruelty behind her action in leaving him in that place without a goodbye. On the car ride back home she'd talked about how her father had lost his will to live after his wife had abandoned him and his teenage daughter. How he had not left his bedroom for a week and when his boss at the paper mill had called to see what had happened, Liza had been the one who had to answer the phone and lie that he had come down with the flu. Promising he would be in as soon as he was able, she spent twelve hours in the sour stink of his self-neglect, coaxed him out, brought him cold chicken and whiskey to do whatever she could to find the father inside him she still recognized.

For a time he managed his life through a balance of drinking and sleeping pills, left Liza to raise herself. Until, some years later, whether by accident or intent, that uneasy balance between alcohol and drugs was lost. Some carnival of sedatives, antidepressants, and Canadian whiskey carried him into several weeks of midnight delusions and he became violent, more violent than his daughter had ever seen him. Windows broken, the dog choked and kicked, walls perforated by his spastic jabs. One night he became convinced that she'd hidden his whiskey, woke her at three in the morning and made her hunt through the trailer in search of the phantom bottle. He told her he'd kill her if she didn't find it.

It had been a neighbor then who had called the police, reported the threats screamed loud enough to be heard three doors down. They came and shone their long flashlights in his face, asked where his daughter was and if she would come out and talk to them. Liza had told them nothing of what had happened but the men had seen enough to understand what they were facing. An ambulance appeared with its team of paramedics. They wrestled him flat to the backboard, trussed him there and took him off for clinical observation. He was gone for six weeks.

Liza tended herself and the house in that time. Attended school, cleaned the broken bits of their home as best she could. She read and worked and lived, and when her father came back from the hospital neither of them discussed what had happened because the past had nothing to do with what would become of the future. And Liza had believed that. That made her who she was.

It was three weeks after they'd checked him into the nursing home when they received the call that her father had passed in his sleep and the shift nurse wanted to know what funeral arrangements the institute should undertake. Liza told them to do nothing until she got there, hurriedly packed her photography equipment and then left. She had not asked Stratton to come with her.

THEY PARKED in an open lot at the edge of the university campus and hurried up the street toward the warmly lit museum lobby. Easterday immediately saw them and excused himself from a conversation with a tall ursine man wearing horn-rimmed glasses so that he could usher them in.

"I'm glad you made it in. I was worried when I saw how the weather was turning out," he said.

"I put my life in the hands of a skilled driver, so there was never any doubt," Stratton said, smiled.

Easterday politely laughed.

"It's good to see you again, Rain. Are you excited to see your aunt's pictures put off to their best advantage?"

"Hmmm? Oh, yes. Definitely. I'm certain you've done a wonderful job."

"I'd like you both to meet someone before we head in. Someone who was a great admirer of Liza's work. He's a photographer himself."

"Of course," Stratton said.

They went over and shook hands with the bearded man Easterday had been talking to when they entered. His name was Roger May, a name Stratton recognized as one of the Appalachian photographer peers Liza had said she admired. He was disarmingly soft-spoken and friendly, and it pleased Stratton to hear his opinion of Liza's work.

"She was something else. She did things that shouldn't have worked, but they did," May said.

As they were talking, Stratton was distracted by two of May's tattoos, one on each powerful-looking forearm. On one was the outline of West Virginia and the other Kentucky. Some script was beneath each, though he couldn't make out what it said.

"Do you mind my curiosity?" he said, pointed at the markings.

May looked down, tugged the short cuffs just above each elbow, traced his fingers over the skin to replicate the loose and looping scrawl.

"This one here says A GOOD MAN IN WEST VIRGINIA. And this one says BUT THE BADDEST MAN IN KENTUCKY."

They all laughed.

Stratton said, "Something tells me there must be a story behind that."

May was about to elaborate when the doors to the main gallery opened and as if by a single mind, the attendees all began to filter in to see what had attracted them here.

The gallery was lit sparely, so that as you entered it was like advancing on images set at the far end of a dream. He and Rain and Easterday walked together at first, but Stratton soon found it was impossible to look at the pictures and maintain physical perspective, so that they naturally drifted to what drew them in and he moved through the exhibit alone.

He spent a long time with Liza's early work. *Open Season. Wedding without a Minister. Granny Noonan. Twice Sewn Stitch. Big Dark. Winter Light.*

He had not known her then. Her photographs as a student still showed that early influence, that loving debt to Sally Mann, though Liza's photographs were of strangers, not close relations. Even then she had felt the need to efface any suggestion of sentiment. Restraint was written into her very genetics, it seemed. Still, there was a distinct appreciation for beauty in these pictures, in their kind light and strong angles. He had remembered these photographs as he would people in her past, companionable ghosts who lived beyond his direct experience but who still exerted a certain idea of her life before him.

Further in there were the pictures that had made her famous. The portraits and even somehow the landscapes that conveyed not just suffering, but a kind of desire or need for that suffering. *Scorched Home Place. Last Wish at the Well. Two Fork Cemetery. Black Woods.* The natural shadows that seemed exaggerated despite their fidelity to realism. These were what others thought of when they thought of Liza. Often, he had gone along with her while she meticulously arranged the equipment and gauged the shifting light. He could only remember how painstaking she had been when she composed these pictures, how brutally technical. The essence of her art had been in her self-conscious style, in her obsession with controlling the viewer's interpretation of the world. What the critics and her admirers had not seen was the quiet toll this exacted, the gradual erosion of what was so lovely in her down to the hardest center of her talent. But that was the concern, to chip away until the sharpest point could be exposed and used like a weapon.

After a half hour by himself he found an empty viewing bench and sat. The people moved around him like minor figures in a film, as if they were set to a piece of sad music in his own head.

"Do you mind if I sit with you?"

He turned at the sound of the voice. It was Liza's young lover, McElmurray. Stratton waved his open hand to say that he was welcome.

"I wondered if you would come."

"I had considered not, but . . ."

"Yes, it would have been difficult not to come."

"Are you sure it's all right if we talk?"

"There's no reason why we shouldn't. Have you seen all of these photos before?" Stratton asked.

"Many of them, yes. But not all. She rarely wanted to talk about her pictures with me. I sometimes felt like there was a part of her that was ashamed of them somehow. I'm not quite sure what I mean by that. Is that strange?"

"It's how things were. There's little we could have said or done to change that."

Rain entered their field of view. Stratton watched her pass through the yellow swelling of soft light as she moved down the chronology of images and then along a wall he could not see. The lost sight of her was a lonely and low hurt.

"Have you seen the final room yet?" McElmurray asked.

"No, I haven't. This is as far as I've come."

Without discussing it further, they both stood and went on to the adjoining room, guided by some compulsion that neither could have named. Though the precise lighting was the same as before, the effect of the color photographs was starkly different. They were not withheld images as before, but were distinct representations, with all the hue and strength the eye would bear. Stratton approached them as he would some animal that might startle. In every frame Liza was there. She was there like he had wanted to remember her.

"There's one you haven't seen," McElmurray told him. "I had decided I didn't want to let it go when we met before. But I realized that this wouldn't be complete without it."

They walked to the back wall where the single portrait hung. A self-portrait. Untitled. It, like the others, was in color, though it was a picture of Liza sitting at a table in front of a body-length mirror. The camera was not placed to her eye. Instead, she held it casually in place on the tabletop. She wore a loose white blouse he didn't recognize. The walls behind her were smoothly white, undecorated. The only object that he recognized was a copy of the book she had written about photographic technique. The spine was turned so that the viewer could easily read it: *The Deceit of Light*.

But it was her eyes that condemned him. He saw them there in the dimensional trap of the mirror, the place where only an aspect of her could be glimpsed, only a splinter of her understood. He recalled once how she had told him that one of her art professors had claimed the reason people read tragic books and sought meaning in art was that it provided a kind of inoculation against the pain we experience in life. She, however, had disagreed. She had answered the professor that such a use of art was unethical. She believed the purpose behind such work was to make people more sensitive to their own suffering, to have respect for it. Otherwise, everything was in service to human will, and anyone who knew the world knew that was impossible. Seeing her now as he did, Stratton realized that Liza hadn't been relentlessly cruel in her pictures. She had been relentlessly hunted, and her only hope had been in taking terrible moments and turning them into paper.

"Thank you for bringing it," Stratton said, shook McElmurray's hand. "Thank you for what you've done for her."

The young man tried to find something to say, but he could not before Stratton turned and went back out to the main gallery.

THEY DID not say much as they drove back home. It had stopped snowing, but the moonlight picked up the brightness in the softly rounded banks. Stratton sipped a coffee that had grown cold, knowing that he might as well, with the chance of sleep already far gone. He watched the changed landscape, marveling as he always did at how intensely new and perpetual a storm rendered things.

They said goodnight at the front door, but he did not go up. He followed her down the hall and stood there where she'd left the door open, paused at the threshold before stepping inside.

She had undressed down to her underwear and a T-shirt and crawled into bed. He dropped his jacket in a chair, sat and untied his shoes then moved in close beside her, their heads on the same pillow, though she was turned away from him.

"It would be okay if you wanted to," she said.

He touched her bare arm and slid his hand until it found her waist, stayed there. His entire body was a distant country to his mind just then. Easier to remain motionless for that reason. Easier to say nothing and allow this quietness to be enough. He closed his eyes.

27

THREE DAYS later Rain was prepping for the dinner shift when she glanced up from her work to see Loyal sitting in his truck in the parking lot. She hadn't seen him since he'd come to the house before the bad weather to apologize for the argument they'd had at his apartment. That in itself was strange. In the past he had called her daily, and though things had been hard, it was odd that he hadn't reached out. Perhaps she had hoped things would end gently that way and a part of her had pushed it to the back of her mind. Perhaps too she didn't like to admit that some of what he said was true about how she had begun to allow herself to feel about Stratton. But that was her own concern, and she didn't like him showing up here like this while she was working. Surprise then turned to something else, and she found her hands moving more quickly and brusquely over their tasks. When she was finished with everything, had wiped the counter down and still he hadn't come in, she told the cook she was taking a quick break and stepped outside to see him.

He was sitting with the driver's window down smoking a cigarette. He didn't look at her when she approached.

"Pretty cold to sit out here with the window cracked, isn't it?"

"It doesn't bother me."

"You coming in or you just going to sit out here?"

"I'm just waiting on you."

"Well, you're going to be waiting a while. I've got about another three hours before I get off."

"That's fine," he said, flipped the butt past her. It went in a brief and smoldering arc. "I'm not in a hurry."

"All right. As long as you understand that."

He nodded, lit another cigarette, and let the smoke crawl from his mouth.

She went back behind the counter and waited on a couple with kids. As she stood there while they ordered, she could see Loyal sitting and staring. He remained like that through the course of the night, his only change coming when he would reach the end of a cigarette and light another.

When her shift ended she took her coat from the back, punched out, and left without telling anyone goodbye. The night had gotten even colder. The pavement was slick from ice and she had to be careful as she crossed to open the passenger's side of the truck and slide in.

"Well, I hope it was worth the wait," she told him, turned the heater vents so that she could get some of the air.

"Mind if we drive while we talk?"

"Not as long as you bring me back here when we're done. I've still got my own car to drive home."

He put the truck in reverse and eased from the lot, turned on the highway headed toward town. The streetlights came over them in paced intervals, the periodic glow like drops of measured time.

"You're acting strange, Loyal."

"I guess I have a right to."

"Why don't you tell me what this is about, then?"

"I figured you might want to tell me. Give me some way to make sense of what's happening."

"What the hell are you talking about? If this is more of your bull-shit about Stratton, then you can turn us around right now. I'm not going through that again with you."

"It's not about Stratton. Not directly, anyway. Why don't you tell me why I would stay away? What would pull everything out from me like it was never real in the first place?"

"I don't have any idea what you're talking about, Loyal."

His fist struck the dashboard so hard that she jumped.

"Cut the bullshit! Tell me then you don't have a husband that's out there looking for you. Tell me that I imagined that shit."

"Oh, God."

"God doesn't have a fucking thing to do with it. I come home from seeing you and this sonofabitch gets the drop on me while I'm going into my own place, shoves a pistol in my back and tells me to go in so we can talk or he'll put a couple of bullets in my fucking spine. Me, I think I'm being robbed, but as soon as he gets me up there he has me sit down and he starts telling me this wild ass story about you and him and how you were on the road together, husband and wife, making do however you could manage, to include selling your ass and whatever else. I thought it was crazy. I thought it had to be, but he had an awful lot of details, an awful lot of conviction."

"What did he say he wanted?"

"Oh, that's good. I'm glad to see you're at least not trying to pretend it's not true."

"Fuck you."

"That's a nice mouth for one of the few friends you got. Why don't you sit there and listen to me, because I've got something you will probably want to hear. After this sonofabitch got finished telling me his story, he told me that if I came back around you he would make sure I never did it more than once. But I followed him after he left, saw him get in his piece of shit car and tear ass out of town. It made me curious, after all, where this sonofabitch laid his head. Thought you might like to know too."

They sped through town and up past the ConAgra plant with its military-looking gatehouse and lurid lights, then shot the long dark corridor of the riverside road. When the headlights hit the clumps of frozen snow they cast back holes of white in the peaceably dark woods. The moon was up and it showed the massive mountain country ahead, stamped against the sky.

Loyal doused the headlights and slowed, though he remained on the road.

"See that down there," he said, pointed to a meager pattern of fire beyond some undergrowth. "He's got his camp set up down there. Parks that old black police cruiser in there and stays all night for the last three nights. I've been coming out here to make sure."

A quarter of a mile down the road he turned around in the end of a dirt driveway and steered back toward town. This time his lights were on and he did not slow as he passed the camp.

"I don't know what you want me to say, Loyal."

"That's fine. I didn't expect you would know what to say. It's all busted to hell, isn't it?"

She was unsure if it was a question in search of an answer. He continued to talk, though she only heard pieces of what he said. Mostly versions of what he had said before. His love for her and the desire to make everything right between them, regardless of the price. Even as she sat there and listened it was like recalling a memory.

He parked on the street bordering his apartment, shut the engine off.

"Why'd you bring me back here, Loyal?"

He wouldn't look at her when he spoke.

"Because this is where we make the decision, Rain."

"What decision?"

"I've got six hundred dollars up there in the apartment. I've got a couple of suitcases too. You can have one of them and we can get the hell out of town tonight. No more questions asked. Just get away from whatever has followed you."

He had leaned his head against the driver's window. She could see the split reflection of him there. She could see his handsome face cut in two.

"I can't do that."

She tried to touch his hand but he drew away.

"Don't do that," he told her. "It's fine. I knew it would be this way."

And while there was something in his voice that troubled her, some distinct change in how he spoke, she did nothing to stop him as he cranked the engine and drove her back to the restaurant.

She said goodnight and got in the Bronco. He spun out of the lot, tires barking, before she could get the engine to run. She sat over the wheel for a long time like it held some final solution she couldn't grasp.

Once she made it home Stratton had already gone up to bed. She let herself in and quietly shut the door. She called his name once. Not Stratton's but the other, the man who still claimed her, who had come back for her. She let the sound roll out of her, as if it were a sadness she'd kept inside for too long. She should have feared him, she realized. And she did. But it wasn't only fear. The answering silence affirmed that she was alone. Of course, that was what she should have hoped.

She sat up in bed trying to read one of the books she'd checked from the school library and kept over the break. It was one her English teacher had recommended, *Jude the Obscure* by Thomas Hardy. Much of it was heavy and the sentences read like something turned out by a piece of machinery, but there was a distinct power in the story there, the doomed ambitions in both love and character for both Jude and Sue Bridehead. She liked too the way the surrounding countryside held them, as if the earth contained them, rendered their losses more meaningful because of the common ground they shared.

She put the book aside and thought about what Loyal had said. His choice of words. Selling your ass. The sound of it was like something vile stuck to the roof of her brain. He didn't know what it had been like, didn't understand the human involvement, but he'd decided he understood everything from the vantage point of his disdain. It made her resent him in a way that was far beyond any shame or hurt she had felt as a result of the act itself. Yes, there was that burden, that sadness in the body from having traded away a part of herself, but that remained hers to suffer. She would not let him make that part of his possession. He had no claim on the sharp edges that formed who she had become.

The moon showed through the trees, lay a pale floating lake across the floor of the room. She imagined the surface of it enclosing her. She pulled the blanket to her chin and made herself tight within its glow. She preferred, not a man, but the night to capture her.

28

LOYAL GOT the rifle from his brother the next morning. He told his brother some friends from work were going squirrel hunting up near Waterville and he wanted to go along, drink some beers and shoot the shit. His brother was still fresh from third shift at the Alcoa warehouse and he asked him to sit and smoke a morning joint with him before he took off, but Loyal told him he had prior commitments.

"Prior commitments, huh?" his brother said. "I bet these commitments come attached to a pair of teenage tits. Suit yourself. Here, here's a box of shells. They're a couple of years old, but they should be good enough for government work. You remember how to work that thing?"

"I'm not an idiot."

"Well, let's not get carried away there, but I'll take that as a yes that you do remember. If you see a coon, go ahead and shoot one for me. I'd like to make the boy a coonskin cap."

"I'll see what I can do."

"You do that."

Loyal drove out of the park and a quarter of a mile up the road before he had to pull over and lean out the window to puke on the ground. His heart was erratic and he felt all the skin in his body shrinking in on his bones, all of him squeezed tight by what he meant to do.

"Fuck it," he said aloud, blew his clogged nose through pinched fingers, wiped the residue on the seam of his jeans. "Let's get it done."

When he got to town he wrapped the rifle in a bedsheet and carried it up to his apartment. His brother had kept it well oiled and the action moved freely when he pulled the bolt back to see if a round had been left in the chamber. He released the catch and the bolt clacked home. It wasn't much. Only a .22. But it held several rounds and the report of its firing wouldn't cause much notice in the woods. He opened the ammunition tube and dropped the rounds into place, then closed it, jacked a round in the chamber, checked the safety and lay it across the coffee table. This was still something not done, something that he could turn away from.

He tried to write a letter, to record the rush of anger and fear that had taken up residence in him. It started out well and he thought it was something Rain might understand, but when he gave it a few minutes and tried to read it back everything seemed misplaced and driven by a desire to justify himself when he knew this was beyond anything he needed to justify. He would not write a confessional when what lay before him wasn't a crime so much as a matter of survival. Why would a man choose to grovel about keeping his own life?

He sat with that on his mind for a while as he smoked a cigarette before he went back down to the truck and drove out past the town limits.

He parked off the edge of the road about a quarter of a mile from where the man camped. The sun was still out but it remained cold. Much of the hard snow that kept to the shadows was still in place. His footsteps made a sound like something being put to a whetstone.

He followed a game trail that cut toward the river, looking for likely spots to bring him. Though the winter had thinned the greenery, the undergrowth was thick and prohibitive. There were a few places, though, a few entrances to deeper pools at the bank's rocky edge.

As he neared he could smell the campfire and soon thereafter see the brittle writing of smoke against the sky. He circled around until he could see the black nose of the vehicle and just beyond that the clearing. And though the fire was still burning high and well, he saw no signs of the man. He settled beside an oak as big around as his forearm and braced the stock against the trunk, swept the area with the scope, though he found nothing more. He lowered the rifle and waited.

Some awful span of time passed and still the man had not appeared. The campfire reduced itself to embers. Loyal stood and waited as the needles of bad circulation ran from his thighs and down to his feet. Once he could move without a hitch in his step, he went forward, the rifle extended before him and his finger hugging the trigger.

He hesitated at the tree line before he committed himself and walked into the clearing. His actions seemed bound by their own independent laws. The imperative of searching, of actively hunting, took over. He swung the rifle in wide arcs as he tried to gather in the entirety of his surroundings at once. The campground with its fresh tracks, the veil of hot ash on the charred wood, the muted darkness of the sleeping car. And yet, impossibly, he was somehow alone amidst the center of it. A refugee come to the wrong country.

He lowered the rifle and stood listening to the near wilderness. The strain of the river through the land and the sounds of the birds in the limbs. He walked out beyond the campsite, waited, did not hear the slight gasp as the car trunk opened at his back like a metal mouth.

The man fired a shot that took Loyal midway down his spine, pitched him face first to the ground.

His hands grasped at emptiness. His brain told his hand to squeeze down hard, grab hold of the rifle that had dropped to his side, though he could see that disobedient hand remain inert. Again, he felt himself reach but his body refused. He could only see and breathe.

The man kicked the rifle aside, toed him over so that he rested on his back. Turned over like something on a spit. Something ready to be processed.

The man did not speak. That was good. There was little time to fear what was coming, little time to know the ache of this turn. He looked away as the man raised the pistol and ended it.

29

HE DRAGGED the dead boy to the tree line and kicked dust over the blood that had pooled beneath him. He took the rifle and tossed it in the trunk, then closed and locked it. In the boy's hip pocket he found a half-empty pack of Parliaments and a Bic. He thanked the dead boy for the unexpected gift and smoked, thought of all the flawed paths that had brought him to this.

"I told you, didn't I? I told you not to make yourself a party to this, didn't I? Young buck wants to rut. Damn you. Rut away now, fool."

He walked to the river and retraced the dead boy's steps. He had known he had been planning something, driving the old highway in the evenings without headlights, not knowing how the river threw back those road sounds on the ear. The boy's plan had been clear to him from the moment he let him follow him back to the camp, though perhaps then the plan hadn't yet grown to its completion. Perhaps that had needed time, though it all came to this eventuality, regardless of intent. It had been written by the same hand that had written the details of his blood. Now the story of the boy was over. Forever.

Once he'd found a good and accessible pool, he went back to the car and got out the pry bar and the old spare and a comealong cable puller. He sat and inserted the tip of the bar where the rubber seal met the rim. Once separated, he tossed the tire aside and held the wheel to get a sense of its weight. Lighter than he would have liked, but it was an older full-size wheel, so it should still serve. He carried it over to where the dead boy lay and put it next to him so he could do what he needed to with the dead boy's hands.

First, he unfolded the arms out to each side, palms raised, so that it looked as though the boy were appraising the broad worth of a world he no longer knew. He positioned the sharp tip of the pry bar in the web of the left hand, an inch to the inside, and stepped down on the blunt end until the metal pushed through. He twisted and gouged to dilate the wound. Once satisfied, he did the same to the other hand. He was surprised at how little blood came, how the natural channels and coves of a body could hold what it no longer needed.

The boy was heavy and the trail was not wide or level. He stopped halfway to rest before he realized he could loop the boy's belt around his neck and drag him on that way. It went much quicker then. Much easier. An achievement of reason, he decided.

He went back, fetched the rim and the comealong. He set it at the boy's head, then ran the thin chain through the opening of the wheel and in and out of each of the hand holes, linked it back to its source. After he was certain that the latch had caught, he cranked the lever on the comealong, tightened the weight until it was clasped firmly in each palm. The boy held the wheel like a prize. He sat and reviewed his work for a while, smoked another of the cigarettes, then went back to camp to get something to eat.

He rummaged through the plastic bag in the backseat of the car, found only a single can of Vienna sausages and a box of shelf-stable milk. He stuck these in his jacket pockets and walked back to the river to see to the boy.

He swung the head over the sheer ledge and then it required only a simple kick. Gravity took the boy swiftly down and under. He sat there with his legs dangling over the eddy, cracked the can of sausages open, and ate them slowly as he watched the complicated patterning of water.

30

STRATTON HAD made Rain breakfast that morning, but she had been quiet, remote. He had not asked her why she had been so late coming in the night before, though he suspected it must have been Loyal.

After eating she said she was going for a walk in the woods and asked if he wanted to go along. He declined, worried that she might have asked him out of obligation. But he did make a small thermos of coffee for her to take.

Once she had left he poured the last of the coffee into a mug, put on a piece of music by Debussy and went back to her room, sat on the edge of her bed with his hand pressed to where she had lain. His old hand. Her young body. He thought of the error of time, the fragility of the souls who passed through it. And he marveled at how she had given him something worth valuing again, something that had drawn him back toward life.

He heard a crow caw from the oak tree in the front. A belligerent scout demanding his daily tribute. Stratton closed Rain's door and went to the kitchen to gather what scraps there were and carried them out, flung them into the bare yard. He stood and waited. The crow cocked its head, hunched, then glided down to inspect. Stratton told the crow to go on, to not be spooked. The crow flashed its slim reptilian eye and waddled nearer before calling the others to their meal. His eye continued to blink like a pulse.

He spent a little while in the office reading and watching the crows eat. Just as they were finishing, Rain walked up the drive. She paused and searched the house, one hand shading her eyes. When she saw him sitting there watching her she raised her hand.

He would remember this best of all. The seeming peace of the moment, the naturalness of her coming home and the unselfconscious grace, as if her movements were something he would have scripted.

Stratton began to lift his hand in turn when he noticed something behind her. She too suddenly recognized approaching disorder. The dark shape of a speeding car wrenched in from the road and shuddered to a halt fewer than a half dozen feet from where she stood. A moment later a wild-looking man tumbled from the passenger's side, curses in his mouth as he gripped her by both arms and raised her to her toes. She threw all of her weight against him but still he kept his hold as he dragged her toward the car.

Time went to pieces then. Stratton ran down the hall to get to the front closet, but his inner vision remained on Rain even as he juggled the shotgun and spare shells in his arms, knowing that she could be gone before he could reach the front door. He could see it all unfold. He could see her going, see her slipping out of this world. The loss of her because he failed to protect, to anticipate.

He cleared the front door with the shotgun pointed at the treetops. He pulled the trigger and the boom was followed by the silver rattling ricochet of pellets as they struck the edge of the roof and rebounded. The man staggered back. Rain finally broke free and ran for the corner of the house. Stratton pumped the shotgun and leveled it, running toward the man to close distance. He pulled the trigger once more but he had held too high and most of the birdshot went over the man's shoulder, though a few slight scratches opened along the man's jaw.

The next two shots came simultaneously. One from Stratton's shotgun, the other from the man's bright snub-nose. Stratton felt the force of the bullet snap his knee. The next moment his foot struck the ground and all the following weight bore down on the joint that could not hold. The impact of the earth slammed into him. Still, he held the shotgun and could see the man had been hit, was holding his left eye with his free hand and trying to find him with his undamaged eye. Stratton rolled behind the car's front wheel for cover as the man fired wide.

The man found cover in the tree line, but Stratton could still hear him there, the sounds of deep hurt done to him. Groans and profanities. The chaos of kicked leaves and rattling undergrowth, as if some beast had realized its snare and was trying to shake free. Another quick shot dug into the dirt and a second hit the tire he crouched behind.

"You walk on out of here on your own," Stratton called. "That'll be it. You try anything more and I can't answer for it."

"Shut up, you stupid bastard! I don't mean to be killed by fucking birdshot."

"Well, those first three might be birdshot. Next two are slugs."

"Bullshit they are."

"You can find out if you want to or you can move on."

"I don't think I'll be doing that. You've got something I came for."

Stratton chanced a glimpse around the big front wheel, sighted the man less than fifty feet away behind a forked walnut tree. He braced his good leg, rolled swiftly up to the hood and fired into the tree line. The slug punched a hole through the trunk half a foot above the man's head.

"Goddammit!"

"I'll give you another chance then."

"Fuck you. You've got one left."

"You sure about that?"

Stratton fished three more shells from his pocket and loaded them. Each one made a crisp snap as it clicked into the shotgun tube. He sat there for a while, let the man think. A short time later he could hear him moving, though he knew it wasn't to put distance between them. He leaned as far as he could without exposing his profile to get another view. Movement flashed beyond the poor concealment of branches. The man meant to get around the back end of the car and deprive Stratton of cover. He would be able to do it too, given enough time. He slid to the back end of the car, leaned his shoulder against the fender, his hurt leg folded behind.

Stratton rose on his good leg and fired into the woods, racked the pump and fired again, slammed metal into the brush and trees, and some of it into flesh too. He saw the man lurch as the slug tore into tissue just as the pistol fired into him, spun him by the shoulder.

He put his back to the car and felt the wet and strangely cold scrim of blood along his arm. Pain came in and he thought he might bite through his bottom lip. The doors of his body had opened and this awful thing inside was what clawed out. He waited there, tried to hold the living parts of him inside while he listened for sounds of what had come to kill him. He caught his breath and waited. A sound of something slow and receding, staggering steps going back into the woods. When he heard nothing more he peered after, saw that the man had vanished.

31

SHE RUSHED down from the house clutching a towel, pressed it to his shoulder to staunch the flow of blood, told him the ambulance had been called, would be there soon. His color was bad but his eyes were clear, awake. He wanted her to remain beside him. She saw that the shotgun lay just beyond his reach. She said to stay still, then picked up the shotgun and walked into the woods, ignored his shouts to stay.

The blood on the snow was pronounced and arterial. It wrote itself out in flecks and long arcs. She paused and touched her fingers to it, wiped its strange oils on the inside of her wrist where her pulse jumped. She had no doubt of where he had fled. And, of course, she would have to meet him there to finish things. They owed one another that.

The ruins of the old place surprised her. There was a difference in how the collapsed shape appeared in the snow. The angled roof had nodded closer to the ground under the unaccustomed weight. The blood led her on.

"You better put that shotgun down, Little Bit," he called from within.

She settled the weapon flat on the ground, held her hands before her.

"Come on, then," he said, his voice thinned by labored breath.

She advanced, aware of the sudden cold and silence of what surrounded them.

She went up the front stairs and stepped carefully across the
spaced boards of the front hall. The house ached and complained
at her passage.

"You're headed in the right direction. Come on in."

His voice was its own spirit in the house. The invitation could
have belonged to the walls as much as they did to this man she'd
once called her husband.

"Where are you?" she stopped and asked. In the long silence that
followed she thought perhaps she would be spared this confron-
tation, but he called her name and she went on toward the back
bedroom.

He was braced in the back corner, his legs splayed and the blood
coming brightly out of his chest like a fatal decoration. He coughed,
waved her in with his hand that still held the pistol. She moved
across and sat a few feet away. He coughed again so that he doubled
up in pain and had to wait for several seconds before he could
speak.

"I'd worried the chemicals would still be bad in here, but it's just
me dying."

"There's an ambulance coming. You just need to let me help
you."

He laughed, though it caused pain.

"I imagine I've had about all the help from you I can stand."

She tried to move closer still, but he raised the pistol to warn
her away.

"I don't mean to be moved by you so you better get comfortable
where you're at. You don't have the first idea why I came here, do
you? You think this was about me trying to get you back? I'm going
to tell you something, Rain. There was never any meaning in it. I
wanted to shape you, I wanted to make you believe in something
that was impossible . . ."

A fit of coughing overwhelmed him. He leaned to the side and
spat, held his hands to the side of his head as if he could contain
the substance of what he thought by simple physical pressure.

"I've always wondered something," he continued, looked her in the eye. "I've wondered how successful I was, how much you believed. Do you still call yourself by the name I gave you? Can you give yourself to someone else as easily and completely as that? Can there be better proof of what I can control?"

She said nothing.

"I'll admit, I didn't expect it to go like this. I didn't mean for it to cost as much as it has. But that couldn't be helped. You'll find out about that, but I don't have time to tell you what got us here. That's something you'll get to carry. If you can carry it. It's hard to know what you can endure."

"I've had to carry plenty," she said, though her voice was as quiet as she could make it.

"That's fine. You think you have, but you still have more to carry. You'll understand that. I do have one thing I'd like to ask of you. Something I've wanted to hear so that I can remember what it sounded like. Can you remember who I was? Can you tell me that? Just one time I'd like to hear you say my name. That name you used to call me when you said you loved me."

When she said nothing he put the pistol in his mouth and pulled the trigger.

32

THE STATE police pulled Loyal's body from the river by the end of the week and he was cremated the day after the autopsy. His brother held no service, and though Rain had wanted to go and say something to him, she had not been welcome. There was little to be said in any case. A young man dead for no reason. It got a story in both the local and Knoxville papers. His picture had run with it, but the print job had been poorly done and the image, doubled and faded with bad color, made his handsome features look strangely grotesque.

Stratton was back home from the hospital by then, mobile with a cane, his right shoulder slung and prescriptively numbed. He tossed out the paper with the story concerning Loyal before Rain could see it, though he suspected there was little doubt someone else would bring it to her attention.

He had grown worried about her. She slept late and did not leave the house except to go straight to work and then home again. She ate even less than he did. He had called Wendy to come and check on her, but she had only sat with her for a quarter of an hour in the front room before she'd claimed a headache and excused herself to the solitude of her bedroom.

When it was time for classes to begin she attended for the first week, but it was clear to him that she had begun cutting shortly thereafter. He quietly went to the registrar's office and had her administratively withdrawn so that her grades wouldn't suffer.

The first week of February he received a call from the real estate agent. The couple who had viewed the house in the late summer had finally managed to wrest enough money from their relatives to finance and wanted to make an offer. Stratton told him that it was unnecessary. Though the agent told him the offer was far more generous than he had the right to expect and to consider before he rejected it, Stratton firmly said no, that he didn't believe he needed to hear any solid figures. He knew it was unequal to what he would need.

In early February the robins came. Perhaps a hundred of them, a busy rust-colored troupe that sprang and sang and tore their living meals from the dampened earth. They electrified the yard with their clamor. He remembered how excited the sight had made him over time. Each year they came and swept over the property with a premonition of spring. He would watch and whistle to them and they would ignore him in their full-throated lust for their own concerns. Liza had once tried to take a picture of it to please him, but she too had been struck with the natural delight of their visit, and she had laughed and watched them too, held his hand while they witnessed the little lives at work and play. They had happily forgotten the camera hung over her shoulder.

He went back into the house and called for Rain. She came quickly from her room, fearing that he was hurt and needed her.

"Come on," he said, smiled, took her hand.

He eased the front door open and they moved with great care to the edge of the porch rail. The birds were a spirited and nervous chaos. Stratton whistled and Rain did as well and the robins went on heedless of the human sounds pretending to be something else.

They ate together that night, that last night, sitting together over soup and wine in front of a pale fire. He was tired and told her he was going to bed early. She said that she would stay up and watch the fire until it had gone out. He thought of kissing her, of saying something that wasn't entirely what he felt, but instead he went up without saying a word and fell swiftly and deeply asleep.

When he woke the next morning he knew that the house was empty. He went down and, to be sure, knocked at her door before entering. She had placed Liza's picture of the girl on the pillow and beneath that she had left a simple note.

This is your home. I need to find mine. Love, R.

He folded the paper and took it with the photograph to the main room, lay them both on the table, her words put there with the picture as its subtitle. He thought of how he might fill the house.

He went to the piano and began to play.

Acknowledgments

I want to thank Gillian Berchowitz for her belief and fidelity to this book. To her team at Swallow Press, especially Nancy Basmajian and Samara Rafert, I am indebted for their scrutiny and enthusiasm. Also, to my agent, Christopher Rhodes, my deepest gratitude for carrying the fire.

To Michael Farris Smith and Andrew Hilleman for taking time away from their own writing to contribute their words.

And to all those who've helped me through their friendship and support. Thank you to Deborah Bernhardt, Frank Bill, Jesse Graves, Thomas Alan Holmes, David Joy, Marilyn Harris Lewis, Roger May, Chester Needham, Roy and Julie Nicholson, Jacob Pichnarcik, Mark, Denise, Merritt, and Silas (Stubby) Powell, Erik Reece, Jon Sealy, Wayne Thomas, and Kim Trevathan.

And to April, my trenchmate, who has shared this book from Then to Now.

About the Author

Charles Dodd White is the author of three novels and a short story collection. He has been recognized for excellence in Appalachian Writing with the Chaffin Award. He has also received a fellowship from the North Carolina Arts Council. He lives with his family in Knoxville, Tennessee, where he teaches English at Pellissippi State Community College. He is at work on another novel.